T0203171

CRADLE

A MAX FEND THRILLER

CHRIS BAUER

SEVERN RIVER PUBLISHING

Severn River Publishing
severnriverbooks.com

This is a work of fiction. Names, characters, businesses, places, events and incidents are either the products of the author's imagination or used in a fictitious manner. Any resemblance to actual persons, living or dead, or actual events is purely coincidental.

ISBN: 978-1-64875-629-0 (Paperback)

ALSO BY CHRIS BAUER

<u>Blessid Trauma Crime Scene Cleaners</u>

Hiding Among the Dead

Zero Island

2 Street

<u>The Maximum Risk Series</u>

Cobalt

Cradle

<u>Standalones</u>

Scars on the Face of God

Binge Killer

Jane's Baby

<u>with Andrew Watts</u>

Air Race

Never miss a new release! Sign up to receive exclusive updates from author Chris Bauer.

severnriverbooks.com

To Terry, my personal cradle of civilization
Love you to the Moon

NASA:
"We are going to the Moon to stay."

Teenage girl's cardboard sign at a traffic light,
Philadelphia, PA:
"Tired, hungry, looking for my dad."

PROLOGUE

April 2021

Cleansing and warm, but not comforting. A heavy downpour, too heavy, the torrents of water pounding the midnight shadows on the river, difficult for her to see ten feet in front of her. Agustina Gómez, thirteen, raised her gloved hand to swipe at her face and the bill of her baseball cap, about to enter the Rio Grande. The river was angry. Two months into their journey from their village in Perú, they were exhausted and hungry, but now, with them so close, they were exhilarated and determined. Her uncle kept her in front of him as they waded in, redirecting her by her shoulders each time the chaotic water got the better of them, him under a floppy bucket hat, her wearing a beat-up midnight green ball cap with a Philadelphia Eagles logo. The waist-high river pushed hard at them, left to right. If they lost their footing and couldn't right themselves, it could drag them under and keep them there. A midnight crossing was better for evading Texas law enforcement, which was their intention, but in this much of a rainstorm it was dangerous. She turned to look past her uncle's shoulder. Her father and baby sister were still on the Mexico side, at the river's edge.

"You must not worry about them, Agustina, you must keep walking," her tío Ernesto called in Spanish. "My brother will start after we cross."

Exhausted, she and her uncle pulled themselves out of the river and onto the bank, their waterproof backpacks intact. She didn't sit, instead removed her cap, shook it, and resettled it on her head so she could better see back across the three-hundred-foot width of river to the other bank. Her father, his backpack larger than her uncle's, now gathered up her two-year-old sister in his arms. They entered the water. Agustina and her uncle watched.

Headlights suddenly switched on behind them on the Texas soil, two sets that pierced the thick downpour. An announcement came in English then in Spanish through a bullhorn. "This is the United States Border Patrol." Behind the voice were an SUV and a box truck.

She'd heard about them, heard they were pleasant, just overworked because so many families like hers were looking for a better life in America. Still, she didn't want to meet them in the flesh. She wanted, instead, to go directly to peruano—Peruvian—friends in a small homestead a day's walk from the border. That hope was now dashed. Doors slammed, and three figures in yellow raingear passed through the vehicles' high beams, approaching them on foot. The agents spread out, one man calling at her uncle in Spanish, telling him to stay where he was, also telling him to make sure "the chiquita does, too."

Her family's plan A, because of Title 42 Covid restriction expulsions and the US government's zero tolerance policy, was to cross the river, evade capture even though many immigrants welcomed it, stay with other peruano immigrant families in Texas, request asylum, and start new lives safe from the peruano drug lords. Or plan B, if necessary, at least for Agustina per her papá: Enter an Immigration and Customs Enforcement detention center if caught by Border Patrol, request asylum, then wait for papá to find her after he and baby sister Gaby crossed the river.

Border Patrol ushered Agustina and her uncle to the rear of the box truck and checked through their backpacks for contraband. Their bags passed muster. An agent spoke to her uncle in Spanish.

"Name."

"Ernesto Gómez. I seek asylum."

"Her name?"

"Agustina Gómez. She seeks—"

"I know. Asylum. Her age."

"Thirteen."

"She looks like she's no older than ten."

"She's short."

"Are you her father?"

"No, I am her uncle. Her father is coming later. Her father and me are cowboys from Perú."

Prodded by the agents, they slid their backpacks into the dark of the box truck and climbed in. Agustina faced out the back of the truck and squinted, attempting to better the sheets of rain that pummeled the swollen river. Her father, with her sister Gaby in his arms, had returned to the riverbank. He waved to Agustina, a weak, apologetic effort. She waved a gloved hand weakly in return, tears welling up. Maybe later tonight, or maybe tomorrow, after the rain let up, her father and baby sister would make the crossing, and they could all be together again.

She hadn't known what to expect, what this long, tortuous trip might do to her physically or emotionally. Or how she'd feel when she finally arrived, stepping onto American soil this first time, doing so without her father and sister by her side.

She knew now. She felt frightened, lost, and alone.

Twenty minutes in the dark, inside the moving box truck. The bumps and dips had Agustina and her tío Ernesto and the four other border-crossers seated on the floor clutching each other to keep from knocking about the cargo space. The bruised, planked flooring inside the big metal box was unforgiving, smelling of sweat and other human fluids, the rain continuing to fall hard, pelting the truck as noisy as ball bearings bouncing off a tin roof. The truck stopped, its ignition turned off, and soon the back door creaked open. A bright floodlight high on a utility pole illuminated the truck's cargo space on a slant. Border patrol agents with flashlights beckoned them forward. The asylum seekers jumped onto the macadam, squinting against the floodlighting.

She and the others were in a paved parking lot, again getting drenched by the rain. An agent waved at them to turn around and face the entrance to the building. Above them, a sign in English that spread across the front of an overhang in bold silver letters announced their location: RIO GRANDE PROCESSING CENTER. One story, gray-brown, drab, no markings other than the entrance sign. The agents conferred. Soon after, a female agent gestured to Agustina and the other minor, a teen boy, for them to move forward. She spoke to them in Spanish. "You and you, come with me."

Agustina objected. "Mi tío..." she said then called to her uncle, her hand reaching out. "Tío! Tío Ernesto!"

The agent scolded her, laid a long Maglite across Agustina's extended arm and pressed it down, then grabbed her wrist. "You must listen to me, miss," the agent said, still in Spanish, her voice gruff. "He is not your parent. We don't know what he is to you. You can't go with him. Things will not go well for you if you do not listen. Do you understand?"

"Sí."

The agent nodded. "Good." She gestured at Agustina and the other teen for them to walk. "Let's go. We're first."

For the second time tonight, Agustina glanced back to where she'd just come from, at someone she was leaving behind, this time her uncle. Her frightened look was met by his nod of encouragement. He touched two fingers to his lips and extended to her a kiss, ending with a sliver of a smile. She returned the kiss, but she couldn't manage the smile.

Oh, to be able to give her uncle and her father and her sister just one more hug.

"Keep moving," the agent said, pushing her forward.

The rain. The monstrous, driving sheets of rain shimmered in the amber shafts of parking-lot lighting, hammering the scrub prairie outside the detention center's entrance like a monsoon. Puddles and rivulets gathered not quite everywhere, spilling over onto the pavement. Agustina entered the building. An hour later, after finishing cups of chicken noodle soup, she and her teen friend had pillows and silver Mylar thermal blankets in their hands. The agent led them to two empty holding cells in another building, padding on the floors for beds. These were the cages she had heard about from her papá.

"Niña," the agent said to Agustina, "unpack and get settled. You will be here for seventy-two hours. After that, may God have mercy on you."

She squeezed Agustina's shoulder in sympathy, pulled the gate closed, and locked her in.

"I am here, papá," she said to herself. "La Ballena can no longer hurt us. But please find me, papá. Please. I am so afraid."

She cried herself to sleep.

1

January 2024, almost three years later
Nazca, Perú

The cargo-configured Boeing 747-400 began banking, lowering to an altitude of 1500 feet. "We are here," Jesus the pilot said into the headset. "Behold, señor Fend...The Flower."

Max Fend, in the copilot's seat, leaned closer to the windshield to get a better look during the flyover. "Copy."

Revealed to his right on their approach was an ancient geoglyph, one of many in the Nazca Desert, catalogued first by explorers in the fifteenth and sixteenth centuries, then rediscovered in the early twentieth century. Since then, the rediscoveries kept coming, more glyphs found as recently as 2022. Max had seen them all in books and on video, but never in person. More than 350 were now catalogued.

"That's The Spider," Jesus said. "We're coming up on The Monkey. We'll fly over The Hummingbird, then I'll show you The Condor. We will buzz as many as we can on our way to Pisco. They're spread over two hundred miles. Quite a display that the Nazca people made for our Heavenly Father."

Jesus Quispi, the pilot, not his real name, had a decidedly spiritual view of life, the world, and the geoglyphs. Max's long-time CIA handler, Caleb Wilkes, had alerted him to Jesus's major Christianity bent. "When we made him one of our covert Peruvian contractors," Wilkes told Max, "he went full-throttle New Testament on us, going with '*Jesus*,' the mother of all religious aliases. Be prepared for an earful."

Conversely, from Jesus's perspective, Max was billionaire Max Fend of Fend Aerospace, no alias, impossible to hide his identity, so Max hadn't. But it was this persona, Max's celebrity, that begot his role here, the main cog in this elaborate sting. Max's notoriety had intrigued their mark, drug lord Balea Xolo of the Peruvian cartel—the "X" soft sounding, more like a "Z"— who'd expressed intense fan-boy appreciation for Max's guile in convincing the world of his benevolence when, in fact, according to what Xolo believed, Max was also a contraband arms and technology dealer. Someone willing to sell American military and aerospace equipment and secrets, even his own company's, to the highest bidder, on the black market in addition to over the counter. Rumored info that was so outlandish, and humorous, and romantic that Xolo apparently decided it must all be true. It made this drug cartel head willing to agree to a seven-figure deal on the dark web to acquire, from a celebrity billionaire, what Xolo was after.

After the capture of Mexican drug kingpin El Chapo and his extradition to the US, Xolo was now numero uno on the US Department of Homeland Security's list of cartel criminals needing neutralizing. And Max and his CIA handlers had designed a ballsy sting in this regard, their current work in progress, signed off by the Drug Enforcement Administration, Homeland Security, and the US military.

"We're coming up on another glyph," Jesus said. "After this one, I'll take us back up to eight thousand. Señor Fend, these glyphs tell a story. These people felt very close to the Creator, wanting to pay homage to Him in this way, to display His creatures like this, for Him to see from above. I am energized each time I see them."

Max got it. These images were created by an ancient people and held in high esteem by them and Perú's current inhabitants, homages to a long-ago time, maybe even to ancient planet jumpers, if one believed any of the "space-traveling aliens" hype around them. But these beliefs were not among any that Max held.

"Now we go to the airport, señor Fend," Jesus said.

Capitán FAP Renán Elías Olivera Airport in Pisco, near the Pacific Ocean. A commercial airport with lofty international aspirations, used by Perú's military as well. It was also a favorite of the Peruvian drug cartels.

"What about the glyph we talked about?" Max asked.

"Yes, señor Fend. The Whale. It's on the way, and coming right up."

"I'll let the team know. Again, Jesus, call me Max."

"Roger that, señor Max."

Max checked his starboard view and flipped the switch on the headset to address their passengers. Jesus began another banking approach.

"Hello. This is Max, your copilot speaking. Remove your belts, find a starboard porthole, and behold the namesake of our target. I call your attention to the geoglyph on the right known as The Whale, this desert etching more than two thousand years old. First we see The Whale, the glyph, then we capture The Whale the man, a pox on the Peruvian people."

Balea Xolo, known throughout Perú and most of the Americas as La Ballena, "The Whale," was a man of significant height, girth, wealth, and power, with Perú's unitary, semi-presidential representative democratic republic under his thumb. Along with La Ballena's expected in-person receipt of his darknet purchase, Max and his team expected some form of Peruvian military presence at the airport. That was why the air freighter carried ten US Army Special Forces combatants strapped into the below-decks cargo hold in break-glass-in-case-of-emergency status. Trent Carpenter, career US Army and best friend to Max, was number eleven among the Special Forces personnel, a personal request on Max's part for Trent to be assigned to this mission. Both he and Max had emotional skin in the operation.

"Thirteen minutes away from our airport encounter," Max announced. "Return to your hidey-hole seats and saddle up, team. We are going in."

The exchange between Max's pilot Jesus and the one air traffic controller on duty at the airport was in Spanish. The twenty-six-year-old Boeing 747 freighter was on its final approach to the airport's lone runway, nearly 10,000 feet of asphalt and concrete. Long enough to land it and long enough to depart it, with the team hopefully able to do both in one day, after a successful mission.

The con had started on the dark web.

Fortunate Son, we want to make a significant purchase. A direct message to Max.

"Fortunate Son" was not Max's choice for an alias on the darknet, it was Wilkes's. A slight dig at Max's inherited wealth, both in monetary and intellectual terms, acknowledging that his father, Charles Fend, all but retired now, was the original brains behind Fend Aerospace. Max agreed to the pseudonym, a fan of Creedence Clearwater Revival's song by the same name. But in this instance the alias had been unnecessary. The customer knew the identity of the person who had the product for sale. La Ballena knew who he wanted for this deal, had sought Max out, and had his organization connect with him.

Speak, was Fortunate Son's typed darknet response.

One of La Ballena's consiglieres, who'd been steered in Max's direction by a CIA operative's boots on the ground in Perú, was on the other end of the conversation. The return message: *We want a 747-400 freighter.*

A few beats before Max's answer. *That's a tall order.*

Can you do it? came back.

I will get back to you.

For others in the business of acquiring illegal arms and specialized equipment below the radar, the answer would have been an immediate no, that's too large a request, you'll need to buy it through the commercial markets, pay full retail, and accept whatever you get in return. Per Wilkes's input, La Ballena had heard that answer from other deep web dealers.

The answer needed to be a yes from Max if they ever had a chance of completing their mission.

The reality: Max was now the topmost dog in a massive American public aerospace company and was in the unique position of being able to deliver what would appear to be a black-market commercial airliner.

Two hours later, after the CIA, Homeland Security, the DEA, and Max had conferred, Max messaged him back.

26+-year-old bird, 400 Freighter, YOB 1998, 16000 hours, top condition, one of *my own. A steal at $6.2 million. 10% deposit. Delivery in 5 months. You're welcome.*

So here they were, delivering on the ask five months later. The time it took to shake loose the aircraft, provide the identification stats, the full specs, gather all maintenance records and work orders completed over the twenty-six years of the aircraft's life, and package the info for the buyer. Plus erect a false wall in the rear of the aircraft's main deck cargo hold, assemble the clandestine players for the sting, and perform repeated transfer simulations and full dress rehearsals at an undisclosed American airport. The show was now on the road to the buyer's requested point of sale in Perú, to close the deal hopefully *not* to the liking of La Ballena, but more so to the liking of the US Department of Justice. Capture the drug lord and deliver him to an American court of law for the heinous drug-related crimes and gang wars he conducted in-country Perú and in the US, and thereby end his brutal hold on the Peruvian government. He'd been a large reason so many indigenous Peruvians were leaving his country and trekking long distances, looking for asylum in America. Another reason for their exodus was economic, as in America was the Promised Land.

Capture Xolo, not kill him, were the orders. The DOJ—the US— wanted to remove him from circulation but also learn more about his massive network.

Stationed offshore Pisco, Perú, well beyond the 200 miles Perú declared as their territorial waters, a US Navy aircraft carrier with a squadron of Marines, including pilots, was on standby if things went wrong.

On the 747 with Max, Trent Carpenter was not behind the false wall in the main cargo hold with the other ten Army Delta Force players. He was the only upper-deck passenger, sitting directly aft of the flight deck. He would perform as one of two visible Max bodyguards, per the prearranged agreement with La Ballena's people.

When Wilkes asked Trent's Army Delta Force CO to assign him to the special mission detail, the CO complied. When Trent received his orders, he'd answered his CO with a full-throated "Sir, hell yes, sir." Trent had lost his brother Josh, Max's best friend, to a heroin overdose. Trent was a hater, to the highest power, of drug kingpins. If things went sour, he would eliminate any and all opposition to the attempted La Ballena capture, or he would die trying.

"We're cleared for landing, señor," Jesus announced. Pilot Jesus was here also as Max's second bodyguard, per full disclosure to La Ballena. The bodyguards would be the only two people allowed to leave the plane with Max—the only two people allowed on the plane to begin with—per the arrangement.

"Roger that," Max said.

The 747 taxied to a stop, the engines powering down. Cars on the perimeter of the runway inched up nearer to the nose cargo door, a feature of the large freighter. One car, a second, then a third and a fourth, their engines idling.

"The second and third cars are armored," Jesus said, viewing them through the 747 windshield. "I can tell the way the sun reflects off the glass, plus I've seen La Ballena's fleet before, in Lima. But these will not be our only welcoming committee, señor Max."

An assumption that was immediately affirmed. A military vehicle arrived behind the three cars. "Lightly armored Humvee is now in the mix, people," Max broadcast to the onboard team.

"Copy" and "Lima Charlie" came back on the headset, from Jesus and from Trent in succession. Civilian clothes, dress shirt, sport jacket, and no tie, Trent had body armor under it all. The rest of the upper deck was empty, the main deck cargo area empty as well, all the way back to the faux rear bulkhead. Behind that fake wall, filling ten temporary jump seats with exterior visibility through two cargo-hold portholes, was the rest of the mission's Army Delta Force team.

"Loud and clear it is, Trent. Shall I open the hatch, Captain?"

"Roger, señor Max."

"Okay then. Here we go."

Max, Jesus, and Trent removed their headsets and replaced them with earbuds. All was allowed per the terms of agreement with the buyer, including firearms. *Caveat emptor* ruled, the nature of deals made on the black market.

A side exterior hatch on the main deck opened, moving out of the way. Waiting for them there was a passenger stair truck that now pulled in closer to the hatch, the stairs ready to receive disembarking passengers. A La Ballena soldier exited the truck and leaned against it, his arms folded.

Max placed the call.

"Buenos días, señor Xolo," Max said into his phone. "We are open for business."

"Sí, buenos días, señor Fend," came the voice on the other end. "I will cut to the chase, as you Americans say, as we are both very busy men. May I have permission to come aboard?"

A hesitation on Max's end. He lowered his phone. "You copy that, Wilkes?"

Wilkes sat among an unannounced roomful of people in CIA HQ in Langley listening in on their exchange. Renee LeFrancois, Max's significant other and his CIA asset partner, was a listener as well, but from a location in Quebec, where she was doing NASA work.

"Yes, Max, we're analyzing," Wilkes said. "One moment." Then, "Copy on the voice, Max. Voice recognition says ninety-eight percent match on La Ballena."

Max raised his phone. "Permission granted," he said to La Ballena. "I'll meet you outside." Max and his Peruvian customer closed out their call.

The driver of the second armored car, a stretch sedan, hustled to a rear door. Two beefy men exited, both dark skinned, one bald, one not, both carrying AR-15s. They straightened their dark suits and stood at either side of the open car door. The third man out was shorter, also in a charcoal suit, a handgun in a shoulder holster dangling inside his jacket. The last to climb out was a tall, heavy, older man, fifty-ish, with a full head of black hair in need of a haircut, a deep tan, a cheeky face, and a hefty body in a roomy navy tracksuit. He brushed himself off before resettling his sunglasses on his face. He waved the other men ahead of him. The shorter bodyguard fell in behind.

"La Ballena, tall fat guy, maybe six-six, in the tracksuit," Jesus said. "He's even bigger than I remember him. Same sloppy long hair."

"Copy," Max said for both his 747 and Langley audiences. "I expect we're supposed to be surprised he's doing this, him personally coming aboard. Your take, Wilkes?"

"Agreed," Wilkes said. "Maybe meant to take you off your game. Stay on your toes."

"We'll meet him at the bottom of the airstairs. Trent, care to join us?"

Max and Jesus left the flight deck, Trent with them, resetting his AR-15 against his chest, Jesus with his hand closed around the semi-auto 9mm in a Belly Band holster above his belt. They descended the ladder from the upper deck to the main deck, then down the airstairs to the tarmac. The La Ballena entourage arrived.

"Señor Fend," La Ballena said.

"A pleasure meeting you personally, señor Xolo," Max said. "Would you care to have a look inside?"

"In a minuto. Please stay out of the way while we do a walkabout. I thank you for accommodating my request for the new paint on the aircraft exterior, señor. I will take a photo of it now, I like it so much."

Horizontal red-white-red markings in the shape of a flag, Perú's colors, were painted below the pilot side of the windshield and on both sides of the rudder. The rest of the aircraft was a flat black, per the buyer's request. With the photos out of the way, La Ballena put his phone away.

He and his crew of three walked the aircraft perimeter. The short one with the dangling shoulder holster was apparently more than a bodyguard, pointing out technical things to La Ballena in Spanish as they inspected the exterior of his intended purchase. The aide looked over his shoulder at Max, kicked one of the plane's tires, then chuckled at being so clever. The group continued their walk, La Ballena's aide commenting throughout. Max and team waited for them at the bottom of the airstairs. The group returned.

The tire inspector-aide glanced at his boss, looking for permission to speak. La Ballena nodded. "We are ready to look inside, señor Fend," the aide said.

"After you, señores." Max swept his hands toward the stairs.

Max, Jesus, and Trent followed them back up the airstairs and inside to the 747's main cargo deck, below the flight deck. Max's stomach churned, some from anxiety, some from giddiness. A line from a poem reared itself front and center in his head, a suffix to his hospitality as a host.

...said the spider to the fly...

From the main deck they climbed the ladder to the uppermost deck of the plane, the flight deck, a lavatory, and the galley on the left of the ladder, six passenger seats on the right. The aide entered the flight deck first, then La Ballena, Max and Jesus hanging back. At this point, Max realized the aide was also a pilot, his gesturing and handsy review of the dash the give-away. They descended the ladder again to the main deck, where they beheld the great expanse of an empty 747 freighter cargo hold. La Ballena and his aide conversed in Spanish, were pleased so far, his other body-guards remaining stoic, their stares at Trent daring him and his AR-15 to rain on their parade. Trent sniffed once then ignored them. Max spoke to La Ballena as they walked through the hold, between the cargo rollers.

"Tell me, señor," Max said, looking to reduce the tension, "what do you have in mind for this beautiful aircraft? More humanitarian efforts? Red Cross deliveries? Helping the indigenous in the Amazon?"

"No offense, señor Fend," La Ballena said, his look aggravated, "but that is none of your business. When does your ride home arrive?"

"When we consummate our deal," Max said, "it will be here."

The troupe walked the length of the hold, arriving at an aft wall that stretched the full height and width of the plane. The aide raised a hand to place his palm on it, feeling its metal constitution. He ran his fingers along its attachments to the bulkhead, the left side then the right, then he eyed the seam attaching it overhead.

A US government and Fend Aerospace cooperative effort, the wall was an invention that had fooled engineers invited to look the plane over during refurbishment. Max held his breath while the aide-slash-pilot continued his inspection. Jesus hung back, just out of earshot of the group. Max heard him whispering furtively into his earbuds. "Something is wrong."

Trent, the Delta Force squad leader behind the wall, their other listening audience in Langley and Quebec—they all would have heard the comment. Max waited on a follow-up.

"This is not La Ballena," Jesus said, barely breathing it. "He's a double. La Ballena has a tiny tattoo behind his left ear. A tiny Nazca geoglyph of The Whale. When this man's hair moves, no tattoo."

Max spoke quietly into his earbuds. "Wilkes?"

"Copy. Hold," Wilkes said, heard by all. "We're checking the signal on the La Ballena phone, the one that verified his voice." Five seconds later, "We see you, and we see other phones next to you and elsewhere on board. The one attached to La Ballena's voice...it's maybe forty yards away."

Jesus, standing well behind them, swiveled his head toward a porthole, again whispering, "The first armored car."

La Ballena's aide moved his hands over the wall, interested in a vertical seam, one Max knew was perforated for a jack-in-the-box surprise release of the bulkhead's contents if and when the time came.

"This wall, señor," the Peruvian said, his fingertips inside the seam. "It is a modification. What is behind it?"

"A prior freight company's doing, in the service of animal transporters, to segregate the live cargo. We decided to leave it. Don't worry, señor Xolo," Max chuckled at the La Ballena double, "the cargo space has been cleaned."

"I do not like it, señor Fend," the aide said.

They were inside an airplane, and airplanes were not impervious to bullets. They were about to be found out. This was bad—very bad—hand-to-hand combat bad.

The countermeasure had to be quiet, with no shots fired. Max moved closer to one of the bodyguards, Jesus moved close to another. Max watched Trent as he read the room, watched him grip his AR-15 tightly to steady it, and watched him cozy up to the fake La Ballena. There could no false moves, Trent could not call attention to himself—

Nothing to see here, folks, just whistling past the graveyard, la-la-la, soon it'll be over, won't hurt a bit...

Trent's left hand found his Ka-Bar in a sheath on his waist and settled on it. Max and Jesus did likewise with their own sheathed, smaller knives.

"Now," Max whispered.

Trent swung his long gun out of the way, ripped his knife from its sheath and drew it across the fake La Ballena's throat, slitting it from behind, a gush of blood streaming onto the man's chest. Max drove his knife into one bodyguard's neck, Jesus crammed his knife into another's. The fourth man, the aide, drew his handgun. He squeezed off three shots, *zip-zip-zip*, little noise. They all connected with Trent, driving him back, knocking him to the floor. Jesus was on the aide in a flash and muscled the gun from his hand, raising a knife to his throat.

"Jesus, don't!" Max yelled. "We'll need him—"

An out-of-breath Max descended on Trent, flat on his back on the cargo deck, wincing in pain, struggling to pull himself upright.

"The body armor, three hits to my chest, Max. I think I'm clean elsewhere..." He coughed, issued another status, "Ribs—bruised—owww..."

Max helped him sit up then stand. Trent doubled over, hands on his knees until his breath returned, then he vomited.

Trent was a lucky man, Max able to see all three slugs in the body armor. Max turned to their hostage, Jesus aiming the man's own gun, a silencer attached, at his chest, Jesus's knife away. A shove put the aide on the floor, stomach down. Jesus handed Max a phone.

"It's his. He has body armor on, too, señor Max. What he did to Trent, I can do to him with his own gun if he doesn't cooperate, ring his bell a little, no danger to the plane."

"Yeah, well, let's not make that necessary," Max said, hovering. "Your name, señor."

"I am Captain Bueva, you treacherous weasel," he said, his tone defiant, "and you, señor Fend, are a dead man."

"Sure, a weasel and a dead man. Got it. Listen, your boss's car hasn't moved. He doesn't know what went down in here yet. We'll let you live, señor, if you cooperate. By the way, we're keeping the plane. Jesus here will soon get our bird all started back up and ready us to fly the hell outta here.

"You are going to call whoever you need to call and act like yourself, señor, or you end up like your associates here. You will tell him everything is good, your fake-ass La Ballena is happy with his purchase, and we're about to show him how the nose cargo door works. Then we're all coming out of the plane to finalize the transaction."

"No comprendo..."

"Well, you need to *comprendo*, and I know you do. I also think you know what's behind this wall."

Bueva's lip quivered, blinked hard, and spoke through gritted teeth in English. "You will never get back in the air, Fend. What you do not see are the surface-to-air weapons. What is it you call them? Stingers? If you try to leave in this plane, señor, we are all dead."

"The stingers—they're in the Humvee?"

Max watched the man's face further assess his dire situation, saw his cheeks droop and his resolve dissolve. "Yes. Two are in there," Bueva said, "and two are behind the terminal building, in case the deal didn't happen."

"Good to know," Max said. "Super. We're going to take our chances. Copy that, everyone?"

The "everyone" included Wilkes and company in Langley. Given Max's warning, with Wilkes's direction, a carrier-based Marine F-35 jet distantly offshore of the beautiful town of Pisco would now scramble. Asking permission of local governments was not a CIA specialty. Denial that anything had ever happened was.

Max watched Trent pull himself together, still stretching, still grimacing, readying for what was now the inevitable. Max nodded at him, making Trent speak into his earbuds. "Delta squad leader Sergeant Minky, you copy?" Trent said.

"Sir," came a disembodied response.

"Show yourselves, Delta."

A large section of the false bulkhead punched out and flattened itself on the cargo deck. Ten combat Delta Force operators burst through the opening, five of them carrying rocket launchers—RPGs, rocket-propelled grenade launchers, or bazookas, in civilian parlance. They stepped over the two bodies on the way to assembling themselves in the hold.

"These are our orders..." Trent said.

—————

The call went through, their hostage, Bueva, speaking in Spanish, Jesus listening closely, his knife next to the man's throat. He'd called the organization's consigliere, not La Ballena, keeping up the pretense that Xolo was on the plane with them.

"Sí...Sí, La Ballena is ready to exit the plane, Consejero. We will do so from the nose cargo door, so he can see it in operation. He tells me you are to arrange for the remaining funds to be transferred..."

While he spoke, the nose cargo door beneath the flight deck began its painfully slow lift. Three of the four nearby cars stirred, as did the Humvee, the vehicle doors opening, the men inside beginning their exits. With enough nose door clearance gained, four Delta Force operators hugging the bulkhead sprung into position and discharged their RPGs. Four nearly simultaneous *pfffts* preceded four exploding vehicles, including the Humvee, with additional Marines using their automatic weapons at the open nose hatch to obliterate the men who'd exited their vehicle. The one armored car omitted as a target remained intact. They wanted La Ballena alive.

Delta Force operators descended rappelled on ropes from the nose, hit the ground, and assembled left and right of the car. Two operators with rocket launchers ran down the airstairs and set up to face the armored vehicle head on.

The black sedan's engine revved, the transmission slamming into reverse, spinning into a one-eighty. One bazooka fired. Its ordnance disintegrated a rear wheel and most of the rear axle when the vehicle came out of the maneuver, the interior of the armored car unbreeched, the car dragging to a stop. The second rocket launcher maneuvered into position to do the same with the front end.

Trent was the first to arrive broadside of the sedan's rear door, his AR-15 steady, waiting. Max joined him, his 9mm drawn. Max's phone rang. He answered, already knowing who it would be.

He listened to La Ballena's pitch. Max responded with his own instructions on how the vehicle would empty, then, finishing up, "You have my word, señor."

Max spoke into the earbuds to the mission team. "He's coming out. All the doors will open, firearms and other weapons will be tossed out. The driver will exit first, will have his hands raised, the bodyguard riding shotgun exits second, same MO. Rear right door, another bodyguard will exit, then the consigliere will follow him, both out the same door. Rear left door, La Ballena, will be last. Delta team, Jesus, all of you—no one discharges a weapon unless we're fired upon. I gave him my word, plus we want him alive. Everyone copy?"

Max heard their responses in duplicate in the earbuds, from Jesus and Delta squad leader Minky.

Trent, standing next to Max, remained silent.

"Trent, good buddy, you okay with this?"

A pregnant moment, then, "Copy," Trent said, his jaw clenching.

They both wanted La Ballena dead, but because their government didn't, it wouldn't happen here.

Doors one, two, and three of the sedan opened almost in unison, followed by the ejection of multiple firearms, knives, and machetes, item by item. Door number four stayed closed. The occupants of doors one through three slid themselves out per Max's instructions, but after that, no more activity, no movement, nothing, La Ballena still inside the vehicle.

Max spoke into his earbud to the team. "My guess is he's waiting for a cavalry rescue. We'll need to hurry him up. Delta, can you order a rocket launcher into position to provide some incentive?"

"Roger," came the answer. Two Delta operators, one with a rocket launcher, repositioned themselves broadside of La Ballena's closed rear door. The bazooka went to a shoulder, the rocket for it cradled in two hands, ready for insertion in the stovepipe.

A distraction overhead. Two high-pitched, raspy ba-*booms* in succession tore open the blue sky directly above them, screaming ordnances from a fighter jet. They delivered strikes to targets behind the airport terminal, incinerating them, or at least the billowing smoke insinuated they had.

A tense moment, their new prisoners lowering their heads in defensive postures on the runway, covering their ears. With the shelling stopped and the fighter jet receding, the prisoners straightened up.

"La Ballena's last two stingers, behind the terminal," Max heard in his earbud from Wilkes, "they're gone. Get a move on, Max. The Peruvian Air Force hasn't mobilized yet."

Max called La Ballena's phone, but no one picked up. Max nodded at Delta Force's Sergeant Minky who hand-signaled his operators with the rocket launcher facing the crippled car. The one operator loaded the rocket.

Max's phone chirped. He raised his hand to signify a halt to the squad leader.

"I am coming out," La Ballena said to Max and ended the call.

The last car door opened. A handgun skittered onto the runway asphalt, away from the car. Their mark exited, his palms raised and open to show his hands were empty.

"Put your toys away," La Ballena said. "I am here."

La Ballena, drug lord billionaire. He'd had a serious lapse in judgment in trusting another billionaire, Max Fend, to consummate this clandestine deal. But he also had the Peruvian military in his pocket. The window to close things out and put their 747 back in the air was tight at best. An enemy military response was maybe minutes away.

Delta Squad leader Minky gestured at two of his operators. They rushed La Ballena. Twenty seconds later his wrists were in cable ties behind his back, the operators hustling him forward. Max spoke to him as they swept him across the runway to the airstairs, everyone on alert.

"Your remaining guards will not be eliminated, señor Xolo," Max said, breathing hard, his chin pointing at the four angry men standing at gunpoint near the incapacitated armored car. "Our operators will disengage with them shortly. As for your señor Bueva here..."

The tire-kicking Peruvian pilot-slash-bodyguard, guarded by Jesus, stood at the bottom of the airstairs truck looking terrified.

"Captain Bueva," Max said to him, "we're not taking you with us. You're free to go."

La Ballena spit in Bueva's face on his way past him then called him, in English, a leprous dog who'd soon be put out of his misery.

Overhead a fighter jet razored its way across a cloudless blue sky, a US Marine flyover, Wilkes said in their earbuds, hanging out just in case. The Army Delta Force operators collected the weapons from the runway and shoved them into La Ballena's crippled sedan. Sergeant Minky gave the okay, and one final bazooka blast destroyed the vehicle.

Max checked his phone and spoke. "ETA Houston is approximately twenty-three hundred hours local Houston time, señor Xolo. That's roughly seven hours thirty minutes from now, with one stop in Venezuela for refueling, where we'll pick up some US federal air marshals. Next stop for you after that will be a US federal supermax prison."

2

Philadelphia, Pennsylvania

She walked the panhandler runway alongside cars stopped for the red traffic light at the intersection, Eighth and Vine streets in downtown Philly, near Chinatown.

Gus, pronounced *goose* in Spanish, and short for Agustina Gómez, was five feet in raised heels if she had any. She was careful not to let her red mittens interfere with her hand-scrawled message as she walked. Her cardboard sign had large, legible block print in black: *Tired, hungry,* plus today's closing argument, *running for president.*

At fifteen, Gus was already a semi-pro at this. Frosty breath, her hair tucked under her Philly Phanatic plush green dangle hat, her large, heart-shaped sunglasses had frames that blinked in red, flushing her waify Latina face. Today's outfit included a torn, mint-green neck scarf. She gripped a plastic bucket, also in green, a piney color to go with the holidays, with a gray handle, also plastic. Not much of her was visible beneath her accents and her outerwear.

She mouthed her primary message to each motorist behind their closed windows, inside their heated cars. "Spare change please, spare change, anything and everything helps."

Eye contact worked, especially with tourists, and especially if an occupant was female.

"Sí, muchas gracias, ma'am..."

"Sí, God bless you, miss..."

No lawn chair or stool, else the motorists would think she was lazy, not working hard enough for their charity. She certainly never showed her phone, or prospective donors would verbally deride her for not being authentically destitute and homeless. A valid objection, because she wasn't.

She did the math constantly in her head while she worked, tallying how good the take was for the day so far, for a Saturday, for the time of day it was, for the weather, for the costume, for her props, and for the last line of the message on the cardboard, comparing these variables to those from her other begging efforts. In this outfit, and today being cold but bright, and this day of the week, with this message, Gus would clear $200, maybe $225, for four hours of work. Over fifty bucks an hour. Money she couldn't make anywhere else because she was underage and a Latina immigrant. Unless she wanted to become a sex worker, and she'd never let that happen.

Both days each weekend, two other days during the week after school, other times when she could fit it in, and at different intersections around Center City Philly—after over two years at this, she knew what she was doing. Saving money plus collecting the data she needed to make her next day of panhandling more lucrative at collecting and saving even more money. If she ever had a chance at completing college entry applications, her essay would tell them what she'd learned and earned as a panhandler, and schools would fight over her. Or so she fantasized.

But for now, she was accumulating a stash, and she had a plan for it. She'd put the plan in motion very soon.

Tomorrow's sign would be *Tired, hungry, looking for my dad.* Her best closing line, an attention getter, and always good on a Sunday, when motorists and tourists were feeling the most benevolent and more spiritually vulnerable. It would be a $300 day, maybe $325. This sign's last line was also the one that meant the most to her, the one truest to her cause, with Gus intending to find her peruano father and sister, wherever they were, or find confirmation that she should stop looking for them.

Her English was accented but good, and her Philly vocabulary was growing, even the new additions. Like *jawn*, Philly's all-purpose, all-occasion stand-in for every noun in the English language.

Gus checked her Barbie wristwatch. It was close to five p.m. Quitting time for today. She packed up, folded her cardboard sign, stuffed everything into her backpack, and said a prayer for her missing family, the bag stirring up memories bad and good, from Texas, the Rio Grande, Mexico, and farther south, all the way back to Perú. She emptied her take from her bucket into her bag, slipped the bucket over her bicycle's handlebars and the backpack over her shoulders, and climbed onto the seat. Next stop, farther into town, would be Macy's on Market Street, a store she hadn't been to in months. Her high-end Barbie wristwatch would need to go into a secret pocket in her backpack, away from today's monetary proceeds from the street corner. She'd stolen the watch at her last Macy's visit, at the height of Barbie-mania.

Gus locked her bike's wheels into a rack. Not a high-end bicycle, but an old, silver Schwinn, a garage sale special, something no one would want to steal, but she locked it anyway. She removed her mittens. Under them were her latex gloves. An affectation of sorts for her, but there was more to it.

Macy's occupied the first three floors of the Wanamaker Building, a historic Philly landmark. Gus headed to Customer Service and handed over her backpack, taking a token for it in return. To the jewelry counters next.

"Hi," Gus said to the lady behind the counter.

"What do you want?" the clerk said. Gus's Phanatic hat screamed "weird" and "no money," her visible blue latex gloves screaming "weirder."

Beautiful fake tan, good makeup, good high-end pageboy haircut, blonde from a bottle, fifties, and not cheerful, she read Gus as someone needing shooing. Ten feet away, another fifty-ish female counter person assisted another customer, a well-dressed man. That transaction was the one piquing Gus's interest, not any transaction that could come from, hypothetically, Gus's exchange with this uptight clerk whose pursed lips highlighted her wrinkle lines around them.

"That men's bracelet," Gus said, pointing inside the counter display, "is that costume jewelry?"

"No."

"How about that one?"

"No."

"I have money, you know," Gus said, not that she intended to spend any of it.

"I sincerely doubt you have enough."

"Where is the costume jewelry?"

Gus waited, her clerk harrumphing, Gus listening closely to the nearby conversation, the well-dressed man and the counter clerk discussing price. The black-gold tennis necklaces the clerk showed him were beautiful. Over two thousand dollars each.

"Another part of the store," her salesperson said, "try Juniors." The clerk eyed a female shopper at the corner of the counter and stranded Gus, no words in parting.

No problem. Gus wasn't there to buy anything, but she was there to acquire something, anything, of value. She'd heard the price of the tennis necklace in the man's hands, not the one he'd lost interest in and that the clerk had left unattended on the counter longer than she should have.

Gus wandered the aisle, engrossed in her phone, straying from the straight and narrow, a zig here, a zag there, moving closer to the necklace, her peripheral vision engaged to the max. Four steps away, three, two—she would snatch it up quicker than a frog could catch a fly...

The forgetful clerk retrieved the necklace before Gus could strike, Gus late by a split second. The young pro that Gus was, she didn't flinch while she surfed more of the counter space, still interested in her phone, reaching the corner of the counter, turning left, then left again, a third left, then a fourth, circumnavigating the perimeter until she arrived where she'd started. The transaction between the well-dressed man and the sales clerk was finishing up in front of her, the merchandise changing hands. Gus continued her meandering, slow stride, her head still buried in her phone, until she bumped into him.

"Sorry, sir."

A hustling Gus made it to the store's revolving door front entrance but not through it. The hand on her shoulder belonged to a burley Latino store detective in plainclothes. He spun her around, the short, five-feet-nothing Gus barely reaching his chest. "Empty your pockets, miss."

"But..."

"Empty them, or I search you."

"You can't touch me, I'm a kid, I will scream—"

"Spare me, chica, you're on video pickpocketing that man. Empty them."

He found a Macy's jewelry box with a tennis necklace in it, $2,200 retail, in her jeans pocket along with the Customer Service token for her backpack. "Let's go. Security office."

In the office, monitors showed footage from too many cameras for her to count. The door stayed open to maintain propriety. The store detective sat her at a table and leaned against it to deliver the bad news.

"The police have been dispatched, kiddo. The man you pickpocketed is pressing charges. Some advice to you, chica. First, the cops will be majorly pissed at having to book you, Miss..." he checked her ICE ID, "Gómez, so don't misbehave in their squad car. They won't like that. Second..." he reached behind him and pulled her backpack forward, "we retrieved your bag from Customer Service. We went through it. There's money in there, loose, I'm guessing a coupla hundred bucks in small bills and coins. Your sign, too. You shouldn't be walking the streets asking people for money, young lady. Someone will hurt you."

The doorway behind him filled with a female Philly cop and her partner. The security guard pushed Gus's backpack at her. "Here, so you don't forget it again."

A cop intercepted it while his female partner produced a set of handcuffs and pulled Gus to her feet.

"I woulda come back for it later, señor," Gus said, her smile sweet and innocent. It preceded some snark. "I always do."

"Stay out of my store, chica. You're now banned."

3

Microwaveable meals from the 747 freighter galley. Sliced turkey, stuffing, mashed potatoes, some green beans. An All-American dinner, refrigerated leftovers from commercial flights out of Houston over the year-end holidays. Max had spirited them in from airlines Fend Aerospace did business with. Bottled water, coffee, cans of soda, and as a special treat, Lone Star beer in longneck bottles. The National Beer of Texas. The team had cases of it belowdecks, a reward for everyone for the flight home in anticipation of celebrating a job well done. Mission accomplished, and with La Ballena in custody and no good-guy casualties, the team, with the exception of the two federal air marshals picked up in Venezuela, imbibed. La Ballena ate what they all ate, but he had to settle for water. There would be no aid, and minor comfort only, to the enemy, a Department of State mandate.

A complainer for the whole trip, their prisoner did so in excellent English. Too hot, too cold, too thirsty, a headache, I'm hungry, and "you guys will all be dead after my hombres get through with you." The aircraft was seventy-five minutes from their destination, ETA 2250 hours at George Bush Intercontinental, north of Houston.

La Ballena, in leg irons and cuffs, was locked down and belted into the seating behind the flight deck. Spacious, with plenty of legroom—delivering on the minor comfort aspect—and on other 747s, this qualified as first class, but on this one, these were the only commercial passenger seats. An air marshal accompanied his visits to the lavatory.

The first two bio breaks were uneventful. "I need to use the bathroom," La Ballena called across the aisle, for visit number three. The air marshal produced the keys for his lockdown in the seat, unlocked the chain that connected their prisoner to the floor, then unlocked the one that connected his feet to his hands. Outside the lavatory, the marshal unlocked the handcuffs. The lav door remained open, no privacy, security demanding transparency. Plus he was a murderous-SOB-drug kingpin-warlord, so at the federal prison level, the air marshal taunted, "You'll need to get used to using the can in front of an audience, Mr. Whale."

La Ballena finished up his business, washed up, checked himself in the mirror, then held out his wrists pending re-cuffing. The marshal fumbled the reconnection, a momentary lapse in coordination. La Ballena was quick to react. His hands got predatory busy, moving in a blur to the deputy marshal's throat, pulling him into La Ballena's face where he sank his teeth into the Fed's nose, ripping at nasal cartilage while feeling for the marshal's handgun. His hand connected, but the strap holding the gun in its holster didn't budge—

The second air marshal tackled him, crushing La Ballena against the bulkhead where the marshal wielded his baton against the prisoner's head, knocking him out in two blows, then delivering more for good measure.

Trent was out of his seat and hovering, his Ka-Bar drawn, when Max arrived alongside their prisoner. One air marshal's face was buried in a blanket, bloody from the deep bite to his nose, La Ballena's mouth and chin bloodied by that bite. Blood splatters on the floor and on the second marshal's jacket and hands came from the skull-cracking he'd delivered to their prisoner, now unconscious.

Trent administered first aid to the marshal's nose, a deep gash that would require surgery to repair one if not both nostrils, pressure keeping the bleeding down until Trent could attach wadded gauze then adhesive tape to hold the gauze in place. Max and the second marshal dragged La Ballena across the aisle.

When they were finished, La Ballena was re-secured to his seat, his head bandaged. They encircled his body and the fully reclined seat with duct tape, turning him into a fat, gray mummy in semi-repose.

Later, their prisoner begged for another visit to the lavatory. No one seemed to hear him.

At 2300-plus hours, almost midnight, Max and the team's Con Air mission ended. The 747 taxied to the tarmac near terminal E, George Bush Intercontinental, then shut down. Two ambulances awaited their arrival. One would be dispatched to the nearest hospital to repair a US marshal's torn nose. The second had an hour's drive north to the Polunsky Unit supermax prison in Livingston, Texas, to deposit La Ballena directly into its infirmary. His pants were soaked in urine and filled with feces. Post his attack, every time he'd asked to use the lavatory, they said it was occupied.

Now close to one a.m., with an audience of US marshals, the 747 pilot Jesus, copilot Max, and the offloading Delta Force, two ambulance techs cut La Ballena out of the rest of the tape and hauled him off the plane. They stripped him naked and sponged him down with cold water from a bucket, wrapped his head in gauze, and pulled an orange jumpsuit onto his large body. The leg irons and chains and duct tape returned. Strapped tightly onto a gurney, they rolled him to the rear of the ambulance where he would join a motorcade of four police on motorcycles and additional US marshals in two sedans.

La Ballena lifted his bandaged head while the techs collapsed the stretcher. He found Max among the crowd. "I will never forget this humiliation, señor Fend," he managed, adding an if-looks-could-kill sneer.

Max nodded. "I won't either," he said. "This is epic."

"You will not be able to hide from me," La Ballena added. A deputy marshal climbed inside behind the gurney and told their drug kingpin to shut the hell up. The door sealed them in.

"Adios," Max said to the closed door. "Happy matriculation into our prison system."

The ambulances gone, Max said his goodbye to his pilot Jesus, who was about to catch a flight out as a passenger, returning to South America. Max congratulated Sergeant Minky and his Delta Force team, all waiting on a military helicopter transport.

"I suppose it's back to the day job," Max said to Trent. Trent would hitch a ride with the Delta Force. "Where are you headed?"

"Fort Sam Houston in San Antonio. Orders are pending."

Trent's gaze at Max was penetrating. He gripped Max by the head, pulled him in close, forehead to forehead, eye to eye.

"I so wanted to waste him, Max. I don't know if I can be talked off that ledge the next time I get orders like this. Love you much, brother."

He'd had six hours sleep in his Turtle Bayou, Texas, long-term house rental, a six thousand square foot, six-bedroom hacienda on a dozen acres with a view of man-made Lake Aranuac. At the moment, because Renee was traveling, Max was the house's only occupant. He stood in front of a TV towel-drying his head at nine a.m., watching a press conference from Livingston, Texas. It was news of La Ballena's capture and transport to a supermax prison for holding, as reported by the Department of Homeland Security in conjunction with the Drug Enforcement Administration.

Last night, Max was too tired to celebrate their successful mission so he decided to do it this morning over breakfast. He popped open a cold bottle of Lone Star then removed the towel on his head, his hair dry enough. He settled into the sofa shirtless and sockless, his gym-maintained body in gym pants, a beer in hand and a new bag of Doritos on the sofa. His feet on the coffee table, he paged through his phone, listening to the TV news in the background.

"Balea Xolo, alleged Peruvian drug kingpin, will be arraigned today on seven indictments from seven different federal courts, including one here in Texas," the Department of Justice attorney said. "Drug trafficking, intent to distribute, conspiracy association..."

Another notch in Max's CIA belt as a freelance contractor. His handler, Wilkes, tried to call him multiple times in the past twenty minutes. Max didn't pick up, didn't want to hear from him, wanted some time away from the Feds. He'd pass on hearing the kudos, thank you, because Wilkes's attaboys often preceded a new covert request. A love-hate relationship between them, the love part a more recent development, the hate and resentment part growing from the Agency asking him to do the impossible time and time again. Max was currently overwhelmed with Fend Aerospace's participation in NASA's Artemis mission, working here in Turtle Bayou as an off-site arm of the Johnson Space Center contingent out of Houston. Max decided Wilkes and the Agency needed to give him some room today.

The press conference DOJ attorney stayed with his drone-like delivery: "...money laundering, organized crime, illegal possession of firearms, kidnapping, murders in multiple cities..."

One person he did want to hear from was Renee, who'd been hanging out with Canadian astronauts in Quebec, working with the Canadian Space Agency on NASA's *Gateway*, a space station that was expected to orbit the Moon in support of the Artemis program. Renee, with Canadian and US citizenship, was on Fend Aerospace's payroll as a contractor, was also on the Artemis project, and was on Max's mind as his long-term girlfriend, whom he hadn't seen in a week. And like Max, Renee LeFrancois was still on the Agency's payroll on a project-by-project basis. Unlike Max, she wasn't a billionaire, so receiving a paycheck still meant something to her.

The Artemis mission: return to the Earth's moon in 2026 and begin to colonize it, with long-range plans to use it as a springboard for travel to Mars. Fend Aerospace's NASA partnership included working on the Commercial Lunar Payload Services program—CLPS—and the development of autonomous commercial lunar landing modules. NASA's version of interplanetary FedEx, UPS, and Amazon Prime combined.

The DOJ spokesperson concluded the presser. "Mr. Xolo's arraignment will be in Houston. That's all we have for you now."

A grand jury. After the seven indictments came the elaborate government-orchestrated sting that included Max Fend in the lead. Up next for La Ballena, arraignment and a plea, then jail with no bail. A trial expected to produce multiple convictions, long prison sentences, then incarceration for the rest of his life, or maybe worse. Unlike with the extradition of Joaquín "El Chapo" Guzmán from Mexico to the US years earlier, no deal was necessary with any country's government to keep La Ballena from facing a death sentence for multiple murder charges in the state of Texas and elsewhere. They'd done an end run around the Peruvian government, found him, conned him, and now, following what Wilkes said to Max in uncharacteristic frankness on the mission's front end, "We learn what we can about his operation and its reach, then we hope to fry him."

Max's phone buzzed. He looked at his screen. Not Wilkes. Renee. From the depths of hell to nirvana in a split second.

"Hey, Wonder Woman. Crushing on you, *eh*, this very minute, honey. How's the Canadian Space Agency, *eh*?" When she didn't bite at the poor joke, "Seriously, when does your flight get into Houston? I'll have someone pick you up."

"Someone?" she said, disappointed. "My plane arrives at two fifteen this afternoon. Why not you?"

"*Me. I'm* the someone. Gotcha, hot stuff. Or at least I'll be in the car," as in Max had a driver lined up for the short trip.

"Good to hear. The Canadian Space Agency is great, and the astronaut assigned to the program is great, too. By the way, someone I have here wants to talk with you."

"Hey. Getting all chummy with some studly Canadian astronaut royalty, are we? Sure, put him on."

"Hi, Max," Wilkes said.

Bait and switch. No click on the phone, Wilkes had been part of the call —Renee just hadn't announced him. She snickered, then raised her voice. "Got *you*, Max. I'm hanging up. See you at the airport."

"Not funny, Renee," Max said before she dropped off. "What do you want, Caleb? I am super busy with Fend Aerospace responsibilities today."

"Sure you are," Wilkes said. "You're probably holding a beer, eating potato chips, and watching the press conference."

Max put the beer bottle down. "Am not. Look, no new missions for a while, Wilkes, okay? In case you didn't know, we're going to the Moon, and my company's in the middle of it. And I'm not eating potato chips."

"Doritos," Wilkes said.

"Fine. What do you need from me?"

"I, too, have someone on the line with me, Max. Hold on."

Max heard Wilkes's phone change hands. When it stopped moving, he was greeted with a deep, cultured voice. "Hello, Max, can you hear me?"

Oh my. Not just any deep, cultured voice.

Max stood, suddenly felt underdressed and under a microscope, regardless of knowing that the cameras in and around his estate rental were all secure and not transmitting any part of him anywhere he didn't want them to, and most of all, not to the one place he was now concerned this phone call had been sent: the White House.

"Mister President?"

"Speaking."

Another internalized oh-my. New US President Matthew Vaughn. RIP beloved Former President Faye Windcolor. Cancer, while in office.

"I guess we can't put one past you, Max. I just called to thank you for all your support and personal involvement in La Ballena's capture. For your in-person participation, your deep pockets, your perseverance, and putting your life on the line. You're the only billionaire I know who's this hands-on with doing anything like this. So well done, and with no casualties, either."

"Thank you, Mr. President."

"You're welcome, Max. The punishment never equals the crime, especially when murders are involved, but La Ballena will be made to pay for them either by spending his life behind bars or by copping a squat on Old Sparky. You did good here, Max Fend. Hopefully all else is good with you as well."

Frankness and the occasional crude comment—Max liked that in his presidents. "Yes, Mr. President, we're good. You're welcome."

"Wonderful. I have to get back to work, and you do, too, putting people on the Moon. I hope that translates to another congratulatory call from a president on that accomplishment, too, and I hope to be the person making that call."

"Me too, Mr. President. Thank you."

The president left the conversation, leaving Wilkes and Max the last two on the call.

"Okay then, Max, I've gotta go, too. Oh, wait, I almost forgot...There's something else I need to bring up with you."

Surprise, surprise. Another mission in the queue, damn it. Max could sidestep the request by hanging up, or he could decline it. A billionaire could do either, and it was something he often thought about but rarely did.

"What?" Max said, resigned.

Max's doorbell chimed.

"That will be a case of Lone Star, no strings attached. My treat," Wilkes said. "Gotcha."

4

Gus was forced to remove her outer clothing at the precinct. They also had her backpack, with its small false pocket, something she'd sewn herself, the idea and its creation learned from an internet hack. It was a DIY inside another pocket where she kept emergency money. Today, it hid her Barbie Rolex. She peeled everything off, mittens, blinking sunglasses, scarf, dangle Phanatic hat, and her well-worn Eddie Bauer waterproof safari coat. She was down to her Lady Gaga T-shirt, jeans, sneakers, and gloves.

"Don't steal any of my money," she said. "I counted it."

"Sure you did," the police sergeant said, lifting out a few crumpled dollar bills. He returned them and zipped the bag up. "Relax, Miss Gómez, we'll keep it safe." He waited. "You're not done."

She made eye contact with him as best she could through the glint of his glasses. "Not taking anything else off, perv."

"The leather pouch attached to your waist, plus those latex gloves—off," he said. "Latex gloves under mittens? Wait, I get it, you're a Latina Doogie Howser. Sorry, never mind, you have no idea who that is. Finger-prints first, then we do a mug shot. Take the gloves off, then the prints, then you give me the pouch, then we do your close-up."

The cop, older and paunchy, centered a live fingerprint scanner about the size of an iPad on the desk behind Intake. "Step behind the counter, miss, and we'll get this done. Gloves off."

She'd never been fingerprinted before. She didn't want to do this.

He turned the scanner on, revealing its blank green screen. He wiggled his fingers, beckoning her compliance. "It won't hurt a bit, miss. I promise."

One thing that always worried her, with good reason, was showing her hands. Gus peeled the first latex glove off, slipping it past her wrist then pulling it off her fingers, the sergeant not paying attention, busy shuffling papers. She peeled off the second, folded both gloves, and placed them to the side. On reflex, she balled her hands up tight, her fingernails digging into her palms.

"Open your hands, miss," he said. "Place your palms down on the desk."

She sighed and uncurled her fingers. Her hands sweaty, she pressed them against her jeans to dry them. Palms now flat on the desk, Gus glared at him, expectant.

The sergeant's eyes stayed focused on them for an extra beat. "Whoa. Jesus. What do we have here?"

Gus quickly re-clenched her fingers, tucking them back inside their palms.

Supernumerary was one name for the trait, polydactyly was another. Peruvian immigrant Gus Gómez, not quite sixteen, was a freak to anyone outside her small village of Gente de la Luna, Perú. Six knuckled fingers on each hand. Five perfectly formed digits and a thumb, the extra finger a side-by-side duplicate of the middle or "tall man" finger, the one a person might use to issue the physical manifestation of an F-bomb.

The sergeant blinked hard, resettled his glasses for another look, but couldn't help staring, the rest of the precinct oblivious, going about its busy, chaotic Saturday night business.

He raised his head to meet her eyes, showing more interest in her now, but she knew it was to see if this supernumerary oddity manifested itself elsewhere, an extra eye maybe, three nostrils, maybe something else. She knew the drill. Her hands made people uncomfortable.

"I...I've never seen this before. Wow. Herb, c'mere and look at this..."

She translated his newfound interest in her: *hey, look at the freak.*

Rolling her fingerprints would now turn into a major show for the precinct, other cops crowding the sergeant's desk.

"Thirteen impressions in all, Miss Gómez," the sergeant explained. "You'll put your fingers against this green screen on the scanner, and it will take the pictures. The first impression will be your right four fingers together, in your case, five, the next impression the left five together. Then two thumbs side by side. After that, I'll need to roll each one. Let's go."

The suspense built. Where would the extra two fingerprints go—there were only five boxes for each hand on the digital scanner...

"Give me a second, miss. I need to check something."

Back from his laptop, he reached for her right hand. "Okay. Your pinkies lose out per department documentation. We won't be doing single prints of them. Okay, let's finish this up."

The cop audience collectively exhaled. With the last of the prints rolled, the audience dispersed, the din of the police station returning. But Gus had heard the comments.

Freak. Is the circus in town? Sideshow...Ripley's...

"You'll go into lockup in a minute, miss. By yourself, so relax, you'll be fine. One last thing."

The drama wasn't over.

"That leather pouch. Hand it over please."

Gus laid her hand on the cracked leather bag with a drawstring tied onto her waist, an amulet tucked loosely inside with room to spare. She gripped the leather tightly in her fist, protecting it, her mouth getting moist. She pursed her lips, about to lose her tough little streetwise chiquita persona in a big way.

"Please no, Officer. I, um...please. *Please* no..." A tear formed in each eye, on the verge of spilling over. "It is something I can't lose. It is important to me. Mi familia, my people, I miss them. Please."

The cop hesitated, blinking at her distress, at her trying to control it, Gus trying hard not to give in to the pain. He put down a pen, reached over, and placed each of his large cop hands gently atop hers on the desk, his ten weathered fingers over her twelve, and he squeezed each hand once before holding on to them.

"I'm sorry it has to be this way, Miss Gómez. The pouch will be safe. I promise we won't lose it. You'll be arraigned shortly. When you're released, you'll get it back."

He patted her hands and brought the tiny, five-foot-nothing, teenaged Gus Gómez back around to the front of the counter. Another cop looked at him funny, but the desk sergeant's headshake and sour face warned him to back off—a little compassion never hurt anyone. The sergeant waited for her to hand him the pouch. She untied it from a belt loop, kissed the worn leather, and burst into tears as he accepted it. He did a quick check inside the pouch and removed its contents, a gray-black stone. He catalogued the stone and the pouch and placed them aside.

"Look. Miss Gómez. You need to relax. We've contacted your foster care facility folks already. You shouldn't be here long. But my message to you here is, the best way for you to not have to give up any more of your personal belongings—the best way to stay out of jail—is to not rip off department stores or their customers in the first place. Got that?"

While in the Texas detention center cages, Agustina had been an aggressive, disruptive, angry thirteen-year-old, fighting with other teens, with the Immigration and Customs Enforcement agents, and with social workers. She'd remained in ICE custody more than a week, exceeding the normal seventy-two hours. The female ICE agent had called Agustina to the fence. The agent spoke to her in Spanish through it.

"That hat." The agent gestured at Agustina's ball cap with the Eagles logo, dark green above her black, shiny hair. "It is getting you into trouble around here."

"American football," a perky Gus said. "Super Bowl. Go Eagles." It had been a present from a kind American tourist visiting the Amazon.

The agent narrowed her eyes. "I have news, then I have advice. First, that hat has earned you a trip to Philadelphia with other difficult adolescents. Let Philly ICE deal with you. Second, you need to calm down, muchacha, or they will waste no time putting you on a plane and sending you back to Perú."

"But mi familia," she pleaded. "Papá, Gaby, Tío Ernesto—where are they? I can't go," she said, sobbing. "They won't find me..."

And after more than two years, they hadn't found her, with her unaware if anyone was even looking for her. Her new home became a community foster care facility in Philadelphia, a sanctuary city. In those two years, she'd learned to read, write, and speak English, and learned to work an urban farm. Some schooling in the local high school, some online learning at the foster care home due to Covid. She learned to defend herself, how to stretch and protect limited resources, and how to survive, in an urban environment and elsewhere.

She'd never felt abandoned, but she'd never stopped looking for her family. She was one of thousands of immigrant kids separated from their parents at the Mexico border and sent to foster care facilities around the country. New York, Chicago, Philadelphia, and other big-city environments. More than 5,000 was the number she'd heard, all of them fallout from the country's short-lived zero-tolerance policy. "Paper trail screwups," ICE called the misallocated kids, Gus among them. "They'll turn up somewhere." The screwups turned up all around the country, but so far, many of their parents hadn't.

It angered her, shamed her, toughened her. *ICE* knew where she was, and *she* knew where she was, so far away from her point of entry. Far away from the last time she'd seen her father, sister, or uncle. But when it came to reconnecting her with her family, her ICE transitional care community parents were little to no help, bordering on cruel.

...Deported. Or maybe they're dead. Stop bothering me. This was Miss Deborah, as in Ms. Deborah Desissi, an ICE transitional foster care parent, her patience waning, Gus having worn out her welcome only a few weeks into her more than two-year stay. Early on, Miss Deborah had pulled up an online photo from an ICE database and showed it to her.

Look closely at this, Agustina.

Gus had seen other photos of what the Rio Grande could do, and had done, to some people crossing it, including parents with their babies, but she hadn't seen this one. A father with his arm around his baby daughter, the two of them facedown in the water on the river's swollen bank.

Your father and your sister. Sorry.

The clothing looked right, as did the hair. But with no facial validation, Gus refused to believe this was a picture of them.

"Peruvian drug lord La Ballena captured and brought to the United States to stand trial."

Gus worked on a Tastykake apple pie, the desk police sergeant having given up his dessert for her. She was being processed out of jail. She stopped midchew, mesmerized at a suspended flat-screen TV, reading the closed captions, absorbing what she could. A news reporter's video of a plane landing at an undisclosed airport, taken at night, cutting to a man on a hospital gurney surrounded by other men on the runway...the man's bandaged head and restrained body...him being loaded into an ambulance.

A dream, this video...oh my, this felt like a dream to her, had to be a dream...

A local nonprofit, an immigration watch group the precinct worked with, had handled Gus's release. The social worker and her immigration attorney had presented the paperwork, and her community care home owner, Miss Deborah, was ready to receive Gus. Miss Deborah's eyes drilled her. There'd be hell to pay when they got back to the facility for sure. Gus chewed, more slowly than before, oblivious to the scrutiny, focusing on the TV.

She knew who La Ballena was, what he'd done in Perú, *to* Perú, the good and the bad. What he'd given to her country, and her family—and what he'd taken away from them. She stopped eating the pie, her stomach rebelling. She swallowed away the discomfort.

The sergeant waved her up to the desk. Gus was slow, the TV news story riveting, absorbing all she could regarding La Ballena's capture.

"Sign here and here, Miss Gómez," the sergeant said, then had the immigration attorney sign the document as well. She scooped up her backpack and her personal belongings, gripping her leather pouch tightly, feeling it to make sure it contained what it should.

"Thank you, Sergeant, for the pie," she said, teary-eyed. "And for watching my stuff."

"Stay out of trouble, Miss Gómez," he said, nodding.

Miss Deborah's verbal drizzle in the car was nonstop, directed at Gus's most recent transgressions, talking a return to jail for her, or worse yet, deportation. Gus responded where she needed to, giving assurances she knew she wouldn't need to keep, because she'd decided tomorrow was the day. Tomorrow she would leave. She'd use the Barbie watch instead of the necklace to entice a friend at the community center. The black necklace she hadn't been able to steal at the store was supposed be the gift that would convince him to go. The gift would now need to be the Rolex Oyster Perpetual Barbie pink watch, eighteen karat gold with muchos diamonds and a dial made of pink opal, a stone so rare it was found only in the southern region of Perú. Or so the pawn dealer she didn't sell it to had said to her. Lucky for Gus she'd also "found" the gift-boxed watch in a woman's pocket on her way out of Macy's weeks earlier, which meant that, as soon as tomorrow, this lucky find would transition to her community home acquaintance Yadier Rolando, if she could talk him into leaving with her.

They arrived at the foster home, three brick stories that occupied two addresses on Jackson Street in South Philadelphia. Alone in her room, she opened her leather pouch and removed her stone talisman, much rarer than the pink opal face on the Barbie watch, the talisman also from Perú, from a creek bank inside the Amazon rainforest.

Smooth gray-black on one side, it had a jagged off-white surface on the other. Gus opened her mouth, moistened her tongue, and licked the jagged side of the stone once, her tongue tasting the salt in the fossil embedded in its porous exterior. She kissed it and returned it to the pouch.

Tonight would be her last night in Philadelphia.

She settled into her bed, held the pouch to her chest, and began a quiet, melancholic cry.

5

Sixth District, Philadelphia Police Department
400 N. Broad Street, Philadelphia, Pennsylvania

"Reverse that video," Cornell said. "Restart it. Stop. There. Right there. In her car, on her way to work at the ICE field office on Eighth Street. A Saturday afternoon shift, right?"

"Right," Detective Poole said. His desktop showed four images of the same car in each quadrant of the screen, the car traversing the streets of downtown Philly, street corner cameras picking up its movement.

They found the ICE worker murdered on the street there overnight, around ten p.m., after she left her Saturday shift. Maybe a robbery, maybe not, maybe a drive-by, maybe not, maybe gang-related, maybe not. Caucasian female in her thirties, she was shot twice on her way to her car, at close range. DOA at the hospital. The maybe-nots were winning so far, the police having no leads. The speculation was that it was a disgruntled undocumented immigrant about to get deported.

On the desktop screen, a silver Honda Civic. Her car had stopped at the streetlight at Eighth and Vine. Excellent video. A camera mounted on a utility pole showed the earlier images.

Cornell Oakley, Assistant Special FBI Agent in Charge, Philadelphia, wore a cookie-cutter business suit as standard FBI garb. He was at the police department's Sixth District precinct, working with Philly detectives, getting the lay of the land. The dead female was a clerk for ICE. With her being a federal employee, and the Feds wanting to look at all aspects, Cornell got the assignment.

"This footage is from when?" Cornell asked.

"Yesterday, two twenty-five p.m.," Poole said.

"Saturday. You have her elsewhere?'

"Cameras on the way down Tenth. She took a left onto Vine, the camera at Vine and Eighth picking her up. East on Vine until a right onto Eighth. South on Eighth to the Philly ICE office to clock in. Why are we looking at this, Agent Oakley?" Poole said. "This was all earlier in the day."

"You solve this case yet, Detective?"

"Well, no, of course not. We're..."

"That's why we're looking at it. All of it, because there doesn't seem to be any good reason why this woman was murdered. You have her on these cameras on other Saturdays, or other days, on the victim's way to work?"

"We haven't looked at other days yet. We didn't see the need..."

"Here's the need. If she's taking the same route to work each day, she's seeing the same landscape, the same street vendors, the same joggers, the same girl-watchers. And vice versa. Creatures of habit are easier victims. I'm sure you know that." Cornell leaned into the screen, intrigued by a new character in the frame. "Look at that looney-tune."

Green Philly Phanatic dangle hat, flashing sunglasses, green beach bucket, cardboard sign.

"Maybe she ran across the same panhandlers every day, too," Cornell said. "Wait. Slow that video down. Our victim's actually talking to the looney-tune girl at the corner. Damn, that's good resolution. What's her sign say?"

"It says she's running for president," Poole said.

"A sense of humor. Look, she's leaning into the victim's car window. That's being way too forward. It's like they know each other. I like her here, Poole. Can you guys pull more camera video on the dates coinciding with the victim's work schedule, for that location and others? To see if there are duplicate encounters between her and other people on her route to work, like this one."

"We can manage that. So what are we thinking, Oakley? A dealer?"

"Maybe. For us to find out. If so, I'm not sure who's the customer and who's the dealer here, either. Please snap off some photos of that panhandling kid running for president. We can start looking around."

Back with the detective on the same Sunday, late afternoon, and Cornell was on a roll, feeling good about his instincts. Two weeks of archived video showed a few people of interest. The same senior guy sitting on a bench many of the days feeding pigeons at Tenth and Nectarine, and who on the other days moved to the Vine Street Plaza, Tenth and Vine, with the same MO, maybe even the same pigeons. Their victim's Honda cruised the rightmost lane and slowed down to toss feed out her window for the birds. She held a few seconds to watch the birdseed hit the sidewalk and scatter. The man either waved at her as she passed or gave her the finger, the video resolution not good enough to distinguish between the two. Farther along her route, that goofy kid with the green dangle hat was in place again at Eighth and Vine, twice more on succeeding Saturdays, leaning into the ICE employee's silver Civic, the kid's sign with different wording, but the camera angle not picking it up.

Facial recognition software was in order for the kid. If they could get a good read, it was someone they would need to talk to.

"I'll look for a match in the FBI DBs," Cornell announced.

"Not necessary," Poole said. "We have her here already. One mug shot, in here yesterday, caught pickpocketing at Macy's. She was released on recognizance."

A seventy-point facial match out of eighty nodal points, according to the software. They had her name, address, and immigration status.

"The victim decided to press charges?" Cornell said. "For shoplifting? Against a teen?"

"Hey, his prerogative."

"That's just cruel. Okay then, let's go pick up our person of interest," Cornell said.

6

Max didn't expect needing to deal with more covert activity yet again today, on a Sunday, and he certainly didn't expect it to be from within his own company. A thousand Fend Aerospace employees were assigned to this 80,000-square-foot facility in Turtle Bayou. The brightest technological minds from around the globe.

He marched into a conference room adjacent to one of the labs. Waiting for him there, seated around a long table, were Fend Aerospace's Artemis program leads, department heads of Engineering, Aerospace, Propulsion, Payload, and—

"Who are you?" Max barked. He directed his question at a plump and pimply guy who could pass for a teenager, seated in a uniform at the near end of the table, eating a bagel with cream cheese.

"Grant, from Facilities Security, sir," the bagel-eater said, wiping his mouth. "Third shift."

Max took the open seat next to his chief of staff, Emily Soo. Mid-sixties, matronly, Korean, always serious, Emily was the best damn cat-herding chief of staff that Fend Aerospace had ever had. She'd held the same position for company president Charles Fend, Max's father, for decades, retiring when he did. She came out of retirement to become Max's cat herder for the Artemis project. "Why is he here, Emily?"

"Because he found it."

"*It?*" Max said.

"Yes. Let me start by summarizing the damage reports."

Emily had all the feedback, all the info collected from the department heads. Payload, Propulsion, Gateway Interfaces, Mechanical, Electrical, Mission Control, others—they all reported zero issues from any of the thousands of attempted hacker attacks overnight, routine for almost every night. None had generated any known breaches.

"But with End-Product Assembly, it's a different story," Emily said.

The main event. The reason for Fend Aerospace's partnership in the Artemis program. When fully functional, Fend Aero's *Blue Spectre* lunar lander would deliver NASA-sponsored payloads to the lunar surface, to help build a Moon base capable of human habitation with an eye toward deeper space exploration, including Mars. The target date for Fend Aerospace's first deliveries was November 2024. Twelve consignments aboard a robotic lander seven feet high and twelve feet in diameter. The lunar landing site NASA had picked was Mare Crisium, Latin for "Sea of Crises," in the Moon's northern hemisphere. Flat and 345 miles in diameter, the mare was 68,000 square miles in area. It was where the Soviets' Luna 15 probe crash-landed in 1969, and where the Soviet lunar mission Luna 24 successfully scooped up soil samples and returned them to Earth in 1976.

What was unique about *Blue Spectre* was its incorporation of major advances in artificial intelligence. Once deployed on the surface, it would observe, it would solve, and it would continue to learn.

Emily prodded. "Speak up, assembly team."

There'd been a full breach through a firewall. Hackers galore, rampaging through the files for the *Blue Spectre* assembly specs for the finished product. The breach lasted twelve seconds, the hackers smash-and-grabbing what they could. Equipment tolerances, payload info, mechanical specs, climate control, robot arm capabilities, custom-designed solutions...and leaving trap doors all over the code before the hack was discovered. Destructive instructions that could take days to unravel. The hackers wreaked some havoc and got away with pieces of the machinery puzzle, but—

"Not enough pieces, you're saying?" Max said to Emily. "And not how the pieces fit together?"

"Correct."

"No AI development data?"

"Correct."

"Essentially a bust, then?" Max's gaze went from face to face, soliciting responses, everyone nodding.

"Yes," Emily said, "but they now know more than they did. And because of the FBI arrest, they've lost their way in, which might make them more desperate, maybe even bolder. Fend IT Security discovered she was online overnight, working from home."

"She who?" Max asked.

"Fifi Hu, on our staff and assigned here, on location. Aerospace engineering graduate of MIT's AeroAstro program. Chinese, and unfortunately, we now know per the FBI and Homeland, she was working for the wrong side—China. The FBI walked her out of the facility in handcuffs this morning after she reported for work, just before you arrived. Grant here, from Facilities Security, was the one who went to IT Security when he saw it overnight."

"Saw what?" Max said, looking bewildered at Emily, then Grant. "Exactly what was the 'it'?"

"Um..." Grant's eyes widened. "Yes, see, I, um..."

"He was gaming, Max," Emily said. "No way to sugarcoat it. Part of a multi-person, online, role-play video game. When a screen message flashed across his security shack desktop, in Chinese, while they were playing, he had to decide whether to out himself as playing video games while at work or stay quiet. He made the right decision and reported it."

Max shook his head, far from happy. Would he need to have this guy fired for gaming on Fend computers right after he blew the whistle on a commercial espionage threat? And how the hell did an online video game get through the firewall anyway?

"Sh-she, ah, set the game up," Grant stammered. "Fifi opened the firewall and downloaded it. Only the two of us were on then, her against me. I was playing the game of my life until that message interrupted us."

Emily explained. "Fifi let the game in. They played it nights on end, apparently, him during downtime on his shift, she from home. Her, him, others out there in the metaverse, too, but only the two of them were playing it last night." When she paused, Grant nodded his affirmation. "In the meantime, she also opened the door for hackers to enter through the game, one time only, something we're in the process of confirming, with that one time being last night. She did it on purpose. It was twelve seconds before anyone discovered the breach. She got greedy, left the door open too long, and got caught. We identified her through her gaming ID. And she did it while she was gaming with Grant, and only Grant. A message, some code in Chinese—something that got through from the Chinese hacker universe—and Grant saw it."

The room stayed quiet, waiting on Max's reaction, then waited longer.

"Tell me the message you saw," Max said to Grant.

"See, that's the thing, Mr. Fend, sir. It was all in Chinese, except for the money and the words Cayman Islands. A US dollar sign and six numbers..."

"IT Security went to the FBI immediately," Emily said. "They translated the message. Wire transfer info, account number, a Cayman Islands bank account, the message was meant for Fifi. Grant's initial info—that he was gaming with her and no one else—sealed it for her, that it was her money."

"A Chinese spy on my payroll," Max said. "I'll be making a few internal calls about our background check process for new hires. Better yet, Emily, why don't you—"

"A full process review is already underway, Max."

"Good. Grant," Max said. "Your last name?"

"Trask, sir. Grant Trask."

"What the hell game were you and she playing that you'd risk your job over it?"

Grant picked nervously at his fingers. "*Zombie Chimps From Mars*, sir. I'm sorry. After I make the rounds around the facility, inside and out, it's, like, super boring during third shift. And the game, it's really nuts. And addictive."

Some of the department heads squirmed, averting their eyes, admissions of the game's popularity. Horrible posers.

Zombie Chimps From Mars had spread like wildfire after its release last year. The Artemis project was returning humans to the Moon, then onward to the next space frontier, Mars. How could the game not have taken Artemis project workers by storm?

"Yes. I know about it," Max said. He let that statement sink in while he read the room. "Except I play on my phone, Grant, and at home, and only on occasion. You should have restricted your gaming the same way."

"The firewall was quickly restored and checked," Emily said. "IT's first order of business after the breach. The game's gone from the OS and the databases."

"Fine. Okay. Everyone back to your battle stations, nothing more to see here. Except Emily and Grant, you stay."

The conference room cleared.

"Long story short, Grant," Max said, "we'll need to make some changes. I know, billionaire CEOs don't micromanage like this, but I'm the exception, at least today I am. Emily—"

"One step ahead of you, Max. Grant, he's not going to fire you," she said. Her eyes peered over her glasses at her boss, so like her matronly self. "Are you, Max?"

Max sighed. "No."

"Of course not," Emily said. "Grant, we'll look for something to supplement your downtime toward the end of your shift. That means no more gaming during company time, even on your phone, unless it's during your breaks or at lunch, and *only* on your phone.

"Max, I'm thinking that having him finish his nightly shifts with the IT Security folks might work. They really appreciated his awareness here. Grant has an associate's degree in cybersecurity. Maybe we can have him learn some additional skills..."

Renee hustled her stride up to close the short distance between her exit from the jet bridge to the terminal gate and the waiting Max. She grabbed him by the shoulders, pulled him in for an embrace, and planted a kiss with meaning. An old movie lip-lock, where the kissee's legs would buckle from so passionate a connection. Here, for Max, it produced close to the same result.

"Wow. Missed you, too, Renee."

In the Fend limo with a driver, Max put the privacy shield up. Another smooch and some cooing, but the rest of the encounter was to talk business. Artemis project business, not CIA business, but still all confidential, and some of it classified.

Fend Aerospace's participation in Artemis would help deliver shipments to the Moon as part of the massive CLPS contract. Renee, like Max, was still privately contracted and occasionally covert for the CIA. But even as CIA assets, they weren't cleared to know all aspects of Artemis. None of the program partners were. That meant numerous American companies like Fend Aerospace plus the Canadian Space Agency, the European Space Agency, the Japan Space agency, and other international partners knew the responsibilities within their own lanes, but not everyone else's.

"Barbarians at the gate, Renee."

"What happened?"

"China got into our data files. We had a lapse."

China's Lunar Exploration Program was on target to provide crewed missions to the Earth's moon in the 2030s. It had already made several drops onto the lunar surface. Soft-lander lunar rover/explorer *Yutu* in 2013, for exploration. A second lunar rover/explorer *Yutu-2* in 2019. In 2020 a sample-gathering Chinese lunar-rover mission returned from the Moon with almost four pounds of lunar soil. Additional sample return missions were scheduled throughout the rest of this decade. After that, fully human-crewed exploration.

Renee verbalized it. "They want the AI code, and how it interfaces with *Blue Spectre*, and vice versa."

"Correct. NASA—the Artemis project—is moving faster than they are," Max said. "After the Moon, the Chinese will set their sights on Mars, like we are. We meet with the NASA folks in a few days in Houston. To go over freight content. I'll debrief them on the breach."

"So we'll finally learn what some of the *Blue Spectre* consignments will be," Renee stated. "It took them long enough. It's not like Fend Aerospace is building the next generation lunar lander or anything."

"Some of the payloads, not all. Not unless our clearances get upgraded."

"Any chance of that?" she asked.

"When I tell them we had a Chinese spy on the payroll, and how she let the hackers in—probably not anytime soon."

7

Jackson Street, Philadelphia

Gus opened the door to the roof and left the warmth of the building. Snow and ice covered the wooden roof deck, and she was greeted with thirty or so degrees of frosty January air, but with no wind. Clear sky, stars, a magnificent full moon. Yadier was there, in a chaise lounge chair, bundled in a blanket and a thrift store UPenn football jacket over a hoodie, its red hood raised and covering a black slouchy cap. When they first met at the home two years ago, he'd corrected her mispronunciation of his name to *YAA-dee-ayy*, then told her he preferred Yadi. She'd told him she preferred Gus, as in *goose*, over Agustina. Yadi blew into his hands. His face and eyes were aglow from the iPad in his lap, his knees up and the iPad leaning against them, him doing what she'd expected he'd be doing, watching a football game. Not American football, but rather "fútbol," or in America, soccer. His favorite sport. It was what he'd played in the streets and playgrounds of their native Perú before he came to America, as parentless as she was.

A news story hit his iPad. A repeat of La Ballena's capture in Texas. In a frenzy, Yadi found other video of the capture on YouTube, bootlegged, the video already going viral. Pictures of La Ballena naked, with him getting hosed down on his way to jail. The story, when Gus was first aware of it, had buoyed her. Yadi didn't see it the same way. He cursed at the iPad screen.

"Hola," she said, after he'd calmed down.

"Hola, mi dulce amiga."

"I need to talk with you," her pitch began, with her staying with the Spanish.

"The chair is empty," he said.

She sat on the edge of a chaise lounge and faced him, her folded hands between her knees. In the distance, a burst of cheering from Lincoln Financial Field rose up, the brightly lit stadium visible from their roof, bettering the steady whoosh of passing traffic on Interstate 95 two blocks east. Airplanes with flashing lights neared and departed Philly's international airport. A helicopter hovered near the football field. Their home, a foster care facility, was in a residential block, a double rowhouse that spanned two addresses and had four all-brick stories, with a good view of the city's three professional sports stadiums clumped together, one of them currently lighting up the clear South Philly night. The noise from the stadium delayed the sales pitch she was about to make. They sat together, their silence mandated by Yadi's boisterous iPad and the cheering from the Philly stadium.

The fútbol game Yadi had been watching wasn't live. It was a replay of Perú's final game in the 2022 FIFA World Cup, with Perú losing to Australia. It was what Yadi always watched, Gus knew, when he was depressed, coming up to the roof to watch it, the same game over and over, because he was homesick for his prior life.

That, plus YouTube music videos. Hip-hop, rap, and what he called street thug music, by artists in the US and from back home in Perú. Lots of street thugs in Lima, he'd told her, and they had their own music, and he'd wanted to be one of them. Yadi had embraced the thug life as best he could in Lima and was doing the same here in Philly. Even the drugs, or at least their distribution. His personal experiences were far removed from Gus's and her background and her small village, her's bordering on primitive, at the edge of the Amazon rainforest.

Yadier "Yadi" Rolando, eighteen, taller than Gus by a foot, crushed on her. The prospect of a conquest, she knew. Streetwise and connected back home, he was streetwise in Philly now, too, but only somewhat connected, hanging with a small, tough crowd. He attended church regularly, more than he attended school. His agenda was burglaries, stolen cars, and stolen car parts, and he had a handgun Gus wasn't supposed to know about. He was party to these illegal activities, yet he'd never been caught, had never been subject to police scrutiny. Gus had panhandled, shoplifted, and did some pickpocketing, all of it borne of necessity, nothing as severe as Yadi, yet she'd been caught, and she was now in the system. Her arrest had helped her with the decision she'd made.

His crush on her would make her pitch to him easier. She could control him with it, she told herself. But she also felt she owed him, enough that she would tell him her plans.

"I am getting out of here, Yadi," she said in English. "Tonight. I'm going to the bus terminal for a ticket. I am leaving in an hour."

Yadi put his iPad down to study her. "No. This is a joke. And it is not funny. I...No, I don't believe you."

He swiveled in his seat, planting his feet on the roof deck. "Look here," he said, turning on his iPad again and cozying up to her. "I have some new music and some videos from Lima. They are fantastic. You should listen with me under the blanket, mi reina—"

She shrugged him away. "No. I am not your queen, Yadi, and I can't stay here anymore." It was a statement, not an opening argument. "I was caught stealing someone's jewelry. I need to leave before they decide to put me somewhere else. Or deport me. I need to look for my father and my sister. Tonight, I am going."

"Mi amor, no, no, that is not good. They are dead, your father and sister, gone forever. My family—they are gone, too, maybe deported, maybe dead. If you want to make it in this world now, you need to rely on your friends. Friends like Yadi. Me. I am your friend. I can take care of you if—"

"I know you are my friend," she said. "That is why I want you to come with me."

"You want me, to go with you? *Me?*" he said, skeptical. "The one you ignore at school, even though I watch out for you." His smirk became a scoff. "You are not thinking straight, amiga."

She spoke through his verbal stop sign. "You will need to decide

tonight," she said, ignoring his discount of her offer. "If you don't want to
go, I understand, but I am leaving tonight no matter what."

"You're right, I don't understand. Where are you going?"

"Texas. My point of entry to America. But I need to make stops on the
way, at ICE detention centers. I have a few leads on my papá."

"What will you use for money? Where will you stay? You are fifteen. You
will get hurt—"

"I have enough saved. I will sleep on the buses. I will find the people
who papá said we could stay with in Texas. Papá said they would help him
be a cowboy."

These were the peruano families she hadn't met because she'd been
sent to Philadelphia. She'd connected with them on the internet. They said
papá and her sister Gaby weren't with them, never had been, and they
didn't know where he was. She would go to them anyway.

Gus had a rather large stash of cash in her room, over $14,000. She
would take it and everything that she could carry, as in one of the home's
laptops, burner smartphones she'd already bought, and a few changes of
clothes, all stuffed into an oversized trailblazer backpack.

"The bus does not go everywhere, Gus. How will you make connections
once you get to a city?"

"I will have my bicycle. And I will put out my thumb."

A huff from Yadi here, a puff there, and more scoffing. Yet she knew he
was thrilled by the adventure of it, the sheer wantonness of it, and by her
asking him to join her.

"I am packed already, Yadi. At midnight, I am gone. I will ride my bike to
the Greyhound terminal. The bus I'm taking leaves at two a.m. If you
decide to come, I will have a present for you. But Yadi, you cannot bring any
drugs. No drugs, understand?"

His eyebrows raised, his mouth widening into a smile. "Got it. If I go
with you, no drugs. But you have a present for me? Is it what I think it is, mi
corazón?"

"No, not that, stop it. But you will like this present a lot for sure."

She pulled at his hand to have him stand. On her toes, she leaned up to
kiss his cheek, then gave him a tight hug. A hug she hoped was not a goodbye, because she would need him.

Gus climbed off her bike and walked it to the entrance of the new, temporary Greyhound bus terminal in a storefront on Market Street, Philadelphia. It cost extra to take the bike with her, but she'd need it at the end of each of her destinations. A shout from across the busy street stopped her. It came from in front of a twenty-four-hour coffee shop.

"Gus!" Yadi called in Spanish and waved. "Look what I got!"

He leaned against a beater of an SUV, silver, dirty with some dents, and double-parked with its flashers on. His smile was ear to ear, clearly proud of himself. Gus crossed the street and fist-bumped him at the rear of the vehicle. Yadi fumbled with the keys and unlocked the tailgate, then lifted it by hand. The vehicle was old enough to have preceded the term "SUV."

"I borrowed it. It is our ride. No GPS, so I will use my phone. Your bike will fit in back. If you think you still need it."

"I am taking it."

First her backpack, then the bike joined a long, stuffed duffel and two cardboard boxes of nonperishable food with generic labels. Things she recognized as having come from the community home's kitchen that were also, she knew, "borrowed."

"By borrowed, do you mean—?"

"Yes, stolen. The car was running, the keys in the ignition. Thank goodness the lines at convenience stores are always long, and so many of the people in them estúpido."

8

Cornell Oakley, with Detective Poole and a local uniform, pushed the doorbell for one of the front doors. One twenty a.m. Two other uniforms watched the amber-lit back alley behind the community home that took up two addresses in South Philly, in case Agustina Gómez tried to leave through a back door.

"A reminder, team, that she's only a person of interest, not a suspect," Cornell said into his earbuds, "and she's only five feet tall." Cornell eyed the row homes across the street. "This block has eyes. Let's not create any viral footage here."

"Copy," came back in quadruplicate.

A second ring of the doorbell, then a strong knock. A moment later, the curtains rustled. An older, bleary-eyed, white female opened the door a crack. "Police?"

"Yes. And FBI." Cornell badged her. "Sorry to wake you, ma'am. You are Ms. Desissi, correct? Good. We're here to speak with one of the teenagers under your care, a Miss Agustina Gómez, about a case we're working on. I'm Assistant Special FBI Agent in Charge Oakley out of the Philadelphia office. This is Detective Poole, Philadelphia police. May we come in?"

The girl residents lived upstairs in the left row home, the door the team had selected; the boys were upstairs in the right one. Ms. Desissi acknowledged that Miss Gómez was a resident.

"What did she do?"

"I can't go into any details, Ms. Desissi. She might have seen something happen in Center City, maybe witnessed a crime. We just want to talk with her."

"I'll bring her down."

The main floor of this ICE foster home was more like a clubhouse, spreading across both addresses. The front living space opened into a community dining area followed by a kitchen loaded with institutional-sized appliances. Past the kitchen, two sets of sliding glass doors led to a long deck the width of both houses. The eight immigrant kids who lived here, Cornell decided, were fortunate, the accommodations quite nice.

Ms. Desissi, upstairs now, was taking too long.

Cornell stood at the bottom of the steps and called to the third floor hallway. "Ms. Desissi? Ma'am? Should we come up?"

The ICE foster parent rounded the corner of the stairs and hustled down the steps on old legs. Out of breath at the bottom, she advised, "She's not in her room, not anywhere on the third floor, and she's not on the roof. We do a bed check at eleven thirty each night. She was here then. Follow me. She has a bicycle she keeps under the deck. My husband is on the top floor of the home next door where the male guests have their rooms. He'll meet us out back."

The two proprietors and Oakley's enforcement contingent waited for the husband to open the shed that housed the bike rack. Ms. Desissi looked over all the bicycles, then spoke. "Hers isn't here."

Now came the Q&A, with Cornell and Detective Poole doing the questioning, the home's administrators doing the answering.

...Yes, she sometimes sneaks out at night, but it's infrequent.

...She has a few girlfriends at the high school. We'll give you their names.

...We have pictures of her on her bike. She dresses a little odd sometimes. Her English is excellent.

...Her mother is dead. Her father and sister might be in country, might not, might be dead, might have been deported.

Their surprise visit over, Cornell and Detective Poole were back in their vehicle still parked outside the home, coordinating their next steps. Visit her school tomorrow, check with the girlfriends, circulate pictures of her alone, plus her on her bike, plus her shoplifting mug shot. What they didn't want to happen might have happened already—she might be gone. Maybe her decision, maybe someone else's. Law enforcement would need to scour the city for her, a fifteen-year-old Peruvian female panhandler and pickpocketer, maybe five feet tall, maybe a drug dealer or user, and now maybe a missing person.

A tap on the window of Detective Poole's unmarked sedan, on Oakley's side. It was Mr. Desissi. Cornell powered the window down.

"It seems we're missing another one. Come back inside. We'll give you what you need to know about him. He's been more of a problem for us."

9

Two thirty a.m. Yadi and Gus cruised south on I-95, Yadi keeping to the speed limit. They were almost through Delaware. The good news was, almost everything in and on the stolen ancient Jeep Wagoneer worked—headlights, taillights, transmission, wipers, with some heat, and a defroster, but not the radio. The downside was its appearance—bumps, dents, scratches, and rust. Mechanically okay, and old enough to call a classic, but a classic it was not. It was just old.

"I had a choice," Yadi said. "I could have had a BMW. Most stolen cars, the police don't even look for them. This one they definitely won't."

Their conversation topics so far: money, Yadi's dream of becoming a hip-hop artist, money, music, fast food, money, fast cars, drugs neither of them used but Yadi sold, and more money. Gus's dream of finding her family in one of the ICE detention centers. Gus maybe going to college.

And guns. Yadi liked guns.

"I have one, mi amor, in my bag," Yadi said. "A 9mm. Usually bareback in the waist of my pants. Not comfortable in a car."

"I know about it," Gus said, unimpressed.

Yadi boasted that he'd used it. "To take care of things," he said, but mostly just to intimidate people. Gus made no similar boasts, but she could have. Not about intimidation. About needing to use one back in Perú, at age thirteen.

They crossed into Maryland, the traffic on the interstate light.

"So where is my present?" Yadi said.

"I have it here." She pulled up a sleeve and removed the Rolex watch with the pink opal face from her wrist. "You will need to adjust it to fit, but it is yours. It is very expensive."

Yadi accepted it, holding it up to examine it in a passing truck's headlights. "Wow, a Stolex!" he said, urban for stolen Rolex. "You are *insane*, chica. It is beautiful." He squinted, sharpening his focus on it. Another vehicle passed them, its lights glinting off the silver band and the watch's face. "Wait. Is that...is that *pink*?"

"Yes. It is pink opal. It is poco común. From Perú."

As in scarce. She wouldn't mention anything associating it with Barbie. Not to a male peruano teen who considered himself super macho.

"From Perú? It is wonderful," he said, admiring it. He pulled it onto his wrist. "It is very tight, but I will get it fixed. Gracias, Agustina."

"Please, you should call me Gus," she reminded him, *Gus* sounding like *goose*. "I am Gus."

"Okay, I forgot. But why not Tina, if you do not like your full Christian name? You don't look like a goose," he said, smirking. "You look like a beautiful swan. You are a dulce niña, mi corazón."

"Papá calls me Gus. And mami did, too. Mi familia calls me Gus. I am Gus."

"Sí, it is Gus the swan then, so beautiful a bird. So, Gus, how far is it to our destination? Can you check your phone?"

She retrieved her burner. The first of many they would need to use. She keyed in Bowling Green, Virginia, as a destination, a city northeast of Richmond. "From Baltimore, one hundred thirty miles. Under three hours."

"Your papá is there?"

"I don't know. It is on the way to Texas. I will visit the center, I will show them my paperwork with my alien registration number. I will ask questions, I will see if someone can help me look for him in their computers again. Something might have changed."

She leaned her head against the window, silent, the night landscape rolling by, mile after mile. In the darkness of the car interior, she untied the leather cowhide that attached the pliable bag to a belt loop on her jeans. She brought the pouch forward, to her lap.

Her security blanket. Her amulet. Her connection to her old life, her village, her family. She felt Yadi's eyes on her, his glances at the pouch. She closed her eyes anyway, becoming one with the talisman inside the leather, needing the strength of her ancestors.

...anxious excited frightened lost, a lost child, no parents, no protection, find yourself, protect yourself...

Her thoughts remained scrambled as she drifted off, issues unresolved, conflicts building, threats, separation, pain, wants, needs, this was crazy, a boy with expectations next to her, help, help, help...

Her subconscious fought the nightmares and the pain and the loss while juggling happy thoughts, happy dreams, happy places.

She would find her father her sister would study rocks fossils hands bones her people, love them, love them all, would avenge her mami, would find, would never stop, would search would love would avenge

...would kill—

La Ballena.

She jolted awake, that name making her jump. In her lap, the smooth black stone sat exposed, with her having no memory of having removed it from the pouch, her fingers stroking the fossilized bones imprinted onto its surface, bone fused onto rock, her heart racing, her hand sweaty. Had she said the name aloud? Had she said *kill* before it? Did Yadi hear any of it?

Yadi stayed focused on the highway, unfazed. The name had stayed internal to her nightmare, her quiet pain only.

She hadn't shared with him, would not share, could not share with him, that one of her destinations was the prison that held La Ballena in Livingston, Texas. That sick monster. Yadi mustn't know that her feelings about him were so different from his.

Welcome to Virginia, the overhead sign said.

"I am envious, sleepy one," Yadi said. "I have nothing left from my home in Lima. All my clothes are gone, my pictures, my parents. You, you have that rock, that connection to your village. How old, Agustina—Gus—is it? So smooth. It must be ancient."

Gus returned the stone to the pouch, suddenly self-conscious. She re-tied the bag to her belt loop. So many people in Gente de la Luna, her peruano village, had stones like this with fossilized bones. They kept them as charms in leather pouches and bags, in lockets around their necks, in tarnished gold or silver or other boxes, or on display in their modest homes with religious keepsakes nearby. They knew them only as relics passed down from ancestors, their belief that they were thousands of years old. Aside from revering these stones and rocks that her people continued to find in the rainforest basins—under layers of newly exposed sediment, and on cliffs and mountains denuded of their vegetation in the name of progress—they became more interesting to Gus, with the ancient history they evoked and the ancestors' hands they'd passed through. This one in particular, with a fossil embedded on its surface.

"Ten thousand years," Gus said, a dismissive comment, "maybe more. I don't know. Very old." She tossed a sheepish glance in Yadi's direction. "I will tell you something, but only if you promise not to laugh or make fun of me."

He grunted. "You should already know that I won't. I promise."

She'd forgotten. Of course he wouldn't make fun of her. What he'd done to a school bully who'd made the mistake of disrespecting her uniqueness in Yadi's presence—her extra fingers—had not been pretty. It came from Yadi's gang mentality. A possession thing. Not because he was an especially nice or righteous person. Maybe more so because he wasn't.

"I want to learn about them, Yadi. About these bones. I want to be a paleontologist."

He cast a look, his eyebrows raised. "A big English word for such a niña."

"You don't know what it means, do you?" she said. "It is a scientist. Like the scientists in the *Jurassic Park* movies. That is what they're called. Paleon-tologists. I want to study fossils. Animal and people fossils. They've meant so much to my village for so long, and I want to know more about them. And don't call me 'niña.' I am not a little girl. You confuse size with age and intelligence. That only shows your ignorance."

She'd gone too far, insulting him like that. Street smarts could be as important as internet smarts, but not as important as people smarts, especially now, on this quest of hers. He'd already proven his value. Having a car was much better than being on a bus, and him knowing enough to steal one that wouldn't call attention to itself was even smarter.

"I shouldn't have said that, Yadi. I'm sorry. You're not ignorant. You couldn't have survived in a big American city like Philadelphia on your own by not being smart. Forgive me."

His grip on the steering wheel tightened, a credit to her scolding, both hands on it now, instead of one. Dawn crept over the horizon, filling the car interior with natural light, illuminating Yadi's angry face. At that moment, Gus realized why both his hands were busy. His face showed his determination at keeping them where they were. To restrain himself, to keep the peace, to not come out swinging. Young peruana girls do not call young peruano men stupid.

His grip relaxed, his face softening, his chest heaving less. The bluster was gone. "We need to make a stop," he said in an even voice. "We need gas. And you probably need to pee."

The last part was a scoff, a dig at her gender, but she didn't care. She was sure she'd dodged a tantrum that could have led to a physical response. She would need to worry about not hurting his feelings, would need to accept the culture of it. That teen gangsters were not used to being challenged, certainly not young peruano males. She'd need to be more careful not to piss him off.

10

Johnson Space Center, Houston, Texas

Max drove their Fend Aero cargo van onto the expansive space center grounds and located the Material Evaluation Laboratory building, where many of NASA's Artemis lunar payload contractors were scheduled to meet today back to back to back. For his team, the first group up, it was an eight a.m. meeting.

"Moon rocks, Max," Renee said, pointing. Max nodded, creeping the van up to the Lunar Sample Laboratory Facility, Building 31, and parking. Here was where the review, storage, upkeep, testing, research, and maintenance of all lunar samples from all the Apollo missions continued through the present day.

"I'm happy they asked Fend Aerospace to be a part of this," Max said.

Standard facility clearance protocols in place for the Eval Lab building meant Max, his four department heads, his chief of staff Emily, and Renee all entered a vestibule where they were individually wanded and their backpacks x-rayed. A "research host" counted heads, said "Please keep up," then led them into a cavernous laboratory with the feel of a warehouse. They followed her along the wall to an area cordoned by tall metal shelving.

NASA's Commercial Lunar Payload Services' first and second round of twelve experiments and payloads were announced in 2019, and a large chunk of the third round was announced in 2021. While so many had been announced already, only a few were defined as being for one mission or another, meaning some could be bumped in favor of others. Planned missions exceeded fifty so far and would take the Artemis program well into 2026. Fend Aero had their arms around them, loosely at this point, but tightening daily. Spectrometer deployments, robotic lunar landers for drilling for water and ice below the Moon's surface. This was also a first attempt at "in situ" resource utilization, meaning the feasibility of collecting, processing, manufacturing, storing, and using products made from materials on astronomical objects like the Moon, Mars, and asteroids, replacing the need for materials to be brought from Earth.

The buyers of payload space included research institutes, universities, the Jet Propulsion Laboratory, physics labs, robotics and technology companies, plus NASA itself. The primary delivery mechanisms to the Moon were moon landers. That was where Fend Aerospace came in.

Max spoke over his shoulder as they hoofed their way around and through the large mass of technology. "Emily. Where are you, Emily?"

Emily, late sixties, was the oldest of the meeting attendees from the Fend side. In good shape because she hiked as a hobby, but she for sure wasn't a sprinter. Max drifted back to the rear of the hustling group, where Emily's short legs were pumping hard.

"Emily. Did it work this morning?"

"Yes," she said, her breath short. "Fully functioning."

"New lithium-ion battery, Renee?"

For the mini-model only. The deployed full-size *Blue Spectre* would be using the newest, most advanced solid-state batteries developed by contractors for NASA.

"Yes, Max, new battery with a full charge."

They reached their meeting area, a space used mostly for storage, the first time the Fend team was meeting in this section of the building. They sat at one end of adjacent folding tables, one table leg leveled by a piece of cardboard serving as a shim. No one could accuse the Artemis program of wasting money on high-end office furniture or expensive meetings. Max unzipped his backpack and pulled the top flap out of the way. His product director did likewise with his. The team of six were ready and waiting.

The NASA contingent of four filed in and were quick to grumble about the meeting space. One of the four NASA participants—the lead—was new for this update session. He kicked things off.

"I'm Dr. Vernon Kirby," the only one in a lab coat said, his bushy, gray eyebrows needing a trim, "and the rest of my team of scientists here aren't. Ha. We're not doing introductions, they're boring. I know all of you have clearances for this, plus we don't have the time, and nobody will remember the names anyway. And we'd rather you didn't, because much of what we do here is classified. How are ya? Never mind, no need to answer. Sorry about this space, the facility's booked with contractors today. Damn, it's filthy in here," he looked around at the shelves, "but I assume it was the best we could do. Unless you somehow pissed off the facility scheduler. Or maybe I did. Ha. You should see where we had to put some of the others. Hi, Emily. Long time no see. Let's get started. We're ready to be wowed."

Max's team members didn't exchange looks because Emily had warned them about Dr. Kirby. The doctor was easily seventy-five years old and was easily on a slippery slope, but he was also easily a genius in multiple disciplines, astrophysics, electromagnetics, geology, systems development, and oddly enough, paleontology. A weird combination of disciplines. Emily knew him from her long tenure with Fend Aerospace. Eccentric wasn't a strong enough description, more like outrageously unable to censor himself.

"It comes with age," Emily had warned them, "and having seen too much to give a fig anymore. He might also be losing it. It's tough to tell with some of these scientists. But NASA's making sure they're getting the most out of him during whatever years he's got left."

Max knew the type, having been around engineers and rocket scientists for much of his career. This could also, Max knew, be Emily describing herself.

Max nodded at a Fend team member. "Ted, please start the demo."

Ted Leonard, the Propulsion department head, had a flair for the dramatic. He removed a levered remote control from his backpack, then removed the six-by-six-inch flying drone it would control. He thumbed a directional button. The drone lifted, flew two seats away, and dropped hooks into the interior of Max's open backpack. The hooks snapped onto a miniature version of the Fend moon lander, a scale model of *Blue Spectre* that was seven inches tall, twelve inches square, and nestled inside a custom-made foam package where it slept like a hibernating Christmas ornament. The drone-lander combination shook loose from Max's backpack and flew, rising three feet above the table and hovering. It moved in front of the seated Dr. Kirby, took a bow, then held its position a few moments for the doctor to scrutinize it and vice versa. It followed this routine with Dr. Kirby's three team members. Finished introducing itself, the drone took *Blue Spectre* for a tour of the storage area surrounding where they were seated. When it returned, the mini-*Blue Spectre* disengaged from the drone, floated softly to the table in front of Max, and powered off.

Max analyzed the scientists' faces for reactions. Only a mild interest registered on each, with polite nods and a few raised eyebrows, but nothing equivalent to having been "wowed."

"Well, Mr. Fend," Dr. Kirby said, "that certainly was underwhelming. What else you got?"

"Ted? Renee?" Max said.

A printer in the storage area turned itself on, made noises preparing itself to print, and began ejecting paper.

"Ha! How did your toy hack into that NASA printer?" Dr. Kirby said.

Renee answered. "Open source, Doctor."

"No, seriously, how?" he said, no longer amused. "The code for it isn't an open source arrangement."

"Doctor, respectfully, apparently it's out there somewhere, otherwise *Blue Spectre* wouldn't have found it."

Renee grabbed the printed pages, handed two of them to Dr. Kirby, retained the others. Ted landed the drone and powered down both units.

"Dr. Kirby, would you care to read the output and tell us what the lander's artificial intelligence learned?" Renee said.

The doctor scanned the pages, glanced once at Renee, then took a longer look at Max.

He cleared his throat and read from the first page.

"*Data gathering. Location, NASA Johnson Space Center, Houston, Texas,*

Material Evaluation Laboratory building, office supplies storage. Last supplies inventory completed October 14, 2023."

He looked squarely at Max, annoyed but not angry. He moved to the second printed sheet and began reading.

"Via facial scan of room occupants. Occupant #1, Dr. Vernon L. Kirby, date of birth December 1, 1945, current age 77 years, 2 months, height 5 feet 6.26 inches, weight 171.42 pounds. Medical procedures: Pleural effusion diagnosed April 2023, age 76, in recovery, left lung exterior wall drained but is still retaining fluid. Local pulmonologist Dr. Isaac Flintlock has 86% success is eliminating fluids from exterior lung walls, Occupant #1's current pulmonologist only 61%.

"Rotator cuff surgery 2017, left shoulder, age 72, cardiovascular catheters inserted, two, 2008, age 63, arthroscopic knee surgery 1998, age 53, fractured ankle 1957, age 12, next cardio doctor appointment is May 18, 2024. Hit print for more info."

Max spoke, stopping Dr. Kirby right there. "The sheets Renee didn't distribute carry similar info for your other team members here. They're welcome to have them when we're through with the demonstration. Or you can destroy them."

"This smacks of being an elaborate parlor trick, Mr. Fend," Dr. Kirby said, but not in a bad way, more like praise coming from a magician appreciating another magician's stunt.

"Far from it, Dr. Kirby," Max said. "Adaptive artificial intelligence. Identify that there is a need, search for a solution, implement the solution, then learn from it. We've come a long way, baby."

"And it is in somewhat poor taste, considering HIPAA laws and all, but I am impressed, and I find that I can't look away. Dr. Isaac Flintlock might get a call. And what else do we have here?" He reviewed the second sheet then read from it. *"Table leg fixes, two needed, add .3 inches and .2 inches respectively, custom-made rubber products available at Bob's Custom Rubber Extrusions, Houston, open now, closed Sundays and Mondays, 4.7 overall rating...*

"Ha! Well done, Mr. Fend. Excellent. A passing grade for today. But one issue. What you just did, what the lander's artificial intelligence just collected as information...it will not be retained, correct? Because you cannot retain anything from these discussions. The demo of the lander's capabilities was excellent, but the info it gathered must be destroyed."

"We're already ahead of you, Doctor," Emily interjected. "Ted?"

Ted the drone operator toggled a switch, the mini-lander powering on again. A small door opened underneath, releasing a storage device the size of a dime, which slid onto the table. Another small door opened, this one releasing the hard drive. Ted picked both items up and handed them to Dr. Kirby.

"Yours to keep, doctor," Max said, "but everything's already wiped clean from them. The lander's dumb as a doorknob again. We won't leave here with anything more than what we brought. Less, actually, considering you get to keep the hard drive and extra memory."

"Alrighty then, Mr. Fend," a jovial Dr. Kirby said, "see you next week, same time? And if it's the same place, this table will be fixed after we get Bob from Custom Rubber Extrusions in here to make some leg extensions for it. Ha!"

Renee, as directed, left behind the AI-gathered info the printer coughed up, on the table. Their research host and building guide snapped up the printed pages for shredding. After a quick bio break, they headed out, stopping to have their bags searched at the exit. The day's weather had taken a turn, steady rain pelting them on their way back to their cargo van, a fifty-yard walk. They each lifted their weatherproofed backpacks over their heads to cover themselves, the rain a surprise for all except for Emily, the only one with an umbrella.

Renee spoke as they hustled between the raindrops. "I noticed something in there, Max. Something odd."

"You mean other than Dr. Kirby," he said, chuckling, "and how you upset him with that open source comment about the printer."

"We did cheat on that," she said. "The lander didn't find the printer info on the fly. We'd found it earlier. No, it has to do with him personally. It seems our moon-lander mockup collected more information than it should have. I'll show it to you in the van."

"You'll *show* me? Show me as in how? We zapped the lander's hard drive and memory and gave it to them. They have the hardware."

"I took one of the printouts."

"You what?" Max resisted the urge to get dramatic, not stopping short out in the rain with the facility's exterior security cameras videoing them, instead speaking under his breath from under his raised backpack. "After what I said about leaving with only what we came with? Not good, Renee."

He checked over his shoulder, his team trailing them, a distant streak of lightning splitting the swollen gray sky. The thunder hit as Max waved them inside the cargo van, the pokey Emily last to enter. Max closed Emily's umbrella for her, the short burst of rain easing up already. The automatic door slid shut.

Renee swung her bag onto the floor in the front of the van and waited outside for a word with Max. He shook his head no, not here, then gave her shoulder a squeeze and her cheek a peck, lingering there for a whispered comment into her ear.

"Show it to me later, with no audience."

"I made the call and went for it," Renee said.

Max closed the door to his office, opened a bottle of water and sipped. He paced in front of his desk.

"Sorry, Renee, but no. Not good. You'll be on video. And for all we know, they account for everything that comes out of that copier. Every sheet of paper. This is highly secret stuff. How did you—"

"When I decided which pages to hand Dr. Kirby and which to hold back because they weren't needed for the demo. They would all need to be shredded. One page made me curious, so I kept it."

She'd slipped it into the presentation's manila folder and left the others on the table, then she'd returned the folder to her backpack. "In a stall in the restroom on our way out, I emptied a package of cold medicine capsules, folded the page I took to fit inside the empty pack, and I returned the pack to my bag."

"Renee, honey...sorry, but what the hell? These guys are all on our side. This is not a CIA mission. Fend Aerospace is a partner for the commercial side of the Artemis program. Why would you even think—"

"Agreed, Max, we're partners. But that doesn't mean you turn it off. Can you turn off the awareness, Max? I know I can't. The work we do for the Agency hasn't dulled my senses. It's enhanced them. Here."

She held out the overstuffed pack of cold medicine. "You have the sniffles, you say? Oh, sorry, I'm all out of any meds, Max, but here, take a look at that paper. It might just clear your sinuses."

Max unfolded the page and began reading. On it was AI-researched info generated from the on-the-spot demo scan that the mini-*Blue Spectre* lander did of Dr. Kirby. At the top:

...Origin, coat pocket, Dr. Vernon L. Kirby.

Beneath the heading, a thumbnail photo showed a passport-sized book tucked into the doctor's lab coat pocket, the small book's title peeking out the top, the picture taken by the mini-lander's camera.

Apollo 17 Lunar Sample 73001. Summary.

Apollo 17, the last US lunar mission, completed 1972. Max unwrapped the folded paper and began reading single-spaced bullet points about the mission and about the lunar samples the mission brought back to Earth. Rote research material, all available online, which was the reason the AI could get at it. Some of this material Max already knew, but as he read, he realized the AI's search function had plumbed deeper.

...Regolith rock and dust sample from the mission. Vacuum sealed on the lunar surface. Kept pristine and untouched for 50 years, Lunar Sample Laboratory Facility. NASA officials decided in 1973 the analysis would be better undertaken by future scientists with better tools...

That there was one lunar sample remaining untouched and pristine for fifty years was common knowledge. It had been NASA's decision to hold one tube of lunar material in arrears for future analysis with future tools and expertise.

...Stored in a second protective tube in special cabinet at Johnson's lunar laboratory.

...Undisturbed until March 2022.

...Sample 73001 opened March 2022. Analysis begun.

...Lunar landmark, Lara Crater. Collected December 1972 by NASA astronauts Eugene "Gene" Cernan, R.I.P. 1/16/2017, and Harrison "Jack" Schmitt, DOB 7/3/1935.

...Harrison Schmitt, geologist, scientist, former US senator, New Mexico. Only civilian to land on the Moon. Proponent of lunar resource utilization.

...Lunar sample: 809 grams.

...Photos: none available.

...Carbon-14 dating completed.

...Fact: Carbon-14 dates organic objects up to 60,000 years old. Age of sample 73001 contents per carbon-14 testing: Older.

...Fact: Earth's moon is 4.425 billion years old.

...Conclusion: Sample 73001 age between 4.425 billion years and 60,000 years.

...Dating of sample: in progress. Results review requires category 1.4(e) clearance.

...Category 1.4(e) clearance: for scientific, technological or economic matters relating to national security. Requires top secret code word.

...Top secret code word assigned January 2023: CRADLE. Security clearance required: NASA administrator and above. NASA administrator reports to and serves at the pleasure of the US president as senior space science advisor.

...Lunar sample 73001 composition: info not found March 2022.

...Lunar sample 73001 composition: info not found April 2022.

...info not found May 2022...June 2022...July 2022...

...info not found January 2024...February 2024...

All other Apollo lunar samples had been catalogued and made available for analysis, and NASA's scientists and others were still learning from them. Fend Aerospace's Artemis payload specialists frequently scoured the Moon sample catalogues, reviewing and refamiliarizing themselves with their content. It was part of the ongoing prep for how to handle future specialized consignments. None of the info on sample 73001's composition, dating back to March 2022 when the analysis began, had been posted in the catalogues yet.

"It seems like the AI was trying to solve for something here," Max said.

"Exactly," Renee said. "It's been a long time with no info on that sample. Nothing in the catalogues because whatever's been done hasn't been released. The AI was persistent, trying to reason its way through its status, determined that it still hasn't been posted anywhere public, the internet, open source databases, other databases available online, nowhere."

"Renee." Max would temper his comments, recognizing how eager she was. "This is all very interesting. When that sample's composition does get posted, our team will review it like we've done with all the other samples.

We'll learn more, and we'll determine if there are any new needs for the special handling of other freight. We'll absorb all of it. It'll make our contribution to the program better for it. Aside from that—"

He handed her a bottle of water and an opened package of Ritz peanut butter crackers, and spoke with his mouth full. "Give it a rest. Relax. Here. These will have to do until we have some wine later and dig into more crackers and dip at the house. Try not to take all this too seriously, Renee. It's only space travel."

Renee dropped into a love seat. "Okay, okay, sorry. It's just that—what I see here is, this lunar sample might be taking a different trajectory. Still no published composition detail. No pictures. No estimate of age. No results posted from the testing, that it's older than 60,000 years. The fact that they were doing carbon-14 dating at all, which works on determining the age of *organic* material. The AI stating that the Moon is over four billion years old. I read this all as it's looking to fill in the gap with better age info. Plus it commented that the NASA administrator answers only to the president. It was doing critical thinking here, Max. Add to it that the sample has a super special topmost security clearance. I mean...Hell, Max, I don't know what I mean."

Max sat next to her, sipped at his water bottle, assessing her angst.

"I get it. The insinuation is this sample has to be extra special, right? With a super top secret clearance?" Then, humoring her. "Hell, it's even got a secret code word and all."

"Don't you dare patronize me, Max Fend. I've seen you get passionate about plenty of things in this business, many with debatable importance."

Max reached for her arm and gave it a light squeeze. "All right. How about this, then—here's a challenge. Let's say that assigning it a top secret code word means there's a top secret report out there somewhere that dictated the need for this super-secret special treatment. How about you do some sleuthing and see what you can find? To satisfy your curiosity. How does that sound?" He kissed her cheek and caressed her arm, looking for some warmth in return for his acquiescence.

On the surface, it was a simple appeasement, greasing a squeaky wheel, but they both knew what this meant. It was not a hollow suggestion. If Renee went looking, especially on a dare, her superlative investigative skills and network connections inside and outside government agencies might find something, maybe many things, interesting, worthwhile, or naughty, to Max's chagrin or not. At a minimum, it might provide entertainment for the not-so-idle rich.

"Challenge accepted," Renee said, laying a quick smooch on his lips, "oh ye of little faith and breath of peanut butter."

11

They took naps at an I-95 rest stop, having driven all night. Gus fit snugly into the reclined front passenger seat of the Wagoneer, Yadi spread out in the bench seat in the back. With the SUV gassed up and Gus and Yadi awake and fortified with breakfast sandwiches, they got back on the road by mid-morning. After an hour farther south:

"When we get to Bowling Green, we do what?" Yadi said.

"We go inside the detention center, and I will ask if my papá and sister are there. Or were."

"Can't you just call the ICE people there?"

"I did. I called many of the detention centers. Many, many, many. The people on the phones always say no, they aren't there, but they answer too fast. I don't think they check hard enough. Sometimes they're not nice and hang up on me." She stared blankly at a highway that had no answers. "I filled out some paperwork one time to have them check their computers, and no one ever called back. I want to ask someone to check *all* the detention centers, and I want to be there in person when I ask them. I will ask the same questions at the next one, too, and the next."

She bit back a cry, not wanting to melt in front of him, wanting to look and feel and act strong. "The information could change. Papá and Gaby might show up. I need to keep asking."

"What happened to you with the ICE people in Philly," Yadi said, grimly, "wasn't right."

She'd confided in him, had told him about a detention center lady who said she'd help. She did help, but it hadn't been enough.

"It didn't work out," Gus said, scrutinizing her fingers. "That's why I'm doing this. I need to find someone who will help me."

She couldn't let him know her full agenda. Locating her father and sister was only part of it. The detention center visits were simply on the way. Texas was her final destination. She might get lucky, or she might get a lead that would bring her closer to finding her family. But La Ballena's capture was what now drove her. She needed to get to Texas. Needed to get to him, confront him.

Kill him.

She would find a way.

"She should have done more," Yadi said.

"Who?"

"That white woman at the detention center. She should have done more for you."

"She did. She showed me something. Last week."

Gus opened her backpack and retrieved a black-and-white photo that came from a printer, heavily creased from being folded, closed, and reopened many times. The photo Miss Deborah had showed her. She held it up for Yadi. It was the one of the father and his baby girl facedown on an engorged bank of the Rio Grande, his arm around her, both of them gone. *Your father and your sister*, Miss Deborah had told her.

"That's not new," Yadi said. "You showed me that before."

"I know, but the ICE lady had better info. She had someone make the picture bigger, to show parts of it better."

Gus pulled out other black-and-white pictures, also from a printer. Zoom shots of a small hand, partially covered with mud.

"Look. See?"

He stole glances at each photo as she held it up. "See what?"

"This baby's hand, stuck in the mud. Look close. It has only five knuckles, Yadi. It's not Gaby. She has six fingers, just like me. This is not papá and

Gaby. This is...this is a different papá and baby daughter. A different family."

She choked back her tears again, knowing how terrible this was for that family, knowing this pain, having felt it herself. "I am sorry for these people, but these photos, they are good news for me, Yadi. Miss Deborah was wrong. My papá, he...they might still be alive."

"Sí. Good news," Yadi said, his voice tired. "For *you*."

"I don't understand. What's wrong?"

"What about me, Gus? What am I looking for? What do I want? Any idea, Gus? No, you don't. You never asked," he said, sulking.

She sat still, quiet and reprimanded.

Before she could speak, he barked, "How much farther?"

They were halfway between DC and Richmond, closing in on the Bowling Green center in Virginia. He was right, she hadn't asked. She was friends with him only because they were both teens from Perú, they both were surviving through street smarts and criminality, and she felt she owed him. For Yadi, she knew it was because he wanted more from her. Other than that, she wondered what they had in common.

She checked her phone. "The detention center is thirty-five minutes after we leave the highway. Yadi, I am sorry, perdóname por favor, I didn't—"

"I got my own dreams, Gus," he said, clenching his jaw, with a fist-thump at his chest. "Cars, money, the music. I can do it. I can bring peruano hip-hop to Texas. To America. I will get a job, but I will work the street corners, too. I will lay it down, tell a story, and make some money. I need to work the streets, I like working the streets. Give the people what they want. It will give me connections..."

A street rapper, a karaoke machine, a slick-quick delivery. She'd seen him working it like every other young rapper wannabe, except Yadi also dabbled in the drug trade.

Just like in Philly, she finished in her head. *Coins and connections. And crank. And coke. The connections to all the wrong people.*

"I am hopeful for you, Yadi. But if I find my father—when I find my father, and my sister—I will stop doing things that could get me into trouble. I won't be hanging out with people like that."

"Sí, I get it. You don't like drugs or thugs. But you will need money. You are pretty, but you won't be able to get by on looks alone. Tell me something, amiga. Your hands...when you were young..."

The pictures away, her ungloved hands were folded in her lap. Hearing this, anticipating more on it, she dropped them between her legs and closed her knees on instinct, trying to hide them.

"...did you ever wonder how, or why?"

She blinked, nervous eyelid flutters that ended with her absently looking at her fingers, then out the side window. She exhaled her anxiety, deciding to share.

"Sí. Always. They are gifts from above, mi madre told me. Something special. From the heavens. That is what all the mothers of the village tell all the children who have them. Polidáctilo. Having a second tall finger makes the hand stronger, the grip fiercer, the handshake more important."

"It, uh, also makes you more exótica. More beautiful."

He was interested in her, liked her that way, it was obvious, and it was something she'd had to rebuff before. Part of the danger of going on this quest with him. Teenage boy hormones—cojones—someday, somewhere, she might calm down enough after this quest to give in to the allure of it, but it would be with someone other than him.

She didn't want to have this discussion. She knew she was not beautiful. In her mind, she was a scrawny, tiny teen whose blind ambition was more important than a teen romance.

"This is our exit, Yadi," she said, ending the topic.

Thirty minutes after leaving the interstate, with the time filled with small talk, they left a rural highway and entered heavily forested land loaded with deadfalls, arriving at the Bowling Green, Virginia, ICE detention facility. They parked in the lot facing the entrance. She stared it down, the entrance, and the perimeter fencing.

"They won't let me in unless I'm with an adult," she announced. "You need to go with me, Yadi. You are eighteen. You will need to have your driver's license ready."

"No hay problema. Let's get this done, amiguita."

She put on her gloves again. They entered a waiting room and stood in the queue for a walk-through metal detector, passing through with no issues. Yadi's alien registration number, or A-number, had passed muster, his driver's license validating him as an adult, meaning Gus would be able to enter as a minor, but their visit quickly deteriorated. They were pulled out of line and led to a counter. Behind the counter, the ICE agent was all business, fingers at the ready above a keyboard, his face in front of a desktop.

"Name of the detainee you are here to see," he asked, a white male with Elvis sideburns.

Yadi looked at Gus for guidance. "Óscar Gómez," she said. "I am his daughter. I am with my friend."

The agent eyed his desktop screen. "No Óscar Gómez here."

She feigned surprise, even though she'd expected that answer. "Sí, gracias, can you tell me when they moved him out."

More keystrokes, then, "Never had a Óscar Gómez here, miss."

"Can you check your computers, por favor, for other ICE buildings. I was told he was here, señor. "

"Look, miss, no, I'm sure there's probably plenty of Óscar Gómezes in the system. We can't be bothered checking anywhere else. It's not what we do here." He handed her a postcard. "Contact these people. Mail or email is best. I'm sorry, but you can't go into this facility because there's no one for you to see." He pointed. "Exit over there, please."

Back in the car, Yadi fumed. "That man disrespected you. I am not happy, Gus. Just like back in Philly. ICE is no help."

Gus didn't see it that way. The agent wasn't helpful, but she'd seen and heard worse during her other ICE encounters.

"Yadi. I'm hungry, and I'm tired. I want to find somewhere to stay tonight, not sleep in the car. A motel. I'm looking for one on my phone. I will pay for it."

Yadi agreed. While Gus searched online, Yadi left the car and paced, his hands in the pockets of his UPenn jacket. The right pocket hung heavier than the left, his hand and handgun inside it, the pocket flapping against his hip as he walked.

He was too angry, Gus decided, with too many glances at the detention center entrance.

"Let's go, Yadi, I found a place for us for tonight."

The Shipwreck Motel, ten minutes south of the detention facility. The right number of stars out of five, one, which made it the right price, $59. Also the right direction, south, so they could pick up I-95 in the morning on their way to Georgia. At 5:30 p.m., they were checked in, paying in cash. "I will find us something to eat," Yadi said. "Back soon, mi amiga."

Gus showered, then put on gym pants and a long-sleeved Eagles sweat-shirt. She didn't dare tell Yadi that today was her birthday. There could be no celebration because she felt no joy about it. Another birthday without family. And worse yet, now she was on the run, her destination vague, but her sense of purpose as real and substantial as the ageless stone in her leather pouch. But the "and worse yet" part wasn't a fair assessment. At this moment, right now, this was what she was meant to be doing at this crossroad in her young life. Be out there, find papá and Gaby, and avenge her mami.

The door to the motel room opened, waking her. She checked the burner phone in her hand: 7:43 p.m. She'd drifted off, dead tired, on a gullied double bed, her nearly two-hour nap restless, but still welcome. Yadi marched in with bags of grilled Dairy Queen fast food plus a plastic shopping bag with handles, its contents squared off, a box of some kind. He put the fast food on the tiny table in front of the window and the bag with the box on the faux mahogany credenza, cigarette burns on its edge like every other piece of stick furniture in the room.

"We have another car," he said. "Better than the one we had. A beater SUV but newer, A Chevy Blazer. I parked it around back."

"What's in the box in the bag?" she asked.

"A surprise."

They ate their meal, burgers and fries, Gus making sure Yadi knew the sleeping arrangements, one person in the bed, the other on the floor. She offered him the bed.

"Only if you will join me there, mi reina."

"Yadi, no—"

"Then you will take the bed tonight, chica. You can let me have the bed at the next one."

She'd already been on the bed. Taking the floor might be the better deal, but she went with the arrangement.

Yadi cleared off the table. "Time to see what's in the bag," he said, smiling.

He lifted out a box, square, flimsy, with cellophane on top, tall enough for a cake. Gus looked inside when he set it down. A cake it was, round and made of ice cream, the sentiment on top a generic *Happy Birthday* with no further personalization. How had Yadi known?

He hadn't.

"Tomorrow is my birthday," he said. "We will celebrate it tonight with this ice cream cake from Dairy Queen."

Well. A nice coincidence. Eating a piece of birthday cake would for sure beg a certain question, so she got in front of it before he had the chance to ask. "Yadi. This is crazy but, surprise! Today is *my* birthday."

"Oh my! Ha. That is excellent." He moved in for a hug, and she let him. She told herself what she felt against her stomach was the gun tucked inside his waist, nothing else. She pulled back quickly to make sure there were no false expectations.

Plastic knife, plastic spoons, paper plates, candles, all from the DQ. Yadi clicked a disposable lighter, lit two candles, and they sang "Happy Birthday" in Spanish, inserting each other's name into their respective lyrics, laughing about it.

"You are sixteen now," he said, "I am nineteen. I am now one full year a man. This next year for me will be fantástico. Big plans, Gus. Big plans, wherever we end up."

It was hard for her to imagine these big plans of his with a cake smear above his upper lip, a childlike ice cream mustache, but she let him ramble, let him revel in his dreams of fame and fortune—

"...in hip-hop. It is perfect timing. It is the best time to be a rapper from Perú. The best! Perú, it is now on the map..."

She pointed at his upper lip with him still proselytizing. He took a napkin to the smear without missing a beat in his delivery.

"...because of La Ballena, mi amor! He will not be intimidated. I am sure he will survive this attempt to ruin him. Gus, there are peruanos in Texas and New Mexico. They are distributors, for La Ballena, for others. If I can prove my worth, I can make big money with them..."

"You want to deal drugs? Is that it? I will never be a part of that, Yadi, ever. I know there are peruanos in Texas, but the ones I will look for are not drug dealers."

The underpinning of Yadi's agreement to head south with her, she knew, was his romantic view of him and her in a peruano version of a *Natural Born Killers* joyride throughout blue-collar America. She'd seen that old movie on her parents' TV with Spanish subtitles, but she'd also seen it play out as a child in real life in the rural areas inside and outside the rainforest, where living within the law was less lucrative, less survivable, than living outside it.

Her message delivered, Yadi's expression soured. "I will help you get there, to Texas. I will help you look for your father. After that, we will no longer need to be friends if you don't want to."

He lowered his eyes to gaze at her lap, fortifying them with a sneer. "You, and your leather pouch—they do not have all the answers, chica! Its amulet magic is not strong enough. We are in the real world now. Put your crazy rock away."

The small drawstring bag was there, its bulk in her hands, she with no memory of having detached it from her waist. She raised her chin, defiant, her tone changing.

"A gift from mi madre on my thirteenth birthday. The bones inside, they are 'beginning-of-time-old,' she told me. I am not ashamed that I believe in it. She sacrificed her life for her family, she—"

Gus caught herself, the statement bringing her to tears, angry as well as sad. "She did not like La Ballena!" she said, her voice shaking. "What he did to our country, our village, what he did to..."

She couldn't finish the sentence. "Never mind. I am taking the floor tonight, pequeño. You are taking the bed. This is not a favor. The bed is very uncomfortable."

She'd called him a "little man." She grabbed a pillow, said buenas noches, moved the bedspread to the floor and wrapped herself in it, not waiting for, not wanting a response.

12

Eight p.m. Cornell Oakley and Detective Poole, his police partner again today, were outside the Walnut Street Theatre in Center City Philly. Cornell had had enough of Perú. Its exodus of hard-luck immigrants bused to sanctuary cities like Philadelphia were taxing the city's resources, with Cornell now able to include the Philly FBI office among them. Peruvian teens in Philly foster homes, Peruvian teens stealing jewelry, panhandling, pickpocketing, and now as persons of interest, two teens missing from a community foster home after an ICE employee from the local immigration office was shot dead in a parking lot. It was unclear, but most likely all of the above was somehow related to one Peruvian teen girl by the name of Agustina Gómez. Also missing was a Peruvian teen male, Yadier Rolando, also a community home resident, older than her by a few years, officially an adult. Rolando's background included a rumored affiliation with a local gang who dealt in stolen cars and illegal drugs. And now—

Cornell and Poole stood over a disheveled guy in a Russian faux fur hat sitting on a piece of cardboard a little wider than him, under a blanket. He stroked his long-haired cat while waiting on the charity of others.

"What can you tell us about her?" Poole said to him.

"She's from somewhere else," the guy said, his hair stringy, but his face clean-shaven.

"She's Latina, from Perú," Cornell said, steering him.

"If you say so."

They listened to him describe how good Miss Gómez was at separating people from their money. "She's got that kid thing going for her, know what I'm sayin'? Don't look old enough to be out here doing this, so people stop to check her out. I seen her on lots of corners, but never seen her doing anything wrong, only asking for money, not giving anything up for it, far as I know, ya know?"

Cornell's phone pinged. "Good to know. All right, thanks, pal. We're good." He dropped a twenty into the guy's open suitcase. He gestured to Poole to start walking.

"Wait," the Russian Hat said. "Almost forgot. One thing odd about her, other than she's out here with the rest of us lepers."

"What's that?" Cornell said, listening while scrolling his phone.

"She wears gloves. Them blue latex things, like a nurse or a doctor. I seen 'em on her, more than once."

"Blue gloves, got it," Poole said.

An internal FBI memo with a video had hit Cornell's email. As they walked, his partner checked his own cell for messages. Cornell opened the FBI memo.

Breaking. Peruvian drug trafficker La Ballena flown to Texas by the US Marshal Service, delivered to the FBI, incarcerated Livingston, TX supermax prison. Arraignment will be in Houston. Indicted on multiple murder charges, drug trafficking, RICO. Nicely done, American law enforcement. Kudos everyone.

The video was graphic, the cold, fat Peruvian naked under the airport terminal's bright lighting, a commercial jet in flat black blending into the background behind him. His head bandaged, La Ballena was pulled off a gurney and made to stand shivering while getting bucket-washed, him looking like he'd lost his bowels somewhere en route.

Cornell and Poole passed under the theater's marquis and kept walking, on their way to a parking lot. Cornell watched the video again, then again.

"What's that?" Poole said.

"We caught a big-time Peruvian drug supplier. Some great video here." Cornell stopped so Poole could check it out.

"Right. La Ballena," Poole said, leaning over. "Heard about it. The guy tried to buy a Boeing 747 on the darknet. From Fend Aerospace." He recoiled, Cornell's handheld still producing graphic images. "Wow. That is one ugly video of one ugly prisoner transport."

When Cornell heard "Fend Aerospace," he knew he'd be making a phone call.

───────────

"Your side gig made me call you, Max," Cornell said. Philly detective Poole was gone, his shift over. Cornell was in his own car, headed to his apartment in Center City Philly.

"You on speaker, Oakley?" Max said, no other pleasantries, even though they hadn't spoken to each other in over a year.

"Hands free, in my car, alone."

"Pick up your phone. I'm not talking to you on any speaker."

"So you want me to drive the crazy inner city streets of Philly one-handed at midnight. I thought billionaire Max Fend and I were friends."

"Friends, merciless bastards, comme ci, comme ça," Max said. "If you pick up your phone we can talk, but only for a minute."

Cornell did as asked. After thirty seconds of getting caught up, with no new personal news requiring elaboration, Cornell launched into it. "Are you part of the La Ballena thing? That Peruvian drug lord capture? I hear it involved one of your aircraft."

"I saw that, too. What a good show. Maybe after they put him away, some of the South American illegal drug influx slows. But me being involved? Can't say that I was."

Cornell translated that as *Yes, I was involved, I just can't say it.*

"Fine. So let's try this. Any insights, from your international travels, about why there's been such an influx of undocumented Peruvian teenage immigrants ending up in Philly? I'm running something down here that involves the drive-by murder of a Philly ICE worker."

"First," Max said, "I can't vouch for, and I don't agree with, these governors putting immigrant families on buses and planes and sending them to other states. Second, I was in bed, ready to nod off before your call. You should be, too. It's midnight."

Still a non-answer. "You being in bed at midnight used to have nothing to do with sleep," Cornell said. "You took my call because you knew it was me. Look, I'm trying to fill in some blanks. This fat Peruvian kingpin tries to buy one of your old airplanes, ends up in jail in the States. On my end, a teen Peruvian drug distributor in Philly plus an indigenous Peruvian teen girl go missing from their ICE home right after an ICE employee is murdered. I'm hearing way too much about Perú lately, and now I'm out on the streets with the Philly police trying to find these two missing kids. The boy works at an illegal car parts chop shop, the girl is a panhandler and a petty thief, but she might know something about a murder."

"Cornell. Good buddy..."

Cornell recognized a patronizing tone when he heard it. He pulled into his parking garage, found his assigned parking space, and knew now that this call was a bust. "What is it, Max?"

"La Ballena is a terror in his country. That's common knowledge. He's murdered people, he's rigged elections. He's paid off politicians, and the ones who won't take the money, he's blackmailed into playing along, or he killed them. His drug network is huge, and it reaches across the US. Our media has reported on all of this, the Peruvian media not so much. But I have no idea what connection he has, if any, to any Peruvian teenagers in Philly. Sorry."

Cornell poked the speaker button on his phone, then again viewed the FBI video on the drug kingpin handoff while Max continued pontificating. He froze the frame where the two 747 pilots were visible in the background, both standing behind the shivering, naked La Ballena. The pilots were the only two faces in the video that were blurred to protect their identities, one guy short, one tall.

"That was you in the video, wasn't it?" Cornell said. "The taller of the two pilots, both faces pixelated."

"I'm on speaker again, aren't I? I'm gonna hang up now, Cornell, before I start screaming at you."

"We're almost done, Max. A simple yes or no, and don't give me an 'if I told you, I'd have to kill you.' Was that you?"

"Can't say that it was, Cornell. Goodnight, brother."

13

Allan B. Polunsky Unit, a federal prison, Livingston, Texas

"Last name and number."

Eleven thirty p.m. cell check on Death Row at the Polunsky Unit, where the Department of Justice had decided to put Balea Xolo until his preliminary arraignment. The words came at him from outside his cell door, with only the waist of the person who spoke them visible, gray uniform, black belt, through an open drawer six inches high and twelve inches wide, used to deliver and retrieve meal trays. The voice was female, authoritative, and drone-like, a white woman with a Texas drawl. The same voice he heard delivering the inbound mail at 7:30 p.m. to the other inmates housed in this section. To his thinking, he would never be on the receiving end of any mail because he wouldn't be there long enough.

He knew the times of each of these daily processes because this prison guard had explained their timing to him, in Spanish, although he knew English well. With no clock in his cell, no timepiece on his person, these routines were the only way he knew the time of day.

"Xolo," he said to her. "Four two seven—"

His inmate number was longer. He checked the pocket of his prison issue jumper to finish it up.

She moved three cells away and asked the same question to the next inmate, no inmates between them, only three men housed on Death Row including him.

It was three days ago that he'd seen the supermax prison grounds from the outside, on his way in, his last real view of the outdoors. The prison's putty-gray buildings were trimmed in blue and spread over forty-seven acres. He'd entered the prison infirmary at dawn after arriving at the airport overnight, was released to his cell later in the day.

Death Row was the best arrangement for him, him needing exclusion from the general population for his protection, the warden had told him. He also told him to expect the worst treatment, adding that he, the warden, didn't give a crusty hunk of Pennsylvania plug tobacco about it, "and I hate Yankee tobacco. You're in a dead man's prison," the warden said. "We will enjoy the presence of your incarcerated butt while we can."

In Balea Xolo's head, it all fit. The horrible punishment: duct-taping him into the airplane seat, his remaining airplane ride with no lavatory breaks, the disrespect of being stripped naked, washed and scrubbed like an elephant at the circus when the plane landed, and the ride from Houston north to the prison, sitting him next to a US marshal with garlic oozing from his pores and orifices.

He wanted out yesterday. There would already be a plan to make that happen. He knew this because he'd created it. A good leader always had contingencies if ever taken into custody, within his own country or if spirited away for incarceration in the US or some other country. A complex plan that would take a massive sum of money, connections, favors, and promises, but it did exist, and he knew it would be in progress. In the irony of ironies, the first stage of it was the reason he was here, his attempted purchase of a commercial airplane like a 747 freighter to use in case of need. Max Fend, the double-crossing SOB, had dangled one such aircraft out there, and it had reeled him in.

The routine each day and night on Death Row: awakened at three a.m. for breakfast, tray return at five a.m., lunch at ten, tray return at eleven, dinner at four p.m., tray return at five thirty, mail at seven thirty. Shower every other day. He'd had only one shower so far. Recreation, in a forty-by-forty rectangular cage, alone, under a chain-link ceiling below a tall glass roof, would be twice a week for an hour.

"Hope you like basketball," the white prison guard said when she'd locked him into his cell the first time, "because that's all there's room for, and that's all we got. If you behave, we'll put air in the ball."

His preliminary arraignment had come and gone, where they'd advised him of his charges, no representing attorneys present because none were needed. The formal arraignment, where he would enter a plea, would be "in a few weeks," the warden told him, and would be held in a federal courtroom in downtown Houston. Xolo had given them the name of a US lawyer to represent him. That lawyer was allowed to bring other attorneys, including his consejero from Perú.

That was the amount of time—two weeks, give or take—that his lieutenants would have to get something done. His only communication with the outside going forward would be any guard who might be willing to trade messages. There had to be somebody he could bribe because there always was. He was a powerful crime family head, not just in Perú. The most powerful opiate producer in all of South America, with unlimited access to the product and connections that could get it anywhere in the US. Someone, somewhere in this prison, maybe would bite.

At least one of his guards was female, short and chunky, and without makeup, her face was plain. It matched the emotionless drone of her voice, not only with him, but also with the other guards. Yet with eyes bright when opened wide enough, skin smooth and unblemished, and vestiges of eyeshadow and eyeliner that she hadn't fully removed for one of her shifts—

With his years of reading people while growing his business, he recognized someone with either a self-image problem or the reverse of it, as in absolute abandon. He would focus on her.

The second night, it happened. He received a white business envelope during mail delivery. His name was on it, typed, with a US postage stamp in the corner. On the security camera, it appeared to be a normal mail delivery. His closer scrutiny of the envelope revealed no postmark on front or back, from a US post office or otherwise.

Inside, a single sheet of paper, with printer-generated words in English and no signature.

You help me, I help you. Tell me who to call. I'll pass along info to you as I learn it. Your people give me some product in return.

If it was from Miss Short and Chunky, then his instincts about her were spot-on. Or it was a setup from law enforcement to nab some of his associates. He'd wait and see.

He'd learn her name tomorrow, on his way to his recreation hour.

"Smink," Miss Short and Chunky prison guard said, introducing herself to her new guard partner, La Ballena within earshot. "Last names are better, no names are best. Okay for me to tell our prisoner your name?"

"Go for it," the male corrections officer said.

"This is C/O Jenkins," she said to their escort. "Okay, we're all caught up. Let's go, my pretty," and they were off.

A long walk through gates and baffles, the lanes all clear for him to make the trip with no general population interaction. They reached the Death Row rec area, his first day using it.

"The ball has air," Smink said, unlocking the chain-link door and swinging it open, then, snickering to her partner after eyeing her prisoner's girth, she added, "But you probably don't care, do you? At least you'll get some sun."

The court was equipped with one basketball hoop at regulation height, a clean, full, cloth net attached. Within sight of the court, a large flat-screen TV. She tossed the basketball onto the asphalt and unlocked Xolo's chains and cuffs. The chain-link door to the court slammed shut after he was inside. She locked him in.

C/O Jenkins wandered into a hallway, would return to the rec area frequently over the course of an hour, C/O Smink to do a lion's share of the direct babysitting.

She moved close to the fence, pointing to the bench against the chain-link panel directly in front of her. Xolo sat, which put him within whispering distance. He looked up at the sun and closed his eyes while basking in its warmth.

"The note was from you," Xolo said in English.

"Maybe," she said.

"The product info would be for you?" he asked.

"For a boyfriend. I don't use. Random testing here."

He stood and stretched, then wandered over to pick up the basketball. He was thinking about her answer.

He made a soft toss of the ball upward, just above his waiting hand. The spinning ball came down onto the tip of his index finger, where it stayed spinning even after he sat on the bench.

"Nice trick," she said.

She was sincere, he decided, but he'd start off slow. He'd trust his contacts to do their due diligence. He gripped the spinning ball in both hands and returned it to the floor by his feet. With his hands folded, he began reciting Bible verses in Spanish as cover, then...

"Phone number," he whispered, his eyes closed, like he was praying. "Ready for it?" He waited for her to acknowledge she understood what was coming.

She lowered her head to check her shoes. "Go," she said, then raised her head and turned her back to him.

His hands still folded, his eyes closed, his head still raised skyward, he repeated ten numbers multiple times over, a Spanish prayer in between them. She would need to memorize them, these numbers, the repetition necessary. When he was done praying, he picked up the basketball, bounced it a few times, and showed excellent form while sinking his first shot, a ten-footer.

She shook her head with half a smile, said, "Bravo," then gave him a slow clap.

He took a slight bow, moved farther away from the basket, and sank a three-pointer, all net.

14

Renee had her laptop with her when she marched past Max's admin person, barged into his large office, and planted herself in an armchair. She opened her PC on her lap and made a few keystrokes. Max was eating lunch, alone.

"We have a meeting?" he asked.

"Move your lunch tray out of the way and give me your chair. Wait 'til you see this."

She went behind his desk, slapped the laptop down on it, and took his seat.

"There's a back door," she said, her face animated, her attention on the screen. "In the Lunar Sample Laboratory Facility's database. Why it's there and who created it isn't identifiable, as far as I can tell. The best I can figure is it's there to let someone in and out of the database without being noticed."

"Probably the developer," Max said, chewing the piece of ciabatta that came with his soup. "The very nature of a system back door."

"Fine, smartass. I won't show you where it is, you won't understand. You just need to see what I was able to get from the database because of it."

"Renee." Max looked over her shoulder while squeezing it, tsk-tsking.

"When I suggested that you do research on that lunar sample, I didn't mean hacking the database."

"No worries. I didn't hack it, I just found a way into it. Besides, if we get caught, Wilkes will bail us out. He always does."

"You said 'we.' I don't like 'we.' My fingers aren't making any those keystrokes, honey. This is all you."

"Yeah, Max, but we're a team, last I checked. Here we are. Lunar Sample 73001, Apollo 17. Top secret analysis, code name Cradle. Scheduled analysis findings release date, it says, is top secret and TBD. Summary report of contents is top secret, 'Cradle-level security only,' in quotes. Still no photos of the sample. Sit, Max, and read. I'll add context where I can."

"Read what? You said there's no report."

"No report *released*."

He returned to his chair, Renee hovering. On the laptop screen, a two-page PDF.

Lunar Sample 73001. Introduction and brief history. The Earth's moon formed 4 billion years ago from a massive impact between planet Earth and a Mars-sized object.

...The Moon cooled, a primitive atmosphere formed, protected by a magnetic field, with water sealed inside the coalescing body. After the interplanetary collision, there were a few million years where forms of microbial life could exist on the Moon.

...Five hundred million years later, or 3.5 billion years ago, the Moon's volcanic eruptions emitted billions of tons of gases. A dense second atmosphere formed, with a likely second magnetic field, creating a second lunar watery habitat. The amount of time where this atmosphere and a magnetic field and water coexisted exceeded millions of years.

"I did not know this," Max said.

"Me neither, but I researched it. It's accurate, or at least it's accurate that this is the prevailing opinion of the scientific community about the origins of the Moon. It could have supported life earlier on. There were two windows for it, with millions of years each. Keep reading."

The findings on the results of carbon-14 radiocarbon testing of the sample were next, performed "*to determine age,*" the report said.

"Again with the carbon-14 testing," Max said, intrigued. "To age the organic material, right?"

"Right. Microbes, I assume," Renee said. "We don't know what they're looking at, the specifics of the sample. At least not exactly. It's not mentioned anywhere in what I saw of the database."

Max scrolled farther, reading more info on the summary results residing in the database, in bullet form.

Age: greater than 60,000 years per radiocarbon dating. No quantifiable carbon-14 left.

Potassium-40 decaying to argon: half-life greater than 1.26 billion years.

Preliminary finding: Potassium-40 decay to argon indicates age of sample is 3.5 billion years.

"Billion. That says three point five *billion*," Max said.

"Yes, it does."

"But that would make sense if it's a measurement of lunar rocks and dust," he said. "The Moon *is* more than three billion years old. That fits."

"Yes. But what if it's the age of something contained in the rocks or dust, not the rock itself? The test results here aren't specific."

"If it's something that was once organic and is that old, Renee, it's now fossilized. The equivalent of rock. Or worse, it's been pulverized into Moon dust."

"I prefer to think fossil rather than powder," she said.

"And that's what you personally would think, fossils on the Moon, conspiratorial as you are," Max said. "But that would be self-indulgent junk science speculation, and I'm not interested in getting into a pie-in-the-sky snipe hunt. We'll end up going in circles when we have real challenges solutioning for the *Blue Spectre* shipments in the queue for trips to the Moon. Or rather *you'd* be the one going in circles. This lunar-sample chase is your circus. There's no reason to assume there's proof of fossilized organisms in that sample."

He read the last few lines in the PDF.

Initial analysis of tested sample completed. Top secret Cradle clearance only. Pending review.

"Here's proof there's something majorly out of the ordinary with that sample," Renee said. "It's got the topmost clearance. And what about these frontend points the author of that PDF made about the sample? Why isolate on when the Moon could have supported life? Why lead with it? Why mention it at all?"

She had him. "I...I don't know," Max said. "It's a drop in the bucket time-wise, given the Moon's estimated age."

"A couple of million years is a drop in the bucket, sure," she said, "but a lot could have happened in that time. And who's to say those conditions—the Moon's ability to support life—didn't actually last millions and millions of years, five, ten, maybe twenty? So this analysis is out there, in someone's hands, or it soon will be, while the official results remain unpublished in the Lunar Sample Laboratory catalogue. Results available only to whoever has Cradle clearance."

"Yes. And that's certainly not us," Max said.

"Right. That's not anybody other than the NASA administrator. Who answers only to the president."

"True that, but c'mon, Renee, you need to let this go for the time being. They'll publish those results soon enough and fill in whatever info is missing for the sample. Our plates are full with *Blue Spectre* work, waiting on more payload prospects info."

"Well, we were a hit with Dr. Kirby, so at least there's that," she said. "Although I wonder if the guy is able to find his way home at night."

"He's eccentric, not crazy, Renee." Max stuck a plastic fork in a grape in his fruit cup. "But remember, none of this can be shared. Not what the mini-lander found in his pocket, and not what you just helped yourself to inside the Moon rocks database. Not the who, what, when, or where of any of it. Or NASA will come screaming at our doorstep. Right, Renee? Renee?"

Her fingers danced across her laptop's keys. "Correct. Can't be shared." She raised her pointer finger, wiggled it, then used it to press one more key in slow motion, looking Max in the eye while she did it. "But it can be saved on my drive."

Max's cell phone shuddered at the end of his desk, from a text. Renee paid her respects, heading for the door to his office.

"Hold up a minute," Max said, checking the message. He murmured his displeasure. "It's from Wilkes. Now what, Caleb? Oh. An update on our Peruvian drug czar captive in Texas."

La Ballena. Renee was already up to speed on his capture.

"Wow. How about that," Max said. "La Ballena had a backup target. A secondary source."

"For what?"

"Another commercial airplane. Wilkes says his Peruvian thugs now have their 747 freighter."

Max texted Wilkes back, Renee looking over his shoulder.

Any idea why they want it?

DEA says they're cutting drug deals with overseas countries

Where is it? Max asked.

A Peruvian airport just outside the Amazon rainforest

Where'd they get it?

We think British Airways. They're tracking down all their retired commercial 747s. They can't find one of them

15

Cornell entered his boss's office in the Philly FBI building.

"Sit," she said, "but don't get comfortable. You won't be here long."

In the chair, he faced Special Agent in Charge Patsy Newman, Philadelphia Region, FBI, seated behind her desk. All business.

"You're going on the road, Agent Oakley. To an immigration center in Bowling Green, Virginia. There's been another detention center homicide. We think it's related to what you're working on now. You'll meet up with the FBI office out of Richmond plus some ICE people."

"Related how?"

"Another ICE employee. Detective Poole will continue to work the Philly ICE employee homicide, but we're shutting down the local search for the two Peruvian immigrants..." she searched her notes, "that teen girl Agustina Gómez and," next page, "Yadier Rolando, the teen male, an adult, although not by much. Just turned nineteen."

"So we think they're on the move out of the city?" Cornell asked.

"Yes. Here are some photos of the crime scene taken in the parking lot of the Bowling Green ICE immigrant center. The victim was inside his car. He'd just finished his shift."

She handed him a stack of printed black-and-white pictures. White male, in his forties, long sideburns, slumped against the steering wheel.

Shot behind his right ear, a right cheek bullet exit prior to a windshield bullet exit, with windshield blood splatter.

"Close range," Agent Newman said. "Someone did it from the back seat. No defensive wounds. Looks like he was totally surprised."

"An execution or a robbery?"

"His wallet was on the seat, open. No cash left in it, but there were credit cards. Maybe a robbery, maybe not. Local police are running prints. ICE administration is now checking into his personal things, to see if they can find anything indicating a reason for an execution. Law enforcement will need to get at his home computers to check for leads. That'll be done before you get down there."

"Tell me again why we think it's Agustina Gómez."

"Check the last few photos," she said. "They're from inside the Bowling Green detention center."

Cornell shuffled through the pile. Overhead security camera stills in black-and-white of a teen girl, tiny, and a teen male, much taller by comparison. He held them up to scrutinize them more closely.

"We think that's her and her boyfriend trying to get admittance to the detention center yesterday," she said. "They were turned away."

"Turned away why?"

"For you to huddle up with ICE and local agents to find out. Probably whoever they wanted to visit, if a resident, wasn't available or wasn't located there. ICE is checking the search info from the desktop you see in the picture. The person at the PC talking with them is the homicide victim. They should be able to track down on the desktop whatever it was he was doing for them. They haven't found anything yet. Go home, pack some things, and get back here ASAP. I'll have a car waiting and the name of the Richmond agent assigned to this case with you. Good luck."

Agent Newman had hooked Cornell up. An Extended-Range AWD Ford Mustang Mach-E SUV awaited him in adjacent FBI parking. Silver and black, unmarked, deep window tint, and way cool. The unit's most coveted vehicle. Zero to sixty in the blink of an eye. One reason to love his job was what he was about to do to this brute of a vehicle, which was get on the interstate and floor it with reckless abandon all the way to Virginia. He inputted the Bowling Green ICE address into the car's Apple Play. Three hours twenty-nine minutes away, per the navigation app. It would take that long if someone stayed under the speed limit. He wouldn't. Meeting his FBI counterpart at the detention center was supposed to be in two hours fifty minutes. Ambitious but doable, depending on how often he'd need to badge any state troopers on the way down.

Three stops, each by a state trooper, ten minutes each.

Hi, how are ya, here's my badge. Cornell Oakley, on-the-job FBI agent, time sensitive case, a loaded weapon in my Belly Band, I need to be at a crime scene in Virginia in under two hours...

...in under one hour.

...in thirty minutes. Yeah, nifty Mustang Mach-E, I know, zero to sixty in a sneeze...thanks, no, don't need an escort, have a nice day.

"...you'd only slow me down," Cornell said to himself, completing his thought after the last state trooper stop. He pulled back out into traffic for the final stretch.

Parking for the Caroline Detention Center, Bowling Green, Virginia, was sparse the closer Cornell got to the victim's car. He circled the gathering of law enforcement vehicles and found room away from them, but with a view of the crime scene. A Honda Pilot SUV, the doors and the tailgate open, a plainclothes leaning inside the door behind the driver, a forensics person with tactile gloves and a flashlight, his head down, checking the carpet. Local cops, detectives, and two people with lanyards, whom he assumed were ICE employees. Was his FBI contact here already, waiting for him? Cornell had beat his meeting time ETA by five minutes in the Mustang Mach-E. What a great car.

He made the call to the agent's number, watching the gathering of folks around the Honda. One person, an Asian male, pulled back from the group to answer his phone.

"Chin," Cornell heard in his ear.

"Assistant Special Agent Cornell Oakley, out of Philly, Agent Chin," he said, on the move now, "Incoming."

A handshake then quick physical assessments of each other, with Cornell considerably more substantial in height and weight. Chin broke the ice. "It *is* you. Dude! How the hell are you?"

Cornell was at a loss. "I'm fine. Sorry, but I'm not connecting the dots here. We know each other from...?" The dots suddenly matched. "Oh, right. Walter Chin, Yale football. Placekicker. Small world. How about that? Good to see you. Ah, wait, didn't I—?"

"Yes. You blocked one of mine. Smoked you on the next one, though. The game winner."

Two Ivy league grads, same era, now both with the FBI. A second hand clasp, heartier and with a small chest bump, a little uneven, linebacker to kicker.

"Let me show you the car," Agent Chin said. "No touching. Forensics is finishing up."

The victim's body had been removed. The interior on the driver's side was as advertised in the photos—blood on the seat, the steering wheel, the dash. The windshield held a spider-webbed crack coming from a single bullet exit.

"Cartridge found?"

"Yes. In another car window. Nine millimeter. No shell casing inside the victim's vehicle or out. Fingerprints all over the front seats, probably the victim's, none found in the rear row so far. Completely clean."

"A male shooter?"

"Speculation, but that's the guess. Let's have you talk with the ICE people."

The ICE people confirmed the prior info, what Cornell had in the photos. The persons of most interest were the two teens who'd presented themselves for visitation. The detention center folks had more info on them now, isolating on the searches made from the victim's computer while on his shift, matched with the time they had the two teens on camera. The searches had to do with the person the teens were there to see.

An Óscar Gómez. No detainee by that name at the Bowling Green detention center, but ICE was now looking for him throughout the system. A common last name, more than a few hits on it, scattered in Texas, the southeast, and the southwest. What the search also generated was there was now a "be on the lookout" alert throughout the ICE detention center system.

"If they show up at another center," per an ICE employee, "now that the BOLO's been initiated, we might be able to detain them. We'll keep you posted."

After a few more minutes of the two of them hovering the crime scene, Agent Chin checked his phone. "I'm about done here, Oakley. Let me buy you dinner. We can talk next moves."

16

Robert A. Deyton Detention Center, Lovejoy, Georgia

Mid-afternoon on a gray January day, cool, but not freezing. They were in their SUV in a parking lot, the entrance to another detention facility looming at the lot's other end, Gus in reflection mode.

She knew Yadi shouldn't still be here, in the United States.

Like her, he'd entered without a parent. Unlike her, he'd been a victim of child trafficking then separated by law enforcement from the adult he'd traveled with to the States. More than separated, he'd survived a violent rescue, he'd told her. Horrific carnage from an ambush and rescue by Border Patrol that took his adult traveler's life and the life of the man waiting for the delivery of Yadi, his immigrant teen male purchase.

Like Gus, Yadi had been assigned an immigration attorney and a social worker. Unlike Gus, Yadi also had a court-assigned psychologist, someone he saw weekly, helping him deal with the trauma of the attack, his unlawful entry, and his time as a trafficked child.

Also like Gus, Yadi was here as the result of "entry without inspection," or EWI, an official immigrant status. By all rights, he should have been deported already. EWI immigrants had a year after they turned eighteen to acquire either asylum consideration or another path toward naturalization, or their path automatically moved toward deportation. At nineteen, a year past the age of majority, they were both aware he was on the radar to be uprooted and sent back to Perú.

At the Bowling Green facility he'd given up his A-number and showed the ICE personnel his driver's license. They'd taken a copy of it. The info on the license was correct, his date of birth, his residence address at the ICE community home, even a red heart designating him an organ donor. But the license itself was fake, arranged by an illegal drug trafficker. Someone in La Ballena's massive network of drug runners who needed him to drive.

He'd accepted Gus's offer to go on the road with her, to head south, partly, she knew, from him wanting to travel together with her, and partly because staying in one place would soon lead to deportation. It was also to impress the people in La Ballena's network, he'd told her, as he got further into his dream goal of hip-hop fame spliced with street thuggery, in search of backing and longer-term employment in the kingpin's network, on the radar and below it.

"Are you ready to do this again, amiga?" Yadi said, eyeing the facility entrance. "To suffer humiliation at the hands of these cojones gringos?"

She exhaled, absorbing the reality of where they were. "This is a prison," she said, with sad yet angry tears coming from the realization. She blinked them away, staring at the rows of razor wire surrounding a grouping of two-story buildings. "Oh, papá. You are not a criminal, papá. Sí, Yadi. I am ready."

A private prison facility, not government run, with ICE placing its detention center inside. The entrance served as a hub that led to four spoke buildings, the fencing outside the complex heavy on sharp, concertina wire. She composed herself.

"I will call the ICE people first from the car and ask for some info," she said. "Maybe then they will let us inside."

The female clerk on the phone asked for her name and the name of the detainee she wanted to see. She was kind to Gus, a surprise, actually willing to help.

"Sorry, Miss Gómez, there is no detainee here by the name of Óscar Gómez. Is he your father?"

"Sí, yes."

She told Gus to hold while she checked other ICE facilities online. "You are calling from where, Ms. Gómez?"

"Your parking lot."

"One moment. Many shuttered prisons have reopened and are now used for immigrant asylum seekers, especially in Texas, but most of them have little to no system automation. This could take a bit."

Gus's mind wandered, the two of them still in the car, Yadi poking at another disposable smartphone, keying at an online game. On so gray a winter day, the lighting on the high-mast poles surrounding the lot was operational, flooding the parking area. They'd parked a distance from the entrance in a corner of a lot that was about a quarter full, a grassy knoll behind them. Gus waited on more info from the clerk.

"You're in luck, Miss Gómez. We found a few people with that last name in the private facilities. If you can hold longer..."

"Where?" Gus said. "Please. Tell me where."

"Okay, um, let me see..."

Gus, her eyes on one of stalky light poles, detected movement near the top, a bird, perched below the lamp, its eyes glistening.

A head-swiveling silver owl. No, not an owl, it was a security camera repositioning itself. The glistening eyes were blinking red, and they fixed on their car, Gus now staring the blinking camera down.

"Yadi," she said.

"What?"

"That security camera—it moved. It's watching us."

Yadi craned his neck to look at the top of the pole. He cursed in Spanish. "We need to go, Gus, *now*."

Two black sedans wheeled into a corner of the lot, blocking the exit. Two more sedans appeared from behind one of the building spokes and roared past a guard shack, toward a chain-link gate that rolled out of the way to let both pursuit cars exit the prison's secure area. Yadi started their car. A fourth vehicle, an SUV with a flashing light bar, paralleled the parking lot on an exterior road, made a hard right turn and approached the parking lot exit. Three vehicles bore down on them, tires screeching, the vehicles fishtailing to a stop in front of them, blocking them from moving.

Yadi slammed their beater SUV in reverse, the vehicle stumbling over a concrete wheel stop and onto the grassy knoll behind them, up the knoll and catching air on the other side before dropping hard onto the grass and turning around to face forward. He gunned the engine, passed the front of a day care, sped across an east-west two-lane road, and rumbled over a single set of railroad tracks, Gus holding her breath. They emerged on a service road for a long line of warehouses. Three law enforcement vehicles, sirens blaring, went full throttle in pursuit.

Yadi hit 65 mph in a 30 mph zone, leaving multiple warehouses in the dust, paralleling the train tracks, 72 mph, 75, 80, their SUV shook at the higher speed, 85...

Gus gripped the sides of her seat. "Yadi! YADI! Why are they after us?"

"I'll tell you later!"

Flashing lights, ear-piercing sirens, rumbling engines behind them, their pursuers could overtake them on a wider road but not on this one, a desolate country lane, where they had a chance, but only if this stretch of road could last forever. Ahead of them a sign quickly came into view, announcing what was in front of them: NO OUTLET.

Hard right onto the fork, then back over the train tracks, onto another service road on the other side, then left, gunning the engine again.

"Where are we going?" Gus shouted.

"I don't know! We need to find a different ride—"

"We can't outrun them, Yadi—"

"I KNOW!"

"There!" Gus said, pointing ahead.

Another hard right, Yadi pushing them up an uneven road with iron manhole covers that protruded like stepping stones in the blacktop —*thump, thump, thump*—where they entered a construction site for new homes on a golf course, a country club setting. "*200 acres, 44 sites still available*" among the "Lot Sold" signs, then came the partial completions, then the finished units, then the finished and occupied units, then—

The sky fell on them. A heavy rain from bloated clouds, in torrents, their wipers now moving at top speed, unable to see, they needed to slow down, slower yet, slower, slower, the mud grabbing their SUV tires, the tires trudging through the brown molasses...

In the rearview, lights and sirens and tires slammed into the ponding mud half a football field back, blasting through it until, like them, they slowed to a crawl with little visibility front or rear. Straight ahead, the golf community's clubhouse took shape, framed and under roof, two stories, lights strung inside, exposed siding on six of its eight octagonal walls, sides seven and eight wide open, one in front, one in rear, like a tunnel—

Also inside at ground level, two contractor panel vans and a blue pickup, and now their muddy silver Chevy SUV, its lights and engine off, idling between the panel vans.

Two minutes later, with the rain still assaulting the mud outside as hard as kids in rubber boots stomping rain puddles, a blue pickup truck crept out into the storm, its wipers engaging, their backpacks and one bicycle tossed in with the tools under the cap that covered its bed, their pursuers having lost sight of them.

On Georgia Highway 41 the rain eased up, but Gus's tirade at Yadi hadn't.

"They knew we were coming! You have ruined everything, Yadi. I...I can't look for papá at any more of the detention centers. They are after you!"

Yadi stayed grim, tense, his head leaning over the pickup's steering wheel, watching traffic, traveling the speed limit. For now, they'd lost their law enforcement pursuit.

"We need another ride right away," he said, ignoring her rant. "We can't keep this truck. There. A Dunkin' Donuts." They circled it, and he drove another hundred yards down the road. He backed into a space in a lot next to a U-Haul truck. "I will walk back. I will wait for someone who is in too much of a hurry. You need to calm down."

"*Calm down?* After what you told me you did, Yadi? *Ugh!*"

In the last few minutes on the highway, Yadi had fessed up, giving Gus a full read of their dire situation. First, he'd killed a Philly ICE employee, a death—a murder—that Gus hadn't even known about.

"...she just strung you along at the ICE center, chica, I saw it. She gave you money on the street, but she was worthless. She had no respect for you. I got major street cred for popping her..."

Gus had listened, horrified, her jaw slack.

The celebration of their birthdays, that night, getting the fast food, the ice cream cake...

"Yeah, I did another one. That immigration cabrón who wouldn't let us in, I waited for him in his car. Then I bought us dinner at the DQ...

"You need to know this, chica. They are not only after me, they are after you. You're the one connected to the detention centers." He swung open the pickup door and spoke at a stunned Gus before he climbed out. "When they disrespect you, they disrespect me, and they disrespect Perú. They bring it on themselves." The door slammed. She watched him as he trotted along the shoulder until he reached the coffee shop and entered it.

Lost, she was so completely, utterly lost.

The damage had been done. Her quest, her path to redemption, to a better life full of good intentions, previously tarnished only by petty delinquencies and thefts, was now littered with two murders. ICE, the Georgia police, and who knew who else, were now after them. After her. She sat frozen, contemplating a future that was getting darker, one body after another...

She left the truck, found her backpack in the covered payload and pulled it free. The bike was tangled up among the tools, but with one impatient tug it was out of the truck and standing upright on the blacktop. Her backpack on, she was ready to leave. She turned a slow 360, to get her bearings and decide on a direction out of here. Breathing heavily, close to hyperventilating, she climbed onto the bike and willed herself calm, then she started cycling away...

Except she'd done none of this. She was still sitting shell-shocked, frozen inside the truck.

Another SUV pulled in next to her, Yadi at the wheel, back already. He jumped out of their new ride, a later model. He left the engine running.

"We must unload quickly, let's go. This one needs gas, go, go, go, I will get your bike—"

She did need to go, go, go—without him—but her reality was, there was nowhere else to go, go, go other than with him, for now at least, if she wanted to stay with her plan.

Their new ride, a white Toyota 4Runner of more recent vintage, was one that might draw attention. Their belongings inside, they reentered Georgia highway traffic heading south. They would then head directly west, per the new plan, to Texas, but in the short run, they needed gas and a motel stop—to map their route, to get their bearings, to get some rest.

And to change their clothes, maybe dye their hair or cut it or both, maybe get face tattoos, do something—anything—to change their appearance. And to steal another vehicle, to lower their profile.

Texas—the state where it all began for her. Where she would find her papá, either in a detention center or in a private prison, or maybe, as an answer to his dreams and hers, he'd be working as a cowboy.

But she'd also need to go to the federal prison in Livingston. Where the root of her family's pain, La Ballena, the root of all peruano evil, awaited arraignment. Where she hoped to somehow get an audience with him, see him, scorn him, spit on him. It would be a meeting that would end significantly differently than her previous one with him, when she was thirteen.

They left a gas station, Gus tapping at her phone, searching for another cheap motel.

"You want to see La Ballena," she said, less forlorn now, more practical, more resigned, and more determined. It was more a question to him and less a statement.

"I want to do more work for him. He is a player."

"*More* work for him?"

"He has a network. I was a part of it in Philadelphia. It is all over America. Very big. His people like me because I am peruano."

"It is a network of drugs, Yadi," she said.

"Yes. He is a legend, dulce amiga. A dealer's dealer. He can make things happen."

Yes, he could, she knew, and yes, he had. Extremely bad things.

"I would like to meet him, too," Gus said.

He would remember her from their last meeting. A most memorable one.

She was thirteen when La Ballena had visited Gente de la Luna, northern Perú, on the outer edge of the rainforest, wandering the few, poor streets of her village. He'd pressed the flesh among the village's citizens, here and elsewhere in the region, distributing money, food, clothing. His magnificent reputation had preceded him, and her bright, young eyes had witnessed his benevolence.

King of the streets. A hero. A godfather.

Revered. Then reviled.

Gus's hair was now reddish-brown and still a little wet; Yadi had colored it in the motel sink. She started on Yadi's head, squirting in the platinum-blond hair color. It would be his new hip-hop thug look, would take more time and much effort on her part to get it right, his hair being so black. While she squirted and rubbed, her mind was still on La Ballena.

The fat man was gruff, demonstrative, and covetous, with a swagger that money and power bestowed, but it was also animalistic and predatory. He had been enamored with the history of the village, with the legends the people believed and retold, to each other and to guests, passing them down for eons. Enamored with their unique, supernumerary hands, and the stone amulets they kept in leather pouches close to their person. Enamored with the women, the beautiful women, especially Agustina's madre, smitten immediately with her, during the first and only time they would meet, on his first and only visit to their village.

But not enamored when no one would gift to him, including her madre, a special talisman stone when he strongly suggested someone should, even when money was offered. And totally infuriated when her madre would not ante up what else he wanted from her: her female virtue. With his hands around her throat and her talisman pouch, and a rip at her dress, he took all of it anyway, and he did these things in front of young Agustina, laughing at her as she beat her fists on his back, his face, his head, while he attacked and subdued her madre until he could finish his dirty deed.

A day later, her papá started their trek north, with Gus, baby sister Gaby, and her uncle Ernesto, determined to leave the country.

"Yadi," she said absently.

He uttered a muffled "Yeah?" still leaning over the sink, Gus's gloved hands squirting in more color.

"Will La Ballena stay in that prison for life? Or will the prison people execute him?"

"Neither, chica. If the lawyers don't set him free, then maybe he escapes. Or maybe his people come to get him. That is my hope. That he gets out."

In her head, a similar sentiment. *My hope—my expectation—too*. For a different reason.

La Ballena hadn't left with her mother's amulet. Gus had ripped it from his hand with a shaky pistol pointed at his head before she fled their home.

La Ballena had then slit her madre's throat.

17

Balea Xolo, the peruano drug farmer and merchant, Peruvian La Ballena to many in the outside world, was in isolation, no one to talk to other than infrequent exchanges with prison guards forced to watch him do his toileting or practice his three-point shooting during his recreation time. What he'd shared thus far with C/O Smink while on the basketball court: his upper-class upbringing in Perú, his schooling, his street basketball and fútbol exploits, and his time on the peruano national basketball team in the early 2000s. He spoke these things to her plus he'd provided her with an all-important phone number that gave her access to large quantities of drugs at cheap prices, for her boyfriend's consumption or otherwise. In return, she kept Xolo informed about certain things inside and outside the prison and about the judicial system.

Today's in-progress exchange with her was nominal prison-guard-to-prisoner chatter until she suggested witnessing a TV news story in progress. "A major reference to Perú," she said. Once he'd settled inside the caged rec area, squaring up and releasing shots, she turned on the large flat-screen on the nearby wall, found a local news channel, and increased the volume.

Xolo paused to watch, the basketball under his arm.

"Law enforcement in southeastern states are on the lookout for two teenagers

as persons of interest wanted for questioning in the homicides of two ICE workers, one in Philadelphia and one in Bowling Green, Virginia. The teens are immigrants from Perú who entered the US illegally, either without their parents or were separated from them..."

The images, this story...the niña...

C/O Smink chimed in from her side of fence, speaking cavalierly, adding color to the report while being watched by the security cameras.

"This girl entered Texas without a parent, was sent to Philadelphia, lived there in a foster home, then went on the run. She and a teen friend escaped the local police and ICE personnel in Georgia, at another ICE detention center. Her name is Agustina Gómez. She's looking for her father, also Peruvian, supposedly in the States somewhere."

He remembered the name. The niña with the beautiful madre he'd sliced apart in a rainforest village after he'd finished with her. This child... she'd witnessed the assault, not the murder. A flashback jolted him, vivid detail of what he'd done to the mother, giving him a brief thrill, but it also sickened him, feelings he wanted to stifle in front of his audience here. This guard didn't need to know how personal his attachment was to the teen.

But this Agustina Gómez...was she running from or toward something? Or maybe this was her runaway partner's agenda, the other peruano teen. Efforts by drug runners to get as many young peruanos as possible into cities around America, plus his own efforts via child trafficking and drug smuggling—they were paying off. Something was pushing these two teens toward Livingston, including this niño Rolando, first name Yadier, per Smink. The something pushing them, Xolo decided, was Xolo himself.

He was now invested in their journey. Thrilled they'd made it into the States, and thrilled they were giving American law enforcement a hard time. As for this little girl from that small, backward village, Gente de la Luna, and as for the stones that the village's inhabitants kept as amulets—if she and her boyfriend made it far enough, Xolo would make good on acquiring one, something he was sure she'd still have in her possession. Yes, he'd have her talisman, a good luck charm for him going forward. Powerful rainforest juju.

He wandered from the TV, sank a basket, then another, then moved in close again to the fence and continued dribbling. He entertained Smink with behind-the-back and between-the-legs crossover moves, keeping his back to her, whispering over the ball, dribbling, asking questions—

"What about the other business?" he said.

"They have it," Smink said below the blare of TV, but discernable. "They're making plans."

The "it" was the Boeing 747 freighter. He was sure the plan for its first use, now that he'd been captured and was in an American prison, had changed.

18

A review of what hadn't worked for Artemis I, pre-Fend Aerospace involvement, was in order again. Max and his team leads sat in conference together at their Turtle Bayou facility discussing the first Artemis launch of nearly two years ago. A lot was riding on Artemis—the future of space travel, maybe the future of the human race in the very long run. Fend Aerospace had signed onto this long-term, multi-decade project for those reasons. A project that would require billions and billions of dollars of investment by multiple governments and public and private industry entities around the globe. The meeting packet they were reviewing summarized what was at stake for NASA, reminders of what Artemis was all about.

Artemis. Perhaps the one NASA project, the one effort, that might bring the entire globe together for a single purpose: potential other-world colonization. China and Russia had their own designs, their own programs, and their own challenges. Their non-Artemis efforts appeared, on the surface and below it, to be less advanced than those of the multi-space agency, multi-country Artemis program.

Artemis I was complete. Artemis II, a four-person crewed flight that would take up to ten days to fly humans past the Moon to the farthest point they'd ever been in space, was on schedule for late 2025. Artemis III, after some delays from unresolved challenges, had been scheduled for 2026. It would last thirty days and be the first crewed Moon landing mission since 1972, with the first female astronaut and the first astronaut of color to land on the lunar surface, and they would spend a week there performing scientific studies and experiments. Artemis IV in 2028 would deliver *Gateway*, the core of a new lunar space station, into an orbit around the Moon, serving as staging for deep space exploration, plus it would land another two astronauts on its surface. Artemis V would enhance lunar space station *Gateway* and provide a third crewed lunar landing to make additional scientific studies of the lunar surface, scheduled for 2029. Beyond that, what was on the drawing board were additional Artemis missions stretching out for decades, Artemis VI, VII, VIII, and onward, with NASA and the other agencies putting plans on the drawing board that would take them all the way to Artemis XIII. Among these ambitious undertakings was a trip to Mars.

The Fend *Blue Spectre* team leads, plus Max, Renee, and Emily, talked openly around the table.

The Artemis payload director: "The Artemis I launch delays, hiccups prior to our involvement, were avoidable. Its satellite shipment performances were atrocious." The Artemis I *Orion* spacecraft launched after four delays in November 2022 and deployed ten cube satellites, or "cubesats," from ten different sources for ten different experiments. The experiments ranged from yeast cards for investigating the effects of deep space radiation, to Moon flybys to collect surface thermography, to infrared spectrometers for detecting organic compounds on the lunar surface.

Inside the *Orion* spacecraft itself were three space travelers. Mannequin "Captain" Mooniken Campos, the last name a nod to Mexican American Arturo Campos from the Apollo and Gemini programs, plus two torsos— "Helga," a German Space Center contribution, and "Zohar," from the Israeli Space Agency, the torsos strapped in to measure the effects of Moon travel radiation with and without body protection, Zohar vs. Helga respectively.

The dissatisfaction of Artemis I came from how poorly the cubesats performed. Of the ten 4.4-pound satellites shipped, seven didn't function and were complete busts, resulting in scrubbing secondary payloads from Artemis II. Max and the Fend Aerospace team wanted no such outcomes for any of the payloads associated with the *Blue Spectre* lunar lander. Every item included in Artemis III and beyond would undergo rigorous review to guarantee delivery and functionality.

Which meant that each shipment involved in the CLPS program was a separate project with a separate track, derived from different customers, some from NASA itself. The designs for each were customized depending on customer needs—anywhere from delivering hardware for GPS services meant to provide a navigation source on the Moon for future projects, to NASA's water-hunting lunar robot *VIPER*, to a drill that would provide a better understanding of the resources available under the Moon's surface. So far, twelve payloads had been commissioned, the twelfth identified "within the last few days. There's no detail on it yet, other than it carries a 'top secret' label," Emily Soo said.

"So people are telling you things before they tell me now, Emily?" Max said. "I'm hurt."

Feigning upset over Emily's many connections in the aerospace, aircraft, and NASA communities, Max picked it up when Emily didn't bite.

"'Top secret,'" he repeated. "A common phrase of late, team." He grinned at the faces around the table. "NASA and the Feds seem to toss it around quite freely. Whatever. It joins the other highly secret statuses that some of these payloads will enjoy. We'll handle 'em all with care and utmost security. Does this new consignment have a name, Emily?"

"Yes," Emily said. "Cradle. It's one of NASA's."

Max's grin turned puzzled then he quickly caught himself. He didn't dare look at Renee.

A new term for the team, but familiar to Max and Renee already, for a reason they couldn't say.

"Okay. Thanks, team. So let's get into our updates and go from there, folks. Maybe we adjourn early today. Emily, take us around the room, please."

———

The CLPS team were gone from the conference room, Max and Renee now alone.

He leaned back in the chair, in full analysis mode. "What do you make of it?"

Renee shook her head. "A coincidence maybe? We'd need to understand whose freight it is, who arranged for it. Even knowing that, there still might be no relationship to lunar sample 73001. But it is odd."

Max's phone pinged on the table, Renee's made noise from inside her blazer. They checked their respective texts. "Wilkes," they said together, then silently read the text.

All British Airways retired 747s are now accounted for. We found the one that La Ballena's people acquired. It came from China Cargo Airlines.

"How'd they get it?" Max opined aloud. He keyed his question to Wilkes, who responded.

A more direct approach. A commercial open market purchase through a broker. For $1M. A steal, someone might say. A circuitous transaction trail but we found it because China is involved, and we pay attention to China. We don't like this. It's odd. If we get any more on it, you'll hear

"'Odd,' he says." Max harrumphed. He eyed Renee. "The operative word of the day."

"At least we know."

"But China, out of the blue? A 747 freighter for *a million bucks*? 747s without engines are going for five, six million or more. That's nuts."

He paused, mulling his own words, then, "So here's my assessment, Renee. The Chinese don't care about the price they got for the plane. I'm guessing they care more about whatever La Ballena's drug people want to do with it and how La Ballena might be able to help them, 'help' in quotes, as in exploit the situation. Damn it, I'm so tired of hearing about China."

The US was in stiff competition with the Chinese everywhere, the trade markets, technology, and China was now in the space exploration race to the max and making noise. Pirated technology remained a huge problem, Fend Aero's wide array of databases and systems facing assault by Chinese and Russian hackers daily. China's fifth lunar equipment exploration project in 2020 planted its first Chinese flag there. They'd scooped up multiple pounds of lunar material, some from three feet below the surface, and brought it back. They would have crewed lunar missions by the 2030s. The space race cold war was in full stride.

The coalition of space programs among the US and non-Communist countries led the world in the race to return to the Moon, and perhaps space travel beyond it. The US, NASA, other countries' agencies, and Fend Aerospace all wanted to maintain the relative positioning in the space-technology pecking order, with China and Russia behind them.

But China, working with La Ballena's drug empire in some capacity—what was that all about?

19

Cornell was still in Bowling Green, his boss Special Philly Agent in Charge Patsy Newman on the phone with him.

"The newest sighting of Agustina Gómez and Yadier Rolando was at the Lovejoy, Georgia, detention center, Oakley. A different stolen car. I don't understand how they eluded ICE security and the police—they're only teenagers, but they slipped them in a chase. There's a BOLO out for them, but it's looking like they're adept at swapping out cars at whim, so who knows what they're driving now."

"So what's the play then, Chief?" Cornell asked. "Do I go to Lovejoy?"

"Checking. Hold on." Dead air, then she came back. "Here's the plan. Forget Lovejoy. Nothing there other than some embarrassed cops. Drive to the Richmond field office. It'll take you about an hour. A field agent will drive you to Richmond International. You're getting a flight to Houston."

"Houston, as in Texas."

"Yes, that Houston. It seems these two delinquents are interested in a private detention center near Livingston, Texas. The car they ditched in a Bowling Green golf community had a handwritten list on the floor—a short list of shuttered private prisons that ICE is now using as detention centers, but the Livingston supermax prison also had a checkmark. You're going to Livingston. Agent Chin stays in Bowling Green to work that homicide."

Livingston sounded familiar to him.

"So I leave the car in Richmond," he said, his voice not hiding the disappointment.

"That a problem, Agent?"

"I like the car, Chief."

"Get over yourself, Oakley."

"Right, Chief, okay, done. But here's something."

"Go ahead."

Livingston, still in his head. "That Livingston facility is where the DOJ is holding that drug heavy from Perú, right? It's a supermax prison. Are we looking at a connection here?"

"Hold on."

His boss left the line again, one Mississippi, two Mississippi...twenty Mississippi—

Back again. "You are absolutely correct, Agent. Yes, Balea Xolo—La Ballena—is there," she said. "And these kids are both Peruvian. Damn. I don't know if one has anything to do with the other, but well done, Agent Oakley...a great observation."

"Yes, ma'am."

"Look, Oakley—Cornell—the next time one of those Mach-Es finds its way here, I'll let you check it out. But I'll deny I ever said that, and you might need to remind me. We're done here. You need to get on the road. Your Richmond flight's already booked."

"Yes, Chief."

In the car on I-95 south, Cornell spoke to his vehicle, cooing to it for this, the last leg of their trip together. The lead time on his arrival was short, with him needing to really crank it up in spots, still while needing to stay out of state trooper trouble. He decided who his next phone call was going to.

He had Max Fend's number. He liked that he had it, billionaire that Max was, and he liked that Max would actually take his calls. The calls might not start off well, each trying to one-up each other, which was better than screaming, but they usually ended in a good place.

"You again?" Max said. "And you're on speaker? What do you want, Cornell? And put your phone to your ear, you motherless hump."

"Fine. Off speaker. I called to let you know what's coming your way. The two Peruvian teens I told you about? They're in a stolen car on their way to Livingston, Texas. A wild guess here, not that you'll admit to anything, but we both know who's in Livingston and how he got there. I thought you might be interested. I also thought you might be able to help us out. In case you hear anything."

Cornell waited. Waited some more. Phone dead? Lost connection? "Max? Hello?"

"Hold on a minute."

Cornell heard a click on the line. He knew what that meant. "Great, so *you* don't want to be on speaker, but you're more than happy to record me on your end? Not much of a two-way street here, bud."

"Take it or leave it, Cornell. But I'd like to know more on those kids. Whatever you got. There might be something someone needs to work out somewhere, and your info would help with it. A quid pro quo at some point, if it can be managed. But seriously, I got nothing more I can offer right now."

"Someone something somewhere. That ain't much, brother."

"Yeah, but we're on the same side, right, Cornell? Sip some water, clear your throat, and give me what you got."

It was Cornell's turn to freeze him, and he did. One Mississippi...five Mississippi...

Max chimed back in. "*Please.* How's that? I'm giving you a 'please.'"

With that, they were off and running, Cornell dishing about Agustina and Yadi and their little crime wave, from Philly to Bowling Green to an aborted stop and near-capture in Lovejoy, with Max recording the info to later dissect and ponder. They finished up, life was good, bros forever, yada-yada, until the red lights flashed behind Cornell's Ford Mustang Mach-E on I-95 and he had to pull over.

Sigh. "Hold on, Max, I just got company. Why don't we do this." He went on phone speaker again and put the handheld down. "Stay quiet. This will be for your listening pleasure, and for all posterity."

By the time the white state cop arrived at Cornell's window, Cornell's badge was already out. He hadn't expected he'd need to thrust it in front of the state trooper's drawn gun.

"Whoa. FBI Special Agent Oakley," Cornell said, stiff-arming the badge for the trooper's inspection, then, for Max's benefit, "Why the gun, Trooper?"

"Step out of the car and get on the ground, on your stomach," the trooper barked.

This traffic stop would take a little longer.

20

It took eight minutes for the tense business on Cornell's end to play out, prompted by a BOLO for a speeding, high-end, tinted Mustang Mach-E SUV in silver and black that had been stolen by a Black man. Just not *this* Black man, Cornell Oakley, nor was it *this* speeding silver and black Mustang SUV with the window tint. Max was on mute on his end, in his Turtle Bayou office, still recording the encounter. Cornell having badged the troopers—there were two—and his declaration that he was FBI...it was all ignored as soon as he volunteered he was armed. He spent five of those eight minutes on the grass on his stomach, his hands cuffed behind his back, next to the passing lanes on I-95 near Richmond, Virginia. Cars and trucks whizzed by until the police activity slowed the traffic to a crawl, the state troopers in contact with their dispatcher. The noise from their radios reverberated off Cornell's vehicle, its door open, and with Max listening and recording.

Cornell returned to his car and closed the door, the recipient of a Virginia state trooper apology that would never make enough of a difference, plus grass stains on his suit pants. He announced his reentry, an expletive-laced tirade that culminated with what Max was sure was his fist pounding a steering wheel and a punch at the dashboard.

Four Mississippi, five Mississippi, six...

Max took himself off mute. "I'll send you the recording, Cornell, minus our discussion on the front end. If you'd like."

Heavy breathing on Cornell's end—twelve Mississippi, thirteen...

Max gave him more room to compose himself, waiting for the calm to restore, as if it ever could. The loud breathing slowed then stopped.

"Sorry," Cornell said after a throat clear. "Yes, I would like that, Max. My superiors are gonna hear about this."

A recording they both knew that could have gone a different, tragic way. A recording that in the grander scheme of things would change nothing, but regardless, it was something that would always need to be done until it stopped happening.

"I'm sorry, my brother," Max said.

"I appreciate that, Max."

"Lunch on me, sir, when we can make it work."

"That would be good."

Max, Renee, and their Artemis team were back with their NASA customers at the Johnson Space Center, finishing up this week's process update with Dr. Kirby's team, today in a bona fide conference room. What they'd been promised to receive after they delivered their update, at Renee's urging to NASA, was a tour inside the space center's Building 31, the Lunar Sample Laboratory, to see some of the lunar samples in their natural, scientific evaluation environment. Dr. Kirby would accompany them. They gathered inside the laboratory facility.

"First, our bunny suits," Dr. Kirby said. "We need to keep the containment area pristine."

White cleanroom coveralls, white head coverings, white masks, white gloves, white tape at the base of the gloves around the wrists, white pull-on shoe coverings. Six giant white rabbits walking on their hind legs before they entered a large hutch. The entrance to the inside of the lab was a vestibule area with an air lock. After one minute inside the air lock, they gained entrance to the Apollo Lunar Lab, then into a vault secured by a combination lock.

Lab spokesperson Dr. Karina Archibald, bright, bubbly, and enthusiastic, made her canned points about the facility's history as she led them around the cabinets with the lunar samples. She moved into more pointed info, fact after fact after fact.

"The Apollo program gave us 842 pounds of rocks, soil, core samples, and regoliths, otherwise known as unconsolidated Moon dust...

"Moon rocks don't erode because there's no atmosphere to cause erosion...

"The lunar rocks contain more water than we originally thought...

"The cabinets where the rocks are kept are filled with nitrogen. Each cabinet is marked with its Apollo mission number, and each sample gets a number...

"When we handle the samples outside the cabinets, it's with two pair of gloves—one pair neoprene, and the second pair, which are the gloves that touch the sample, are Teflon...

"The rocks are stored in the vault if not undergoing active study...

"No mix and match of the Apollo samples, except for one cabinet that displays samples from all the missions together for lucky visitors like you to see...

"Requests for analysis come from Principal Investigators, what we call PIs. Anything that leaves this environment comes back needing to be thoroughly analyzed for contamination and kept separate from the material that never left the lab. In so many words, we have new and used pristine Moon rocks, and they don't get to comingle."

The tour was wrapping up. The piece that Max and Renee were waiting for finally came around as a topic.

"Which brings us to one of the smartest things NASA ever did when they first decided how to manage these one-of-a-kind specimens," Dr. Archibald said. "Here, in this containment cabinet, you can see rocks from the last manned mission, Apollo 17 in 1972. The interesting thing about these rocks..."

She launched into the explanation about the fifty-year wait before NASA opened a certain sample tube.

"...is they were vacuum-sealed on the Moon, then stored in a second protective outer vacuum tube inside nitrogen-purged cabinets. When

March 23, 2022, rolled around, Apollo 17 plus fifty years, it was a big day. I can show you one of the reasons why it made sense to wait that long to open it."

One difference was X-ray versus CT scan. She held up two photos of the same Moon rock sample, resident inside the long, vacuum-sealed tubes hammered into the Moon's surface for extraction purposes. The first was an X-ray of a 1972 sample taken with then-current imaging capabilities. The image was two-dimensional only, "2D" being the best the technology could do. The second was from CT-scan imaging done on the same sample in 2019.

"So we have 2D versus 3D. With 3D, you can see inside rocks in the sample before breaking them open. We like being able to do that, before disturbing the soil."

She passed out the photos—very impressive—and collected them after they made it around the group.

"That concludes the tour, folks. Any questions before we leave the lab?"

"I have a few," Max said. He'd ease into things, making nice first. "Let's start with a thank-you for having taken time out of your day to share your expertise. We know how busy you folks are…"

Max and Renee had decided, before they'd asked for the tour, what their goal was for this visit. Get inside, get the lay of the lab, prod for more info, but don't be belligerent about it. What was clear from this visit was there was no way they could get near any of these samples to look at them by themselves, let alone the one that interested them the most, 73001. Max would come at it sideways.

"The lunar sample number for that 3D image—what is it again?" Max asked.

"That's 73002. Apollo 17."

"Right. You know about Fend Aerospace's role in helping Artemis deliver payloads to the Moon, right?"

"Of course," Dr. Archibald said. She glanced at Dr. Kirby. "That's why you're here today. To start a dialogue because you folks plan to help NASA bring us more samples in a few years. It's all about your *Blue Spectre* lunar lander. What I hear is it looks awesome. A robotic vehicle equipped with real-time AI and all that."

"Yes. True," Max said. "Equipped with how our AI looks and functions today. It will update itself, will continue to learn, will become even more awesome by the time it's launched. But about the moon lander's services. Can we request Apollo samples for study? To help us design containers to scoop up similar samples when NASA contracts with us for new lunar missions?"

"There's a process for becoming a PI," she said, "but that shouldn't be a problem. Sure. Decide on the samples—I'll give you more info on what's available for study—then follow the process, and we'll review your requests."

Okay then, time for Max to go for the clincher.

"Great. That lunar rock in the CT scan, 73002. The photo you showed us. We'd like a sample from that one."

"That might take some doing, but the lab will look at the request. It's popular at the moment, among our team especially. But we should be able to accommodate you with something."

"Great. And something from sample 73001."

Bubbly Dr. Archibald ceased bubbling for a split second, almost not noticeable, but the concern was there. Also almost unnoticed was her glance at Dr. Kirby. She continued.

"The results for that sample aren't available yet, Mr. Fend, but sure, put it on the request form, and we'll give it a shot. I do suggest you list some alternative samples that would suit your needs as well, as substitutes if certain samples aren't available. Okay, that concludes our time today." Her bubbles back at full strength, Dr. Archibald closed out the discussion. "And don't be stingy when passing the tip jar on the way out. Ha-ha. Thanks for stopping by."

The bunny suits gone, Dr. Kirby took the lead out of the building, holding court with Emily and the rest of the Fend team a few strides ahead of them. Spokesperson Dr. Archibald had stumbled slightly over the 73001 request, but Kirby hadn't flinched, not even when she'd glanced at him. Maybe there was nothing out of the ordinary for this sample, as in zippo, no story, move along, nothing to see here, period.

Max and Renee drifted farther behind, outside earshot of Dr. Kirby, et al. Renee blew into her hands and spoke with them near her mouth, in between breaths, camouflaging her words.

"It isn't there, among any of the samples," Renee said quietly to Max. "There was no cabinet for it."

"I know," Max said, thinking aloud. "So where's sample 73001?"

Renee's eyes flashed open. She sat up in bed.

"They finished analyzing it," she said.

"What?"

Max had a hundred anxious topics on his mind, and they could, and often did, keep him awake at two in the morning. Or maybe tonight it was the three bottles of Lone Star he'd sucked down while eating half a pepperoni pizza, still answering emails.

"If it's not where it's supposed to be, undergoing more analysis," Renee said, "it means they're finished with it."

"But NASA's *never* done analyzing Apollo lunar materials. Analysis is ever-present and ongoing. It's the reason there's a Building 31."

Renee grunted and grabbed her laptop from the nightstand and started keying. Max did likewise with his phone.

Sample 73001. It was all they'd talked about last night on the heels of yesterday's tour of the lunar sample lab, looking for a reason for it not to be there, for why Dr. Archibald had flinched, as faint a flinch as it was, when Max had asked about it. Even the eccentric Dr. Kirby had stayed stone-faced.

Max, working on his phone, surfed a database looking for US government top secret security categories among the ISOO, the Information Security Oversight Office. Here the category was, again. He read aloud.

"Here we go. *'1.4(e) clearance. For scientific, technological or economic matters relating to national security...'*" He stated the description, knew it was important, but also knew it wasn't specific enough.

"Ha. Amateur," Renee said. "Been there, done that. You're looking public. I'm looking private. I'm glad I saved it."

A mock clearing of the throat. She read from among her files. "Ahem.

From our friendly *Blue Spectre*'s AI. *'Top secret code word assigned January 2023: CRADLE. Security clearance NASA administrator and above. The NASA administrator—'*"

Max interrupted her, laying a gentle hand on her wrist. "Okay. I get it. There's only one level of top secret clearance above the administrator: the president." He sighed. "The White House could be involved. That makes this a stalemate. We need to wait until after they publish their analysis. Prior to that, there's nothing more we can learn."

"Max, Max, Max."

Renee moved her laptop out of the way and hovered her face above his. Her lips found his, and she gave him a smooch. "Au contraire, lover. It won't be at the White House, of course. It could be anywhere, sitting under lock and key, or maybe even in plain sight. But there *is* a certain payload specialist who runs the entire space agency, right?"

A former senator and congresswoman from Texas, who was a former NASA payload specialist as part of the US Space Shuttle program, and the current NASA administrator. The ageless Susan Ignacio.

"Someone who has NASA's topmost top secret clearance," Max finished for her. "And someone whom I've met, through my father. Captains of their respective industries. She and Dad are friends."

"Mais oui, that is correct," Renee said. She retrieved her laptop and started keying. "And as luck would have it, Max, she lives here in Texas. Maybe she'd like to have the billionaire son of her long-term billionaire friend Charles Fend over for dinner for a special in-person mini-me *Blue Spectre* demo."

21

The first helicopter landed, colored a deep blue fore and aft, with Fend Aerospace in small white letters next to the hatch behind the flight deck. Beyond the ranch's pastures that were mostly brown, with some green braving a mild winter, a Texas sundown monopolized the horizon. Max Fend, Renee LeFrancois, and Ted Leonard, Fend Aerospace's CLPS *Blue Spectre* Propulsion director, climbed out as the bird powered down. They gathered twenty yards distant from the main house, heads lowered, copter blades slowing. Suits, ties, a dress, and two backpacks. The second helicopter landed, bulkier, no company identifiers, and often given to comparison to Marine One, the US president's, this bird was a deep-blue and white versus the president's military-green and white. The stairway hatch opened. Charles Fend disembarked, gray hair, white teeth clenched in a determined smile, with Emily Soo, former aide, at his side. Max and Renee greeted Charles with welcoming hugs and quick handshakes. Their aircraft engines quieted, the group walked arm in arm while crossing the front lawn of a sprawling ranch home, at its center an original bunkhouse for a mid-nineteenth century cattle ranch.

Lampasas, Texas, was home to former senator and current NASA Administrator Susan Ignacio. The carved cedar front door opened. Inside stood a lanky octogenarian slightly stooped, pulling the heavy door out of the way, her blond hair its real color and still all there. Her tan blouse was tucked into her jeans, the blouse embroidered in thorny red roses down one arm, the blouse hiding, if Max's memory served, a sleeve-length tattoo of similar red roses underneath. Light-gray orthopedic sneakers covered her ancient feet.

"It's scotch," Susan Ignacio said to Charles Fend, handing him a tall glass. "Emily, you're a cab," and she handed her guest a goblet-sized glass of cabernet sauvignon. The retired senator's slight smile accompanied the cheek pecks she gave them both. "My housekeeper will take drink orders from everyone else in a minute."

"I'll take those," she said to Renee, stuck with carrying the flower bouquet meant for their hostess, Max and Ted Leonard weighed down with the backpacks. The senator lay the bouquet on a Spanish credenza, texted someone, then pointed to her right at a large study off the vestibule.

"Leave your things in there, folks. We'll be back here after dinner."

The NASA Room. She'd been head administrator at NASA for more than a decade, surviving two presidential administrations. All NASA's employees and contractors knew about the room, Max and Renee included.

"Unpack 'em if you want, then come into the living room and get settled. Dinner will be in an hour. Y'all are overdressed, by the way. It's barbecue."

Max and Ted lightened their loads in the big study, unpacking their bags and setting up their *Blue Spectre* model on the incredibly beautiful cedar table anchoring the room. Renee left her laptop bag. They closed the study door behind them and joined their hostess in the living room.

Nubian goats, Great Pyrenees and Karakachan dogs. Her ranch was well known in Texas, breeding the goats for their milk and the dogs for guarding livestock, all her ranch animals for sale. "We all need hobbies," she'd told Max and his dad when they were all younger. "I love my goats and my dogs and I remember 'em all, even after they relocate, and even after they pass. I hope they have memories of me, too."

A Texas girl with Texas roots, she married one of her cowboy ranch hands more than forty-five years ago, a marriage that lasted until her husband's recent passing. A no-BS person, with little pretense and a what-you-see-is-what-you-get attitude. She'd been to outer space as a payload specialist, for God's sake. She'd experienced it all, with state and federal governments, in politics, and the inner workings of the sciences, from the inside and close up, and from the outside and the highest of altitudes.

"This was a short-notice request, Charles, but you know I love you, so I figured what the hell," she said.

"Thank you, Susan," Charles Fend said. "So good to see you."

"Your son here wants to show us what his lunar lander can do, so I said let's do it. I get only highly summarized feedback on Artemis, culled to make it look and smell better, knowing it already looks and smells pretty damn good to start with." She turned to Max and eyed him closely.

"I don't care about stepping in goat pucky, Max, and Charles knows that. Seeing the nitty gritty of these missions at ground level won't hurt. Plus I haven't seen you in a while, young man. You're looking rather sharp. Less carousing's what's doing it, I expect." She eyed Renee. "With good reason, as I understand. Nice meeting you, Ms. LeFrancois."

"Likewise," Renee said. "Renee."

"Susan. C'mon, follow me. We eat, then you folks can 'demonstrate,'" she said in air quotes. She grabbed Charles by the arm and began walking. "How are you, my friend? Are your aircraft still protecting us from ourselves and our enemies during your retirement?"

"We do our best, Susan," Charles said.

"Me too. Everyday. Even at NASA. Especially at NASA. But that's another story."

A slow walker. It was so they could appreciate her home, but it was also from her age. Old feet in orthopedic footwear. With her in the lead, the rooms they passed in the long sprawl of the ranch home had a striking southwestern feel. Terra cotta tile floors, stucco walls in Spanish yellow, curved arches, Frederic Remington bronze statues, sculptures, and artwork.

"Some of the art are originals, some are knockoffs," she said as they wandered past the display pieces, on pedestals, on the floor, on the walls. "I can't tell the difference. The vases that I own, I do know they're all originals. The bronze pieces, not so much. But originals or reproductions, I don't care. They're all magnificent renderings either way, or I wouldn't own them."

Max appreciated the cowboy art and its American Wild West flavor as they navigated the hall. Renee paid more attention to spying into the adjacent rooms, leaning into hallways left and right of the one they were in, glimpsing into the wings of the senator's home, Renee ever the snoop during their slow walk. No interior security cameras were evident, but they were there, guaranteed. As they walked, they encountered no obvious leads regarding 73001. If it were here, it would most likely be in or nearest the "NASA Room," but it could be anywhere inside the large home, or nowhere in it.

"'Bohemia,'" the senator said to Max after the group entered the veranda, pointing at a free-standing claw-footed bathtub filled with ice and bottles of beer. "The oldest and most traditional of the pilsners brewed in Mexico, and one of the finest beers in the world. Frosty mugs in the freezer over there if you're into that."

A large meat smoker belching sweet wood aromas monopolized the center of the open-air veranda, where a Latino male cook, larger than the smoker, was tending it. "That's Jimbo, folks, the best pitmaster in the state, a friend of my late husband, and one of my best buddies. Say hi to Jimbo."

Greetings and waves all around. Beyond the veranda, for a thousand yards plus, came the sprawl of the lovely state of Texas in its natural brown and green habitat, the senator's goats grazing in the near and far distance. The smoker wafted cottony white clouds like a steam engine departing a train station.

"Pig, cow, venison, rotisserie chicken, some corn on the cob, and some authentic Mexican side dishes made by Jimbo's wife, some by yours truly. No goat. My goats are dairy goats only. We eat, we drink, and Charles and I will spin tales of yesteryear's space exploits that will probably entertain him and me only, then we move inside. Sound like a plan?"

They walked back to the large NASA Room near the vestibule, just inside the front door. It would have felt more like a memorabilia room overloaded with Space Shuttle and Apollo program trinkets had it not been for the sculptures occupying its perimeter and the polished Western red cedar table in its center, plus the hanging museum-quality art. One massive bronze piece sat directly on the planked floor along one wall, another large bonze piece along the opposite wall, plus two eclectic porcelain vases opposed each other on the other two sides, both on pedestals. The senator hobbled around the art pieces and told them to grab seats at the rectangular table. The six chairs were carved from the same massive cedar as the table, they were told, and were as beautiful and as exotic as the sculptures.

"The table looks great, doesn't it? I love it," Susan said. "But these chairs are as uncomfortable as the dickens. By design. I want people to get through their business in here, then leave. Sorry, not sorry. Max, son of Charles, you are up."

Max searched the room, its contents distributed evenly around it—balanced was the word—and tidy. Two pull-down screens for presentations, one each at either end—again, balance—and an even number of built-in bookcases containing framed pictures of notable folks like President Vaughn and NASA Administrator Ignacio together, more *Space Shuttle* memorabilia, and more NASA trinkets. Max gestured, the signal for him and his propulsion guy Ted Leonard to grab their backpacks, the stars of the show. They lifted them onto the table.

Max about-faced a moment, a double take at one of the sculptures. "Senator?"

"Yes, Max?"

"Is that one also a Remington?"

"*The Buffalo Horse*. Yes. It's a reproduction of Remington's tallest bronze piece. I paid top dollar for it. The original casting is in a museum in Oklahoma. Or it was until a few years ago when it was reported stolen. That was the reason this reproduction was so damn expensive."

Three feet high, two feet wide, a foot deep. An American buffalo on its hind legs, an airborne horse in motion, wrapped oddly around the buffalo's neck, an Indigenous warrior in a breechcloth above it all, with him in the process of getting tossed headfirst off the horse. The buffalo had ruined the warrior's intentions of running it down. The senator flinched as she glanced at the sculpture.

"Jimbo," she called, her voice raised but not loud. Jimbo appeared in the NASA Room's doorway. "That new delivery. It's ruining the room's aesthetic. Take it to my bedroom, please."

She pointed at the buffalo sculpture. Out of place amid the bronze piece, a shoebox with cable ties securing the lid sat under the bucking buffalo, atop the sculpture's base, upsetting the study's tidiness and balance and the magnificence of the masterpiece. "Easy mistake, but it doesn't belong here. Okay, where were we?"

Max faced the seated group of Ted, Renee, his dad, Emily, and the senator. The demo began, Ted rising to pilot their drone airborne.

It attached itself to the mini *Blue Spectre* lander and lifted off again. The drone plus the lander hovered in front of their host the senator for a theatrical bow, did the same with Charles Fend, then Ted had it wander around the room at eye level, rising and falling as it searched the bookcase contents on and under the shelves. For this demo, they'd programmed the lander to analyze and collect data on inanimate objects only, not gather info on any organisms present, meaning humans, to avoid the HIPAA aspect, or so Max had told his team. Their audience remained quiet during the lunar lander's one-minute-thirty-second performance. Ted landed *Blue Spectre* in the middle of the cedar conference table and the drone next to the lander, then powered everything off.

All their phones either beeped or shuddered nearly simultaneously, even Jimbo's.

Texts.

"Madam Senator and Charles," Renee said, "check your phones, please. We should all have messages. Max?"

Max accepted the handoff. "I'll ask that each of you read from whatever texts you received. The texts will come from sender 'Fend Aero *Blue Spectre*.' Renee, Emily, Ted, and I already know what to expect, so we won't be reading ours. Dad, we'd like to know what the lander discovered about you, the senator, and Jimbo. You first, Dad. A hint, to dispel any concerns you might have, the lander's AI will report on whatever metals and minerals you have *on* your person, not what is inside your body. Dad?"

Charles Fend read from his phone. "*Mr. Charles Fend. Rolex Submariner Watch. Tiffany 24-karat gold wedding band, width six millimeters, pavé set diamonds. Pilot Vanishing Point Marble Green Fountain Pen.*" Charles chuckled.

"*Pants by Gieves and Hawkes British military tailor, pants zipper pull 14-karat gold.*"

The senator spoke, her smile wide in anticipation. "Let's do Jimbo before me." Jimbo stood near the Remington buffalo sculpture. "Dearest Jimbo," she said, "do you have a text from the lander?"

"I do, ma'am."

Her smile broadened. "Let's hear it."

"Are you sure, ma'am?"

"Go for it, Jimbo. Please."

Jimbo thumbed the text back onto his phone screen and read, "*Jimeno Urías. One belt buckle, brass.*"

He looked at his waist and cocked his head in agreement. After a throat clear, he read more.

"*One 44 Magnum Smith and Wesson Classic Revolver, six-and-a-half-inch carbon steel barrel, carbon steel frame, wood grip, 42 ounces, capacity six shots, six cartridges.*"

He glanced at the senator. "That's it, ma'am. The only items it shows. That would be accurate."

Senator Ignacio spoke. "Thank you, Jimbo. As you can tell, Jimbo is a bit more than a pitmaster out here on the ranch. He's part of NASA Security. Okay, let's see what your *Blue Spectre* says about me." She read quietly. After a moment, she spoke.

"It addresses my earrings, my pendant, a pair of nail clippers that I have in my pocket, and it's apparently picked up specks of some minerals from around the ranch, I'm guessing stuck in the soles of my shoes, plus—oops—there's dirt in my fingernails that I thought I'd removed. I'm sorry about that, my friends, I did help to prepare some of the dinner's side dishes, as I'd mentioned earlier. Ha-ha. Busted. I didn't wash my hands well enough. So sorry."

Chuckles around the room. Their phones began making noise again, receiving additional texts, one after another. Renee explained. "The AI took a little longer to analyze everything it scanned in the study. We're getting that output now. Ah, Max, and Ted, maybe we could stop it now from overloading our phones, please. I guess we hadn't thought that part through…"

Ted toggled the controller, and the texts to their phones stopped.

Max's phone had fifty-six texts in the queue, all received in the span of thirty seconds, the other text recipients with similar large numbers. "For your reading pleasure later, Senator. The lander delivered assessments on the contents of your library." Max glanced at a few of the texts, nothing of interest to him. But the senator—

Her face was pale, her eyes narrowing, her mouth turning down. "Sonova—" She caught herself. "What is this?"

They all waited on her next comment. Max glanced at Renee, who remained inattentive to the senator's verbal upset, continuing to read, read, read, absorbing texts with additional AI evaluations, Max reading the same, confirming the senator's vases as originals created by a Polish artist of world renown who used various minerals in his creations. Then came texts about the Remington Buffalo Horse sculpture.

Renee jabbed Max in the ribs, apprehensive, pointing at her phone. "Oops," Renee whispered. They eyed the senator together.

Susan Ignacio lost her composure while reading aloud. "Is this a joke? *The Buffalo Horse by Frederic Remington. Gilcrease Museum, Tulsa, Oklahoma. Reported as stolen in an art heist August 2022. A unique bronze cast. It has no cast number.'* Damn it! What the hell is this, Charles?"

Max and Renee followed along on their phones.

Senator Ignacio read more. "*Originally sold December 31, 1914, by foundry Roman Bronze Works. Modeled in 1907. Type of cast: Original casting.* This is the original? I have a stolen Remington?"

What it was, was an abrupt end to the barbecue, with them still in the NASA-themed study while a fuming Senator Ignacio made a call to the Texas auction house where she'd purchased the bronze sculpture. No harm done—they would replace her reproduction with another auction house copy of similar quality after the FBI collected what the AI deemed as the originally cast sculpture. The *Blue Spectre* demo was over, the results dramatic, entertaining even, the lander unit earning its keep in the program yet again, this time at the NASA administrator level.

Back in their respective helicopters, Charles Fend lifted off, on his way to the airport. Ted, Emily, Max, and Renee returned to Max's Turtle Bayou estate rental and called it an evening, back to the grind tomorrow.

Max and Renee were alone in his hacienda with the fully functional miniature of the lunar lander. The trip to the administrator's ranch had been a bust in terms of learning more about lunar sample 73001.

The NASA Room. The most likely place for the lunar sample in that house, if the sample were there at the ranch at all. They'd come prepared for that expectancy, even though it was a long shot. If, for reasons to be determined, the NASA administrator had sample 73001, not the Moon rock lab, her home was a good guess for it.

"No denying the wow factor of *Blue Spectre*'s AI capabilities," Max said, scrutinizing the unit, sitting outside its custom container, naked on the kitchen counter. A tinker-toy-sized model that cost twelve million dollars to build, the full scale *Blue Spectre* getting its final walk-throughs at their Artemis lab. A red light on the underside of the device flashed, indicating the unit was low on its electric charge.

Max spoke, puzzled. "I thought we went with a new rechargeable lithium-ion battery." He lifted the unit up and flicked open a hinged latch. His tug removed the energy source.

"Fully charged when we left, Max." Renee checked a wall clock. "It ran for over eight hours. A low charge after that long sounds right. Get me the memory. We'll see what we have."

Max retrieved a disk from an internal slot, a coin-sized, silvery metal piece. Renee popped it into an accessory for her laptop and settled into a sofa while the data loaded. They'd left the senator's home without volunteering to purge the mini-lander memory and hard drive. The unit was, after all, there to snoop. Had they been told to purge the results, a sleight of hand would have been in order, a plan B effort engaging the laptop in Renee's bag.

"Eight hours is the high end for the battery charge," Max said. He poured himself some orange juice. "The batteries cost over forty grand each for this demo unit. Designed to survive earthquakes, submersion into liquids, even molten lava. We haven't tested the lava part yet, but we will."

"Max."

"What?"

Renee's eyes went wide, her breath shortening. "Look at this."

Max joined her on the sofa in front of her laptop. On the screen was data gathered by the AI, timestamped at four hours seventeen minutes ago.

Renee's fingers stayed away from the keyboard, she and Max reading the info on the screen. "From the senator's NASA Room," she said. "The lander was already functioning before we did the demo. Before we came back to the room after dinner."

"You bet it was. While we chowed down on the Texas barbecue, our mini *Blue Spectre* was on, scanning the room. Whatever its cameras could see, the AI was analyzing. It's probably still scrutinizing the data it gathered."

On the laptop were separate screenshots plus a long video, as well as short PDF files with summaries on topics like vases and bronze sculptures. Renee paged and paged, Max following her cursor clicks. She pulled up the video. "This isn't current, of course. We're seeing output of what the lander's cameras were seeing at that point."

The video showed slow, circular sweeps of the room, the lander's three cameras operating, their output dividing the laptop screen into three views, eye level, waist level, and floor level.

"Pause the floor-level view," Max said. "Back up. Stop."

She froze the video on the buff-colored rectangular box that had ruined the room's aesthetic, resting on the base of the Remington buffalo sculpture. A NASA logo in black occupied most of the box's lid, a mini-lander camera videoing it from above, at an angle.

On the lid's left corner, a white label with black print. Renee zoomed in, its small numbers and letters coming into focus.

"Whoa," Max said. A chill ran down his spine. He shuddered, then a pronounced swallow, then, "My goodness."

Apollo 17 - 73001

The PDFs that followed showed the AI's attempts at again reaching into open-sourced public databases for more info on the sample, generating a page of N/A responses, still no additional data available, no analysis, no output. Nothing published on the uncatalogued Moon rocks.

"The AI halted its internet search at this point," Renee said. "But...look at this. It found a network and entered it. One nearby the AI." More keying.

"The network *nearest* the AI." She sat up straighter. "My money's on it being the senator's home computer network."

Renee hesitated, them both knowing what the lander's AI access portended. Personal exposure, Fend Aerospace exposure, for snooping into a senator's personal data space. The risks were major. Maybe so, too, would be the reward.

"It's why we were there, Max, right?" She was basically asking permission to continue.

"True that. No second-guessing on this, Renee. But...is this saying her network has no encrypted password protection?"

"Why would encryption matter here? This is the AI that Fend Aerospace will be using on the Moon, Max. And by the time it's ready for the launch, it will be even more powerful. It just needed to *want* to find the password. Because it programmed itself to look for info on that lunar sample, it went after it."

She paged down, clicked on the link *Show password*. The password dots changed to characters, a ton of them, a few hundred or more, some characters Max hadn't known even existed.

"This is, now, officially super awkward and scary, Max Fend," Renee said. "We're living dangerously here, investigating the NASA administrator's home network."

"But this isn't real time, Renee. The breach is already four hours old. It got in and it got out with no repercussions. I'd say we're okay." Max spoke to the screen. "Beer me, oh wise and powerful *Blue Spectre*. Show us the way."

On the screen, a list of network files in origin date order. Renee slowly paged through it. Max squeezed her shoulder and pointed. "That one. Open it."

An obvious choice, the file named *73001 Report*.

"If it had a password, the AI breezed through it," Renee said. "Damn, this thing is good."

The report's contents read like the reports on the other Apollo 17 sample, 73002, which came from the same metal tube, from the same core sample of the Moon's surface. Mare—a.k.a. sea—basalts, consisting primarily of elements that Max and Renee knew from reading the catalogue summaries of other lunar samples. Pyroxene, plagioclase from molten lava, norite, troctolite, dunite. A tiny scoop from the 72002 sample had been extracted, with the NASA scientists staying with their mandate to mostly look, not touch, relying on analyzing the small sample while poring over 3D CT scans of it. Lunar minerals that the analysis said were 3.5 billion years or more old.

The materials listed in 73001, however...a few went in a different direction.

Calcium. Iron and calcium carbonate, *"probably carried by water from surrounding sediment..."* per the summary.

"Sediment, carried by water," Max repeated. "Now that's a surprise."

An observation followed the note about the sediment. *"...and the sediment filled in the porous material observed in the CT scan's 3D images."*

"What porous material?" Max said, thinking aloud.

"Max." Renee's blinking slowed to become a stare. She gripped his wrist and squeezed. "Those minerals filling in the porous materials, coming from water passing through sediment—that's how fossils are made. It's describing the creation of a fossil."

They speed-read the remaining paragraphs. There was a summary, and at the bottom of the report a short conclusion reached by the report's author.

The porous materials were bones. They are now fossils. Dr. Vernon L. Kirby.

They leaned away from the laptop, shoulder to shoulder, their stares pie-eyed, unfocused.

"Fossils. On the Moon," Renee said. "If you remember, Max, I did have that on my bingo card."

"Something on your bingo card that you *wanted* to see, I'll give you that much, but three- to four-billion-year-old bones? Too much of a stretch. The dinosaurs go back only as far as, what, hundreds of millions of years? This analysis can't be right."

"It says here..." Renee did an online search on the web, "dinosaurs go as far back as the Triassic. Two hundred fifty million years. So these aren't bones, Max, they're one hundred percent fossils only, made from bones. According to the report, the porous material filled in with whatever the sediment brought with it. Bones that are now rocks. What's in this sample isn't just Moon dust and rock particles, it has a *shape*. The shape of the bones, left behind after the organic material rotted away. And there are 3D images of it, or them, somewhere."

"Fossils," Max repeated. "Three to four billion years old. Billion. That word again."

"And they're on the Moon," Renee said.

"Yes," Max said. "Not Earth. The freakin' Moon."

"I need some wine," Renee said.

"And the NASA administrator is sitting on this information."

"The administrator and at least one other person."

"Kirby," Max said, "at a minimum."

"My guess is at the maximum, too. He called it, then he probably shut the review down, knowing this had to take a completely different path. But can you blame her, Max? Or Kirby?"

"No. And we need to sit on it, too. For the same reason. Because this could change everything."

22

Amazon's Alexa, reporting through the Echo Dot in Max's bedroom:

"Alert. There's movement at the front gate."

Someone was apparently visiting the Turtle Bayou hacienda at one a.m., with Max and Renee's long, grueling, showstopper of a day behind them. Max shook away the cobwebs and sat up in bed. Renee stirred, but Max grunted a reassurance. "I'll check it out." He pulled on gym trunks and shoes, grabbed his 9mm from the nightstand, and went to the window. He tilted the blinds.

Three sets of car headlights were moving up the long driveway with urgency. They stopped short in front of the garage.

"Alert. There's movement near the garage," Alexa said on the Echo in the upstairs hall.

"Yeah, yeah, I know," Max grumbled. He negotiated the stairs in the dark. A persistent Alexa kept at it. *"Alert. There's movement at the front door."* Then came the voice echoes on all the Echo Dots, downstairs and up. *"Alert. There's movement at the garage door...the patio door...the side door..."*

Reaching the first floor, Max checked his phone for the Ring doorbell camera feed. A man in a suit held up a badge at the front-door camera. Behind him, two more men. If any of them were armed, their guns weren't displayed. But they would have to be armed because, with an entrance like this at this time of night—if not armed, why bother?

He heard Renee's footsteps upstairs. Good. If he could believe the badge, he'd need her down here while he ran interference.

Max arrived at the landing for the front door. He stayed flat to the wall while barking at his visitors through the door to the hacienda's alcove. "I need more info than that badge, friend."

A hesitation, then, "You'll have to take my word that it's the real thing, Mr. Fend. Agent Holland, FBI, the Houston office. We need to talk with you and Ms. LeFrancois."

"About?"

"You know what it's about. Jimbo sent us."

"Too vague," Max said, "and it doesn't work for me. I can't say I—"

"Open the door, Mr. Fend. We need to speak with you. A matter of national security."

Clear now to Max was the lander had *not* gotten in and out of the senator's network without notice. It took four, five—he checked a wall clock—six hours, but the administrator's pitmaster-slash-NASA Security guy-slash-bodyguard had apparently caught up to the AI's breach of the network and chose to escalate rather than contact Max about it. Max reholstered his gun.

"I'm opening the door," he said.

Three FBI agents entered. They didn't hold to the hallway but spread out over the ground floor. The agent who badged him, Holland, whispered words meant for his outside FBI contingent. Renee had already found her way into the kitchen.

"Where's your demo unit?" Agent Holland said to Max.

"My what?"

"That lunar lander demo unit you brought to the NASA administrator's home tonight." He showed Max a picture of the mini *Blue Spectre* taken from a security camera in the senator's NASA Room. "We have a search-and-seizure warrant for it."

A bait and switch. They'd waited for Max to let them in before they announced the warrant. The warrant was now in Max's hands, unread, because he knew what it would say. He stayed planted between the agent and the hallway that led to the kitchen.

"That *thing* is a mini-version of a multi-billion-dollar moon lander for the Artemis program, Agent Holland, with most of the lander's functionality, but miniaturized. It's going back to our lab tomorrow. NASA Administrator Ignacio and her grill guy liked the demo. A lot. What's the problem?"

"Read the warrant, Mr. Fend. Probable cause that your demo unit illegally entered the administrator's private network and reviewed top secret documents, per the senator's 'grill guy,'" the agent said with air quotes. "We're taking it with us. Where is it?"

He pushed past Max and marched down the hallway to the massive gourmet kitchen. Renee was in a far corner, waiting on the drip coffee maker, her back to him. The agent and his associates converged on her, Max following up. She poured a cup of coffee and sipped at it. The commotion made her turn around. Her feigned surprise at the assembly was a good sell.

"Oh. Hi," she said and took another sip.

Agent Holland craned his neck to see past her. "Move."

She stepped aside, revealing a small carafe of brewed coffee. Next to it, the mini-*Blue Spectre* rested atop its white custom foam packaging, the packaging askew.

"I'm making a call, Agent Holland," Max said, his phone to his ear. "To someone I know who can clear this up. If our AI component entered the administrator's personal network, it was unintentional. No harm done, I'm sure. One moment please."

Max spoke into his phone while Agent Holland and an associate did what they could to settle the demo unit into the foam container, struggling to arrange the fit right. Renee cozied up to Max with him still speaking on his phone. She handed him a cup of coffee. He nodded his thanks.

"Your favorite coffee cup, sweetie, clean as a whistle."

He checked it out with a glance. Plain white ceramic cup with a plain white handle, no markings, not a favorite cup, nothing special about it. It might have even come with the house rental. Their eyes met. "So you're telling me the cup isn't dirty?"

She met his stare. "Nope. I cleaned it up right good."

Max ended his phone call with an abrupt "I'll call you back." He focused on his unwelcome guests. "I lost my argument, Agent Holland. We'll let you have the demo lander. For now."

The agent did a poor job of hiding a snicker about Max's perspective that he was granting them permission, as did his associates. The top to the mini-lander container was snugged up, the *Blue Spectre* packed and ready for transport. Agent Holland nodded at his fellow agent, who wrapped his arms around the package. Targeted device acquired. The agents retraced their steps down the hall, toward the front door.

Max called after them. "It comes back in exactly the same condition, gentlemen, or I guarantee you *my* government contacts will be coming after *your* government contacts." The front door closed.

Max sipped at his coffee and put his arm around Renee. "This cup isn't clean, is it?"

"I have no idea. It was in the sink. Maybe?"

"But the mini-*Blue Spectre* now is," he said.

"Info downloaded, emailed, filed away for a rainy day. *Blue Spectre* is spotless."

A hug and a kiss between them. "We make a good team, Ms. Le Francois."

"Indeed we do, Mr. Fend."

"Let me call Wilkes back. I'm sure he has no idea why I hung up on him." Max redialed his contact.

"Caleb. Hey. Sorry for the call before, then the hang-up. I woke you up again just now, too, didn't I?"

"What is it?" Wilkes said.

"It turns out I didn't need you. But we might hear some rumblings from the FBI about the Artemis project and Fend Aerospace's *Blue Spectre* demo for NASA Administrator Ignacio. A misunderstanding. I'll tell you about it tomorrow. Go back to sleep."

"Max—wait. I have some company news. I would have called you in the morning with it. It's about La Ballena."

Max listened, Wilkes elaborating. "That 747 freighter *China Airways* delivered to his people in Perú—we lost it somewhere in the Amazon rainforest. We had eyes on it, now we don't. We never learned what they were planning for it, and now it's a ghost."

Max rubbed his tired eyes. "Okay, well then, that's that. He's still incarcerated, he'll go to trial, he'll get convicted, and he'll go to prison. Or better yet, maybe he gets executed."

"Or maybe his lieutenants are starting their own drug delivery business between China and Perú," Wilkes said.

"Yeah, well, as long as we don't see the plane in our skies, Wilkes, I think we're good."

"Max."

"What?"

"The NASA administrator called the president about your visit last night."

Dammit. Stay calm.

"The president called the director. Your moon lander demo impressed the administrator, according to the president, but she never wants to see it anywhere near her ranch again. She's apparently not a big AI fan. Something about a bronze sculpture?"

"Oh. Right. A museum piece she has in her possession. The AI discovered it was stolen. She was really upset. Just add her to the list of AI naysayers, Wilkes. No matter. As long as NASA pays the invoices and she lets us stay in our lane with Artemis, we'll do our best to stay out of hers. We good?"

"For now. But finding that missing 747 might turn into a new mission for you if it doesn't turn up. Goodnight, Max."

23

La Ballena dribbled the basketball to the edge of the fenced rec area, a shaft of sunlight illuminating the basket, like God was speaking to him, showing him the way. He squared up in the corner of the court for another three from outside the arc. Feet spread, eyes on the target, the ball at his waist, his girth glided off the floor for the shot. He released it at the apex and landed way more gracefully on his feet than a man his size should have.

Swish. A trey, and nothing but net.

The ball found the asphalt and bounced. Gravity made its stake, friction slowing the rolling ball to a stop against the fence. He walked the width of the court in pursuit, a slow gait. He passed his prison guard-slash-snitch C/O Smink, who was on the other side of the fence but close to it, within whispering distance behind the basket.

Halting words and phrases, nouns and adjectives, meant for him only as he wandered past her after each shot. One jump shot after another she updated him, a few gliding, light-on-his-fat-feet layups in between.

"US marshals," she said through unmoving, ventriloquistic lips. "Many."

Swish. Another trey.

He passed her again.

"Armored transport, overland."

Doink. The shot was short, off the rim. *Bounce, roll.*

"Multiple vehicles."

Swish.

"Federal courthouse." The formal arraignment, where he would enter his pleas.

Airball.

"Ambush. Thirty men."

A reverse layup.

"Rescue."

Swish.

"Private airstrip, closed."

Swish.

"747."

Swish.

"Remember me, Xolo."

Airball.

He picked the ball up, let go a sudden, hard, two-handed pass at the fence, C/O Smink on the other side, the ball slamming it, the chain link rattling. She flinched, startled.

His smile at her was lopsided. "Do not worry, señora, I will not forget you."

His judicial hearing was in Houston tomorrow. His men would arrive by 747 at a closed airstrip, would be heavily armed, ready for a war. The Feds' armored vehicles transporting him to the federal courthouse would be attacked. An all-or-nothing effort. His men would make it work.

"Take me back to my cell," he said.

24

Nine and a half hours on the road from Lovejoy, Georgia, to the Pine Prairie ICE Detention Center, another ICE prison, northwest of Baton Rouge, Louisiana. They picked up a 2004 Chevy Suburban at a Church's Chicken in Tuskegee, Alabama, then traded it in for a 2008 Dodge Durango at a Roy Rogers in Biloxi, Mississippi. The Durango's brakes were mushy, there was some rust, and it was a smoker's car, but it had room for all their stuff just like the others, plus it looked bad enough for no one to care, so it worked.

They'd learned their lesson in Lovejoy. They would cruise this detention center, observe it from a safe distance, and make no attempt to enter. Yadi parked their ride on the side of the road next to a swath of forest abutting the shoulder.

"It's on the other side of these trees," he said. "I will stay with the car, mi amor. You do what you need to do, but make it quick. We can't stay in one place too long."

It would be however quick, or however long, it would need to be.

Gus entered the woods wearing her heavy coat, a scarf around her neck, her wool gloves covering her latex ones. She watched her footing as she picked her way through thirty to forty yards of overgrowth, rocks, and sticks beneath the hardwoods and their canopies. She emerged on the other side, the detention center behind an intimidating width and depth of penal fencing.

This was what a one-story prison looked like, one that was also an immigration detention center, heavy on the concertina wire and multiple, tall fences deep. A long building with a corrugated roof inside the length of a fence that ran nearly a hundred yards. A quick check of her phone. Two-fifty p.m. below a clear, Louisiana winter sky. The only creatures stirring on the facility's grounds were guards patrolling this panoramic stretch of prison property.

She was here to check for a pulse. There was no reason for her father to be here, in this facility, any more than there was a reason for him to still be in any ICE facility anywhere, three years after they'd crossed the Rio Grande into the US. But she knew he *could* be, because she knew in her heart he was alive, *counted* on him being alive, somewhere. She needed to tap into the vibe behind this fence, to feel its atmosphere, the warmth of the inmates. Surround herself with the hope that radiated from beating hearts of incarcerated immigrants who believed the American dream awaited them on the other side—her side—of the fence.

But she felt nothing, felt no connection, saw no detainees wandering the spread between the fencing and the detention center building.

She looked to recharge, to tap into the energy, the hope of the detainees, to fortify herself before reentering the jaws of the beast, the state of Texas, the jurisdiction that held the truth about the last of her family, however horrible that truth might be. Would any of the shuttered Texas prisons, newly reopened to handle the immigration overflow, hold the key to her papá's whereabouts? Seeing this stretch of prison yard with empty benches and basketball courts and picnic tables, she felt as empty, as hopeless, as the yard itself. They were two highway hours from the Texas border, and she was unsure of, still second-guessing, what her destination held for her. Redemption? Promise? Reunion?

Retribution?

Gus sat amid a patch of brush and weeds, and she rested, crossing her legs, and planned to linger here a bit, absorbing the melancholy before heading back to the car. She felt for her indigenous pouch, her security blanket. She untied it from her waist, kissed its worn leather, and laid it in her lap. Her gloves off, both sets, she opened the drawstring and set the gray-black stone on top, her fingers testing, appreciating the stone's smoothness. She raised the stone to her lips, kissed it, then turned it over, touching the tip of her moist tongue to its porous side.

She prayed to her mother, to her ancestors. To the tiny ancestor whose bones were embedded in the stone, wedded to her amulet. She prayed to the supreme being.

A bell rang, and multiple doors for the detention center opened. Wandering outside, first piecemeal, then in groups, the incarcerated men, boys, and toddler immigrants found the benches and the picnic tables and the basketballs, shirts coming off for some of them, even in the cold. Within a few minutes she felt it, felt their enthusiasm, their optimism, their courage, their aspirations—their faith that better days lay ahead, waiting for them on her side of the fence.

Gus saw their smiles, and she felt the rush. This was the boost she'd come here for. She could do this.

She left the woods and opened the car door, emotionally squared away.

"Let's go," she said to Yadi.

Texas was oil country, hurricane country, and gun country. Beaumont, Texas, the town they'd just entered, was no different. "Look for a Starbucks on your phone, mi amor," Yadi said.

"A shopping center northwest of downtown," Gus said. "With a drive-thru, near a large Kroger's grocery store. Behind the grocery store are some apartments. With parking."

At the Starbucks, Gus ordered a hot chocolate, Yadi abstained. They drove across the lot to the Kroger's. Yadi idled the SUV in a parking space. He eyed the front of the busy grocery store, then the Starbucks they'd just left, in the distant corner of the lot, then the grocery again. He hand-combed his platinum hair then tapped at his mouth with a closed fist. He was thinking.

"It's a straight line of sight between the two, Starbucks to Kroger's, with no obstructions. No good. Let's look at the apartments."

They drove behind the strip mall and entered another parking lot, a large complex of apartment buildings. From there, it would be a three-to-four minute walk to the coffee shop, around the corner of the strip mall.

"Perfecto," Yadi said. "These people all have guns. They will shoot if they see anyone messing with their car. But Starbucks customers, they are —how did my Philly friends say it, 'more show and less go'? Drink your hot chocolate, Gus. I will go for a walk. When I get back, I will need to explain something that is going to happen tomorrow."

However long it took, Yadi would return with a new ride. Gus sipped and read news stories from her phone.

A breaking news headline. *Arraignment: Alleged Peruvian crime family head Balea Xolo, also known as "La Ballena," will arrive at the federal Courthouse in Houston tomorrow. Multiple indictments, heavy security. US Marshals Office...*

Drug head pariah. Supermax federal prison. No successful jailbreaks from there, ever. To be held there under heavy guard until his trial. Solitary confinement. Aside from legal counsel, there were no visitors. No one could get near him.

Every day, from the moment she'd learned of his capture and transport from Perú to the US, she'd tried to work out the logistics in her head, always coming up short, her in Philly, La Ballena in Texas, half a country separating them. A fantasy of hers was no protective glass between them, no bars, no separation, no protective custody, and one gun. Stick it in his face, obliterate the monster. Ever since his capture, she'd never *not* dwelled on the satisfaction that this glorious act could bring her.

To accomplish this, she'd needed a strategy, so she'd created one. A play that would put her in front of La Ballena at the right moment.

Become a cross-country runaway. Convince a young, ambitious, wannabe thug to go with her, a peruana like her, who'd fessed up already to being on La Ballena's team. Someone who thought he controlled this trip. Someone she could manipulate. It was the play she was making now.

The news of the arraignment might have low-bridged her, La Ballena moving one step closer to a trial, one step closer, maybe, to the death penalty, low-bridging her because his punishment would be at the hands of the government, not her. Instead, the news thrilled her. It was happening now, with Gus no longer half a country away. Beaumont to Houston, a one-hour-thirty-five-minute drive, according to Google Maps. So close. When Yadi spoke with her about this thing that he wanted to explain, she would contain her enthusiasm and act surprised.

Forty minutes now, a long time, waiting for him to return, longer than she'd expected for him to find a coffee-shop mark, if that was all he was doing.

A white, four-door pickup stopped short in the parking space alongside Gus. Yadi powered the pickup's tinted driver's-side window down, Gus doing likewise with her window.

"We are good to go, mi amor!" he said.

She pointed behind him, at the truck's back window. Two molded plastic vertical rails were affixed to the top and bottom of the window frame. "A gun rack," she said. "And it is empty."

"Sí. We will need to be quick. I don't want to find out the hard way about the rifles it holds. Let's get everything moved over."

The back seat loaded, the pickup's capped truck bed with her bike under it, they got back on the highway. Yadi took frequent, paranoid peeks at the rear- and side-view mirrors.

"What I'm about to tell you will be a shock, Gus," he said amid his scattered glances, "but it is a good thing. For you, for us. I received a text—"

Gus would let him talk it through while she rummaged through the glove box, something she'd done in every vehicle he'd stolen, which had supplemented their cash by hundreds of dollars. No money in this one, but there was a surprise. A loaded handgun. She removed it, turning it over in her hand, curious.

"Gus. Chica. Are you listening?"

"Yes. You see this pistol, right, Yadi?" She held it up.

"Yes. Fine, you want me to look at it. Give it to me." He examined it, felt its light weight, eyed its short barrel. "A small revolver. It looks like a woman's gun. See, it holds only six shots. Someone would need to be close enough to shake hands to use it. I like my semi-auto 9mm Glock. Now we have two guns. You can put it back. What I am trying to tell you is I have been texting with a peruano soldier."

"That was why you were so long?"

"Yes. He is no longer in the army. He is one of La Ballena's men, and he is still in Perú. I have kept him updated on our trip."

"Why?"

"Niña! I told you why. I want to do more work for La Ballena. I want to help him, any way I can."

"But tomorrow, Yadi, he will be in an American courtroom. I saw on my phone. La Ballena does not have much of a future." She opened the glovebox again. Instead of returning the gun, she removed a sew-on shoulder patch that had been underneath it.

"Yadi."

"Him in a courtroom tomorrow is what is *supposed* to happen, chica."

Gus patted him on the arm. "Yadi—"

Yadi kept pontificating, flashing a knowing smile. "But it is not what *will* happen."

"What is this, Yadi, this patch? What is a Texas Ranger?"

Yadi grabbed it out of her hand and cursed in Spanish.

"This is not good. This truck—someone who has friends in Texas law enforcement must use that arm patch to get out of trouble! They will want this truck back. Find a motel for us for tonight, *now*. Tomorrow we will be very busy. Things are about to happen. Tomorrow we will go to a private airport, and we will wait, and we will look for a replacement ride afterward."

25

Sunday morning. Yadi's phone alarm, yet another burner, woke them at five a.m., Yadi in the bed, Gus asleep on the floor, their motel north of Beaumont, where they'd spent most of yesterday. She'd given him something to think about, sharing the queen bed with him to start the night, to maintain his interest and his allegiance. They'd slept in their clothes, ready to make a quick, easy exit in the morning, or an emergency exit if needed. Some hugging, some touching in the bed together. When he got too frisky, she moved to the floor.

Yadi opened the window blinds, Gus also awake, a pre-dawn glow on the horizon greeting them. Yadi leaned far right at the window, confirming their transportation was where they'd left it, backed into a space at the end of motel, away from their room. The gun rack was gone, relocated to the motel dumpster. "One less identifier," per Yadi.

Gus hefted her backpack onto her shoulder, Yadi doing likewise with his own, and they tossed them into the back seat of the pickup. Ignition on, heater on, defroster on. Yadi tapped at his phone.

"Twenty minutes away, there is a private airport in..." he checked his phone again for a text, "Evadale, Texas. Our contact says '*Operation begins 0645 hours. Be there.*' The dude is so military. Ha! I'm very excited to be doing this, amor."

The truck heater cranked, the frosty interior warming. They were on the move north on a two-lane road, searching for coffee takeout and breakfast sandwiches. Yadi's expression changed, going from giddy to serious. His sincerity was a harder sell with his boy-band platinum hair.

"Gus. Mi corazón. You know I am always looking out for you, right?"

"Yes. I suppose. Maybe."

"There is no 'maybe,' mi reina."

"Fine. You like me."

"That is why I find it difficult to tell you this. You need to realize you are now no longer welcome here because of what happened at the detention centers."

"Here where?"

"In America. This country. Because of the murders."

"You did them, not me. I only want to find my father and sister."

"Yes, but you are with me and are being blamed for them. You are considered an accessory. If they catch you, you will go to jail. I am in contact with La Ballena's people. They are interested in you. In us. You say you want to see them—see him. That is about to happen for us, mi vida! Then you will need to decide. Stay with me, while we both work for La Ballena. Or go on the run without me, and you will then go to prison when you are caught."

Gus had had it right. What she saw about him, they'd seen, too: he was perfect for manipulation. She was doing it, manipulating him, but so was La Ballena.

She was too far into this to disengage now. They'd made it to Texas. She was the nearest she'd been in three years to other immigrant people, other peruanos, who might help her find her family.

Gus was also the nearest she'd been to La Ballena. He was incarcerated, but he was still dangerous. His people wanted to see her not because they were benevolent. They—La Ballena—wanted something from her.

She gripped her leather pouch and prayed to her madre.

Two birds—two dreams—one stone. There could never be a more perfect comparison.

"I don't know, Yadi. I can't decide this minute."

A lie. None of it included working for La Ballena. She would take her chances on her own, Yadi and La Ballena be damned.

A left turn off Texas 105, onto Airport Road. They paralleled 1,500 feet of greenery on the right and dustbowl terrain on the left, all of it dead-ending with a crushed stone parking lot. They crossed the lot, passing an old two-story building with rust-splotched corrugated metal walls. A long time ago, the building was an airport control tower. Red-and-white-checked curtains in the control tower's windows looked new, or at least not old. The parking lot ended at a low-rise set of aluminum spectator stands. No other cars, no other people. Yadi idled the pickup between the stands and the rusty building, two lanes of entrance and exit to what was beyond it, an airstrip.

"This is not much of an airport," Yadi said.

Gus got onto her phone and checked out a few links. "It's no longer an airport. This tower is a souvenir hut. This is now a place to race cars, but it's closed for the season."

They exited their truck and wandered past the low-rise spectator stands, entering a strip of racetrack blackened by tire skid marks, fifty or more feet of them, on side-by-side lanes of asphalt, two blacktopped airport runways next to each other.

"They call this a 'drag strip,'" she said. "Here. This is what races on it." She showed Yadi pictures of colorful muscle cars with commercial sponsor logos, drag racers with big tires, and aerodynamic motorcycles.

They peered left and right, up and down the strip. Aircraft hangars painted with automotive sponsor logos and large one- or two-digit numbers hugged the runways in the distance. Outside the airport's two-runway footprint, the aluminum stands, and the hangars, the space was surrounded entirely by forest. Very private, but..."There are no airplanes here," Yadi said.

"No airplanes," she repeated, then pointed slightly above his head. "Look. A plaque."

A bronze plaque atop a black pole told the history of the property. A private airport that opened in the 1950s and closed to become a commercial dragstrip in 2002, in operation each racing season. Its runways had been extended during their time as an airport to become the 6,000 paved feet that they were today. The drag strips used less than half of it.

"I texted my peruano contact on the plane, to tell him we are here," Yadi said. "I told him the airport is no longer an airport, and that the runway looked too small."

Gus shielded her eyes from the low sun, swiveling her gaze left to right to get the full panoramic view of the landing strips. "I don't see a problem with the size, Yadi. The runways are very long."

"Not the length, mi amor, the width. The plane...it is very big." He checked his phone. He had an update from his contact. "They are twenty-two minutes away from touch down. He's not worried about the runway. We should wait in the truck. It's warmer, and we won't be so close. Just in case."

Doors closed, with the truck idling and them inside, Yadi was like a tennis fan during match play, his repeated nervous checks of the sky in both directions unnerving Gus. She settled on watching him, studying him, her expression turning grimmer by the second. For today to turn out well for her, it would not turn out well for him.

"I should not have dyed my hair," he said and grabbed the rearview mirror for a look at himself. He ran his hand over his head. "Silver hair works for the Japanese artists. Peruano hip-hop players, I'm thinking now, not so much."

"You look fine," she said, and she meant it, because how Yadi looked wouldn't matter. La Ballena's interest in him was because of La Ballena's interest in her. They had history. This meeting, should it happen, would not be happening otherwise. She just didn't have the heart to tell him.

But she would be kind and stoke his vanity. The least she could do.

"You are unique, Yadi, and they will see that. You will make a good impression."

Over his shoulder, an aircraft approached, no flashing lights, a dark spot that grew larger in a distant sky, moving in their direction, descending.

"Yadi," she said, her eyes following the plane. "They are here."

The roar of the jet engines increased, bordered on deafening just before it touched down. They stayed in the truck, listening and watching the large aircraft whoosh past them and touch down, five stories of whoosh in the blink of an eye, left to right, the ground shaking, the stands rattling, the blast of the engines replaced by the noise of screeching tires with no let-up. Yadi jammed the truck into drive, and they bolted onto the runway in pursuit, trailing the acrid smoke and stench from the burning rubber of the plane's tires, the aircraft threading the needle that was the narrow runway, the tires close to the edge on both sides, in danger of leaving it, the front end shimmying—

Stop, stop, STOP, Gus's inner voice screamed, with them able to see the plane about to run out of asphalt, its nose tilting forward, then tilting more, needing the landing gear brakes and the friction with the ground to fully take hold, then—

The nose leveled off into a safe landing, the plane cruising a short distance more to a stop. Yadi raced the pickup closer to the jet engines, then drove off the runway, back-roading it up to and alongside the dull black aircraft—a 747, Yadi had labeled it—with a small peruano flag beneath the flight deck window. The jet engines powered down then off, and the nose cargo door started its slow lift upward. When the cargo door cleared, a ramp slid out and dropped to the blacktop.

"Look at them go, chica!" Yadi said, excited. "They are in a hurry! They don't know how much time they have..." His excitement dissolved into nervous glances behind the jet and above it, skyward.

"Before what?" Gus said.

"Before the American military comes after them for landing an unauthorized peruano aircraft in the middle of Texas." He tapped a text into his phone and received a response. "We will meet my contact after they've unloaded, but he says it must be quick."

Multiple vehicles drove down a ramp in go-go-go urgency, the jet's cargo hold spitting out SUVs and sedans, camouflaged and plain, plus troop movers, missile launchers, and other tactical vehicles. Then came the commandos in ski masks, Gus losing count, at least fifty, in full combat gear, although not in uniform.

"They are mercenaries," Yadi said. "Some peruanos, some Americans, and men from other countries, other fighters. Very tough machos, and with conviction! Like me! This is so impressive, that La Ballena has this much appeal..."

"They are being paid to be here, Yadi," she said. "It is for the money that they fight," *not because of any conviction,* she finished in her head. They were no better than armed drug bullies.

"Yes! The money! Lots of it for them, lots for us. Because they will liberate a powerful man, and they will take him home. Get out of the truck. We need to be ready."

Gus wanted to vomit, hearing him talk like this about these people. She climbed out and caught up to him. The mass exodus leaving the hold of the plane was nearly over. The vehicles drove down the airport runway in single file away from this monster aircraft, exiting the runways via the same unimpressive road as the entrance, the only paved way into and out of the private airport-slash-drag-strip. A soldier in a ski mask waved Yadi forward but he put his hand up when Gus began to follow. Yadi closed out the distance, talked with the commando, and showed his 9mm. The commando gave him a nod, was then dramatic about directing him in Spanish to get back to his vehicle, and quickly. Yadi trotted back to Gus, the two trotting back to the pickup. Yadi spun the truck around, ready to join the evacuation.

"There is a change of plans, Gus. We are following them and their equipment out of here. We will wait elsewhere until they summon us. After they have freed La Ballena."

The Jeep moved off the runway, and Yadi followed it. Gus, in a state of urgent need, objected.

"I need a bathroom, Yadi. Now."

Their pickup neared the rusty souvenir hut, Yadi complaining, "But Gus, mi amor—"

"There," she said, pointing, "we need to stop there, or it will need to be on the side of the road. It must be now, please."

Four porta-potties extended from behind the old control tower. Yadi drove deep into the tiny clearing next to it. Out of the truck quickly, Gus walked tight-kneed to the rear of the tower, praying one of the toilets was open. She checked each door, her prayer at each one denied.

Ugh. "Close your eyes, Yadi," she called, "privacy!" He complied, and she squatted, making sure he kept his word by staring at him, ready to scold him if he peeked.

She heard the crunch on the stone of vehicles slowly approaching the tower from the runway side. Two four-door sedans in navy blue eased past, oblivious to the pickup and to Gus, advancing at a slow pace. Following the sedans came two logoed box trucks with red, yellow, and white logos that advertised potato chips. They could have only come from the plane.

Gus hadn't missed the faces of the drivers of all four vehicles while she relieved herself.

They were Asian.

26

Bulletproof vest, black helmet, heavy steel-reinforced boots. Xolo objected to none of the protective clothing covering him and his orange jumpsuit. The handcuffs and chains attached to his wrists and feet were a different story—too tight, too restrictive, he could barely walk, his complaints all going ignored. He shuffled forward, passing through multiple prison baffles toward the supermax prison's vehicle garage. He checked the faces of the prison personnel at their posts as he was led past, each C/O tight-lipped and ignoring him, even Smink, his infrequent escort inside the prison. Smart on her part, to keep up the façade. The troupe stopped in front of his transportation, an armored Chrysler SUV in blue and silver. The warden stood between him and the SUV's rear door, the only prison employee to show a hint of interest, his expression dismissive, but his words were not.

"Do yourself a favor and enter a guilty plea, Xolo. Maybe you'll get a back-door parole rather than the death penalty. If you do that, when you get back we'll let you play for one of the prison teams in gen pop if you want. Three point shooters are always at a premium. Even fat ones."

"Back-door parole" meant dying in prison.

Screw you, I won't be back for any of it, was the response in his head, but he verbalized only its two-word front-end in Spanish, which in this part of the country prison wardens understood. The man smiled, didn't react. Xolo knew the message connected.

The warden handed a manila folder to a US marshal uniformed in army-green body armor from his head to his waist, camo clothing everywhere else. Underdressed, Xolo told himself, but it didn't matter what the marshals were wearing. They were dead men.

The geared-up Fed gripped Xolo's elbow and ushered him forward, a nine-a.m. sun greeting them and making him wince, the warmth of the sunshine not a regular experience for him since entering solitary. Warm today, temperature in the fifties, no winter outerwear for him or for his escorts. Xolo took a deep breath. It would be a pleasant ride in pleasant weather—until the surprise.

"Ow," Xolo said, grumbling to the agent leading him to the vehicle, a smaller man. "The cuffs, they are too tight, señor."

"Seriously?" The marshal moved from a gentle hold of his elbow to a firm grasp of his cuffs, dragging him all the way to the armored truck door, the cuffs digging at Xolo's wrists. He put his hand on Xolo's head, guided him into the back seat. "Shut up, get in, then shut up some more." He closed the door, locking the prisoner in.

Such disrespect. Xolo would kill this little maggot gringo himself.

The five armored SUVs left the prison, two in the lead, two in the rear, La Ballena's vehicle centered between them, their destination the United States District Courthouse in downtown Houston. A one-hour ten minute ride per C/O Smink, but also per Smink, the trip would be interrupted.

"Watch for drunk monkeys," had been her last message to him, in Spanish. Because of the message's cryptic nature, that's what he would do.

Prison guard Smink, snitch corrections officer. He'd agreed to a lifetime supply of drugs for her boyfriend, for the help she'd given him, but "lifetime" meant an agreement weighted heavily in Xolo's favor. The free drugs delivery would be frequent, in significant quantities. If her boyfriend didn't OD on them, she'd get fentanyl from Xolo at some point. Free drugs from him were fine in principle, but free didn't mean forever.

The SUV chatter between the two agents in the front seats was lost to him, the miles and miles of four-lane highway whine and thick Plexiglas drowning them out. Twenty minutes into the armed transport—

The Den of Drunken Monkeys, the sign said, eye level, yellow and black, screwed on the exterior wall of a roadside bar that the armed caravan rolled past. The single-story roadhouse was a worn out honky-tonk, beaten down, Xolo was sure, by hard-living cowboys and their rough, chunky women. Per the sign, its blue collar guests could look forward to *Beer-Pool-Darts-Liquor* inside, hosted by top-hatted cartoon monkeys who liked downing shots while posing for bar logos.

Xolo eyed his driver and the second marshal riding shotgun, having isolated on their weapons during the transfer. AR-15s, in the front seat with them, plus two 9mm handguns each, plus a shotgun, plus Ka-Bars in sheaths velcroed to their exposed body armor. On the north side of the road, vehicles on the move blurred past them, but on their side the passing lane was quiet, traffic held up by the two armored SUVs bringing up the rear of his caravan, occupying both lanes.

The Drunken Monkeys hangout came and went. Xolo now questioned Smink's reliability.

Two, maybe three miles later, the highway went hard right and entered a stand of trees choking the road for a quarter mile on both sides. The caravan approached a railroad crossing that sliced through the middle of their path. Lights flashing and bells dinging, the crossing bars were on the way down, all five vehicles needing to stop to let a train pass. The mood in the SUV shifted, the marshals quieting, on alert, speaking into their lapel mics and earpieces. The agents were on edge, their chatter loud. Xolo stiffened, hopeful, was even more excited because of the cliché of it all.

"Where's this damn train?" the shotgun marshal said, impatient, his eyes swiveling. This was taking too long. "Can't see past these trees..."

The marshal issued an order at his lapel. "We've been here too long. I don't see no train. We're crossing the tracks. Everyone copy?"

The verbal confirmations came back. The first car drove around the barrier and approached the tracks—

It abruptly stopped, the second car on its tail also stopping short. A commuter train came barreling through the intersection right to left, its horn blaring, its six railcars crossing a few feet in front of the SUV, inches, seconds, from disaster. With the train past, the gates went up, silencing the bells, the flashing lights blinking out. Xolo heard cursing in the lead agent's earpiece before the SUV's brakes released and the driver put the transmission into gear. He felt the tires of his vehicle *thump-thump, thump-thump* across the railway tracks. All five vehicles resumed their ride, the mini-forest extending another few hundred yards before they would exit it, Xolo disappointed, losing hope that an ambush was still in play.

A white flash came from an ignition at ground level to his left, from inside the woods. He heard the *pffft* delayed by a split second, then saw a man on his knees underneath the weapon on his shoulder, the incoming rocket catching up to the left of the two SUVs in front of him. It hit the vehicle's midsection, cutting it in half, with both halves exploding, the road shaking from the direct hit. A look to his right, another white flash, the second lead SUV suffering as the target this time, blasting it off the highway, the fire from two ignited gas tanks rising, both vehicles raining burning rubber and metal and bulletproof glass and body parts, human and vehicular. Xolo ducked down, making himself as small as he could under his helmet and inside his Kevlar, covering up like a turtle.

Ba-boom, ba-boom, two more hits came in succession, striking the two vehicles behind him, more flaming debris dropping in bits and chunks onto the roof of the only vehicle that remained—the one he was in. The marshals in his SUV had their long guns raised, ready to exit but they held up, the short one shouting into a phone, relaying this disastrous update, adding a realization that had sunk in for him and his partner, that Xolo, in their vehicle, was the only reason they were still alive. The panicky reporting—*Mayday! Mayday! Mayday!*—drowned out the noise of anything on the move outside. Xolo lifted his helmeted head above the window ledge. Armed masked men stood in ready in the brush. He waved to them. One waved back, then gestured for him to get down.

Pffft.

Another surface-level rocket hit his SUV in the front end, left side, demolishing the armor, slamming the engine compartment, blowing through it to an exit out the other side, leaving the interior and its occupants jolted but unharmed.

Panicked responses overwhelmed his escorts' mics, overlapping shouting, pleading for support, no idea how many were out there, damn it, repeating gunfire ricocheting off the armored SUV, the driver's-side and passenger doors taking hundreds of rounds. The back seat was a virtual stronghold, Xolo listening to the gunfire and the exploding rounds, shrapnel and stray bullets hitting his doors, nicking the windows, but none of it penetrating.

The two remaining Feds fist-bumped each other, then, breathing hard, they exhorted themselves, pumping themselves up for what they had to do, which was open their doors, climb out, and go on the offensive.

Fifty was the number that C/O Smink had told him. Fifty peruano commandos and street thugs and mercenaries with military weapons, against ten US marshals with AR-15s in five armored vehicles, the vehicles now in pieces from close-range shelling and automatic gunfire, the marshal contingent now numbering only two. It was a military-style attack against a federal law enforcement escort. The only question remaining for Xolo was, could he survive his own rescue. He ducked down again, awaiting a new barrage of bullets and two more executions.

He heard the marshals yell with gung-ho abandon. They bolted their armored car cover and hit the blacktop running, discharging their weapons. He heard the torrent of bullets in response, pinging and thudding and zipping through their unprotected appendages, the blazing-lead amputations of hands from arms, and arms from shoulders, and lower limbs from torsos, fifty guns versus two, a slaughter at the hands of a firing squad, their agonizing screams quieting in a matter of ten seconds.

The helmeted Xolo sat up and showed his face in the window, keeping his cuffed hands and feet below the ledge. A cheer rose from his rescuers when he raised one hand for a thumb's up. They rushed the vehicle, found a key fob on a marshal's shredded torso, and pressed buttons until the rear doors unlocked.

Xolo stayed seated inside. He barked in Spanish at the first rescuer to reach him.

"Bolt cutters, amigo. Get these restraints off. No one can see me this way."

Shearing the chains had untethered his wrists and ankles, but the cuffs and leg irons remained in place around them. They would need a different solution for them. "Get me to the plane. We have no more time."

He emerged from the armored vehicle to another round of cheers and applause, raising a fist in solidarity to his rescuers. A masked lieutenant squeezed him into the rear seat of an SUV with a driver then climbed in next to him. Xolo hugged him and slapped him on the knee, their ride lurching forward, away from the mess of the ambush and the gathered commandos who made it happen.

"These men..." Xolo waved at the parting crowd of masked faces giving his vehicle room to pass, "you have coordinated their exits?"

His soldier removed his ski mask. "They are on their own, boss, and they are good with that. They have been paid. They will find their way home, or they will stay in America. It is up to them."

Xolo nodded. "How about the other thing?"

Their SUV accelerated, two escort vehicles trailing them.

"The trucks with the Chinese soldiers who came with us—they are headed east, boss. Our arrangement with them is now concluded."

27

A big day for the Artemis program and for Fend Aerospace, leaving no room for Max and Renee to dwell on mini-moon lander demos or a former senator's breached private network or dinosaur fossils that just might be from the Moon. Max, Renee, Emily Soo, Fend Aerospace's *Blue Spectre* end-product team, and NASA engineers were gathered at the Turtle Bayou air hangar warehouse. Ten thousand hours of tests, trials, and simulations by Max's company, plus an additional ten thousand similar hours by NASA. All had been performed onsite inside the hangar in a low-gravity chamber and outside on the open Texas prairie. Two hours of prep, some pomp, some flesh-pressing, and a Fend Aerospace ribbon-cutting had culminated in the transfer of the finished product, the full-size *Blue Spectre* Moon Lander, into a white two-axle semi, no markings, at one of the warehouse's loading docks. Aerospace engineers would add after-market options specific to the first flight when the product reached the Kennedy Space Center, Merritt Island, Florida, where the last payloads would arrive and find homes onboard. After that, more simulations, more testing, and eventual inclusion in one of the Orion spacecraft's rocket stages, ready for Artemis mission liftoff late next year.

"Checkdown complete," a NASA manager said, reviewing his iPad. "Consignments are five cubesats, three university experiments, and one

Voldemort mystery meat package from my employer. A second NASA mystery meat package was aborted for this trip last minute. It didn't sit properly inside its configured compartment. We're notifying the customer. We'll fix that at JFK. Nine seats taken, one on hold until launch date, and two empty seats awaiting customer selection round out the twelve payloads for this mission. What's supposed to be onboard today is, save for the one snafu. Is your guy in the helicopter, Mr. Fend?"

"Copy that, sir," Max said. "*Blue Spectre*'s propulsion chief Ted Leonard. He's there to babysit this trip and add color to the copter's video of it."

Voldemort mystery meat. An item that must not be named, one of a few shipments requiring clearances higher than those currently in attendance.

The journey was Turtle Bayou overland to Beaumont Municipal Airport, forty-three minutes, then a military airlift from Beaumont to the JFK Space Center that would take over seven hours. Many on the Fend Aerospace lunar support staff in Texas would resurrect themselves in Florida over the next few days.

Max and his team huddled together in the temporary command center set up to watch the overland trip to Beaumont in real time. The truck dieseled away from the dock amid hoots and hollers with a multi-vehicle escort. Six Texas Army National Guardsmen in a Humvee, two state trooper vehicles, and one sheriff's helicopter had been drafted to accompany the semi with the lander. Dashcams on all the vehicles streamed live video. A camera mounted on the helicopter delivered video from overhead. And above all of it, NASA satellite imaging could see the entire trip from outer space.

Texas Route 61 North, then it would be US Interstate 90 East. Trees, ranches, farms, open road. The video streams coming at highway level from the Humvee and the state trooper sedans were less steady than the overhead view from the helicopter, but it was still all good. Propulsion Chief Ted Leonard in the sheriff's copter launched into ho-hum chatter about cows and crows and ranchers on horseback.

Max, ten minutes into the transport, spoke to the room. "Anyone holding their breath?" He raised his own hand in response, two Fend engineers joining him. Emily sipped at an herbal tea, Renee at a coffee, both ignoring him, intent on watching the video streams. The convoy left Texas

Route 61 and entered the eastbound lanes of I-90. Max's phone vibrated in his pocket. Wilkes.

Max picked up, no hello, began talking to him immediately. "It's a good day here in Turtle Bayou, Caleb. The sun is shining—"

"Max—"

"...the birds are chirping—"

"Max—"

If Max kept talking, Wilkes couldn't interrupt and harsh his mellow.

"...and we're watching the diesel exhaust from our overland *Blue Spectre* transport as it chews up the miles—"

"Damn it, Max, shut up and listen. La Ballena is no longer in custody. His people just ambushed the US marshals taking him to the Houston federal courthouse for his arraignment."

Max's breath shortened. He stood, wanting to make eye contact with Renee, to discreetly alert her. Something was distracting her, freezing her, the video feed from the helicopter, Max unable to get her attention. He left the conference room, Wilkes still squawking on his phone, Renee getting more animated in Max's wake.

"They're gone, Max," Wilkes said. "The marshals, state troopers, cops, all of them were slaughtered. The Marines are there now with Texas FBI. The armored escort vehicles are in pieces from RPGs, maybe Stinger missiles, and automatic weapons. Plus a Marine helicopter found that Peruvian 747 on a local private airstrip. They dispatched a ground unit to the airport. They're moving on it now."

The conference room door flew open, Renee screaming at Max from the doorway. "Get in here, now!"

He marched back into the room, still on the line with Wilkes. She pointed at the overhead footage streaming from the copter's camera. Max crowded the monitor, then spoke to Wilkes. "I'm hanging up and calling you back on Facetime video, Caleb, so you can see what we're seeing."

Two navy blue sedans had joined the convoy uninvited, were barreling down the shoulder, the first rocketing past the moon-lander truck on the inside, the second paralleling a Texas state trooper vehicle, squeezing the cop car out of the lane and forcing it sideways left, trying to cut it off from the semi. The trooper vehicle accelerated, engaging the sedan, shots fired from the shotgun position at the sedan driver.

"Bulletproof," Renee said. "That sedan, the glass, the car panels are all armored..."

One final push from the navy blue sedan against the trooper vehicle's body shoved it out of position, sending it across the median where it lost control and careened into the westbound lane and oncoming traffic, horns blaring, tires screeching until it was broadsided by a big rig that pushed it down the highway. The copter camera followed them, the eighteen-wheeler braking but not fast enough, the police car rolling onto its side, the rig's big silver grille sparking against the cop car's underside while it slid until the car exploded, flames rising. The copter cam swiveled to catch up with the rear of the speeding, *Blue Spectre* semi.

Audio from heavy gunfire blasted the conference room monitor from the National Guard Humvee bringing up the rear, bullets pitting the rogue sedan's rear window but not shattering it. The sedan's side window lowered. A bazooka rocket launcher emerged, the weapon's stovepipe taking aim at the Guard vehicle, the assailant masked.

Max, Renee, Emily, the entire control room audience gasped and yelled at the feed coming from the Guard vehicle's dashcam, screaming at the guardsmen to brake their vehicle, back up, move, get off the highway, find cover, go, go, *go...*

The Humvee slowed to distance itself but stayed in position, its dashcam audio picking up an order for its occupants to move, move, move, open your doors, exit, the Humvee camera staring down the barrel of the RPG aimed at the windshield. An ordnance ejected from the weapon's stovepipe, the small missile traveling a hundred feet before a direct hit on the Humvee, exploding into the interior, the Guardsmen still inside. The conference room lost it, shouting and cursing at the monitor as the Humvee camera jolted off, the signal gone, the viewers horrified, shocked into silence. Two vehicles gone, the moon-lander truck was still on the move, its dashcam still live.

The other navy blue sedan emerged from the shoulder, entering the truck's dashcam view, passing the truck on the right, squeezing between it and its state trooper lead escort. The sedan tapped its brakes which forced the truck to slow, the sedan braking more, both vehicles slowing—slower, slower, slower—then a full, hard stop. Ted Leonard's reporting from the helicopter was panicked, breathy, expletive-rich, with him demanding his pilot circle back and hover, the pilot complying.

The lead trooper vehicle one-eightied and came roaring back toward the moon-lander truck and the sedan blocking the truck's way.

The copter camera zoomed in. A man in a ski mask emerged from the navy sedan's rear door and walked backward toward the truck, his long gun firing nonstop at the lead trooper vehicle now on a collision course, providing cover in his wake. The rogue sedan's shotgun door opened, a man quickly exiting. He reached back inside and slid out another bazooka. Staying behind the door, its window down, he settled the stovepipe on the ledge. The trooper car bore down on it, Max and team witnessing yet another dashcam flash from another bazooka, another rocket, another explosion, and the loss of another camera signal amid gasps from the team.

Three convoy vehicles gone, three dashcams gone, two left, the moon lander semi and the helicopter. Max and team strained to hear the feed from the semi, their driver's mumbling indiscernible, his cursing not so much. A click, then came the squeal of a hinge.

"That's the glove box," Max said, the room agreeing. Another click. "He locked his door."

"No," Emily said, "he unlocked it."

On dashcam video, the masked assailant from the sedan swiveled his long-gun aim from the trooper car on fire to the truck's windshield, advancing to the left, leaving the truck camera's view. The feed from the hovering helicopter showed the assailant grab at the door handle and pull it open. Before he could pull a trigger, he recoiled from a shot to his face, then another and another, driving him back onto the asphalt, the semi-driver's hands visible in the overhead feed, both wrapped around a hand-gun. The truck lurched forward, the conference room erupting, the pride, the satisfaction, the hope gushing from the team...

The semi's door opened again—another masked assailant, from the sedan at the rear of the truck, was on the running board. He ripped the driver from his seat, threw him onto the asphalt, and shot him multiple times in the head and chest. The truck rolled to a stop, the helicopter still hovering, still streaming video. The assailant with the bazooka from the lead sedan raised it again. This time, he looked skyward. He was locking onto the copter.

"Oh no," Ted said from his copter seat. "Turn off the feed, Max, turn it off now, tell my wife—"

The helicopter audio picked up the explosion, no video, only the prayers of the two men inside while the copter plummeted, then the second explosion on impact, stunning the conference room silent until tears and hugging and consoling began, and until Max raised his hand to quiet them. Still on Facetime, Wilkes would hear him, too.

"Everyone, shhh, please. Listen. There's still audio."

Slam. The sound of a truck door closing. One camera on the dash of the truck was still functioning, voice and video. Its streaming footage showed a bullet-riddled, navy-colored sedan one car length in front of the truck's grille and, beyond the sedan, the burning trooper vehicle.

A second door to the truck cab opened and closed. Two males speaking Chinese had climbed inside, their voices surrendering to the truck's diesel engine revving and blasting its exhaust through the straight vertical pipes rising above the cab, the blasts shaking it. More talk, then a laugh, then one man shushed the other into a dead-air moment. The dashcam video suddenly crackled and blurred, and when the crackling stopped, its feed showed sawgrass, presumably next to the road's shoulder.

"Did anyone get any of that?" Max asked.

Emily Soo answered. "It was Mandarin. Standard Chinese. I understood only part of it, but one word didn't need translation. He said 'China,' in English. He said they're going to China."

Max, Renee, and Emily were doing double duty from the Turtle Bayou conference room, now a control-center war room with ten monitors taking feeds from other war rooms, the Pentagon, NASA in Houston and the Kennedy Space Center, NSA, the FBI, and Wilkes, his location unknown, with him unannounced as CIA. They, among others, were handling both issues: the La Ballena rescue problem and the *Blue Spectre* lunar-lander hijack. Two separate sets of slaughter. Local law enforcement, local FBI, and the US military had been mobilized.

Max, speaking with NASA and a Marine colonel, "Do we have the satellite imaging yet?"

"Coming," a NASA tech said. "The dashcam footage review is done. Here it is, back-to-back-to-back dashcams queued into one stream."

In under three hours the NASA personnel, with Max, Renee and Emily at the Fend Aero warehouse, had been able to assemble the *Blue Spectre* ambush timeline. Streamed footage from seven dashcams and the one camera mounted under the helicopter, the assembled video worked forward from the least amount of camera footage per unit to the most. It began with the two cams on the trooper vehicle forced off the road and hit by the big rig—thirty-two seconds of footage—then the two on the Humvee —forty-three seconds—then the two on the lead trooper vehicle—sixty-one seconds—then the two-plus minutes of single-camera footage from the helicopter, videoing all four ground vehicles. The footage from the dash of the cause célèbre, NASA's semi carrying the moon lander, was last. The dashcam for the truck streamed until the battery died, providing hijack action for three minutes, a nosey coyote for another four, and blades of sawgrass waving in the wind for the next fifty. During the coyote footage, sirens from arriving emergency vehicles soon overwhelmed the audio.

Then came the satellite images, more important now because they could track the truck after the hijack.

"Here it is," a NASA official said. A black-and-white still photo hit all their screens, showing the semi on I-90. "The truck's got company, trailing at a distance, right—here—" a circle appeared on the display, surrounding a car or truck, "and here," a second circle doing the same. "Those are the armored sedans. The next set of stills show the three vehicles here, three miles later, and here again, still together after another four miles or so."

"They stayed on the highway," Max said, "and took the same route the logistics teams had mapped for our *Blue Spectre* truck."

"Still headed toward the Beaumont airport," the Marine colonel said, everyone agreeing.

Four more images indicated that the group of three vehicles remained on the interstate, still heading east, then...

"Nothing else, gentlemen," the NASA manager said. "Nowhere else on the satellite images. We lost them. The satellite's still searching, still imaging the interstate ahead of where we saw it last, waiting for it to show up again."

"That still shot with the last image," Max said, moving in closer to the desk monitor, "there's an intersecting road just ahead of it. Does it have a name?"

Renee spoke up, following along on her laptop. "Google calls it Private Road 106." Everyone viewing the footage was doing the same, connecting the different points on separate map apps on their own devices at both space centers, the Pentagon, plus other locations around DC and Texas.

The Marine colonel was visible on camera, barking orders into a phone. He put his phone away and addressed the viewers. "A squad from one of the Marine contingents we sent is now on the way to that private road. ETA twenty-four minutes," the colonel announced, adding, "Mr. Wilkes, I have an update for you on the other situation."

Wilkes, another onscreen presence, had remained silent. "Yes, Colonel?"

"You're getting your own Marine contingent as well. ETA in under twenty."

"Thank you, Colonel."

Depressing chatter, hand-wringing, and concern permeated the war rooms at all locations.

A captured Peruvian drug lord awaiting arraignment was now un-captured and on the run.

A multi-billion-dollar piece of space exploration equipment was in the wrong hands, probably the Chinese government's, its hijack still in progress. The US president had already called the Chinese president to demand an explanation and had received a denial. The lives lost, and the loss to the Artemis program—the US anger was off the chart. But that story hadn't been fully written. The hijack was only three hours old.

Emily Soo slapped her palm on a table, a eureka moment that quieted the on-camera chatter at all locations. "I figured out what was wrong with their discussion."

"Whose discussion?" Max said.

"The men who were in the truck, in the cab at the end of the ambush, the voices the dashcam picked up. Renee, put your Google map on a monitor so we can all see it."

The Polycom telecon feeds from all locations went silent. A map of the Houston-to-Beaumont corridor popped up on the monitors in all the war rooms.

"Do you ever call the United States by its Chinese name, Max?" Emily asked, out of the blue.

"What? No. I can't say I even know the Chinese translation for 'United States.'"

"Renee, zoom in to I-90 and follow it east. Those hijackers mentioned China, but they weren't going home yet, folks. They would have said they were going to *Zhongguo*, or any of the other proper Chinese names for their country, and I know many of them. They instead said they were going to China. *English*, Max. Who calls their own country by a foreign language name for it? No one. One of them laughed about it, caught himself, then they tossed the dashcam. Renee, hold the frame. There, right there. I say that's where they were headed."

On the map on the screen, the interstate ran through the city of China, Texas.

"If they went down that private road," she said, "it was to get rid of that truck. This is where they were going afterward. They didn't mean to tell us, but they did."

28

They were forced to wait at the bottom of the airplane stairs while they were searched. Yadi opened his coat, lifted his shirt. The large peruano guard removed the 9mm from Yadi's waistband and handed it to a second man before patting Yadi down and finding no other weapons. The second bodyguard pocketed the gun clip then returned the gun to Yadi. He thumbed Yadi aside and beckoned Gus forward. She looked past them, at the plane behind them. A face filled a window, male, dark, expressionless and unmoving, his eyes half-lidded.

Gus had never flown, had never been inside an airplane. Her legs weak, her stomach fluttering, it was all she could do to walk straight these few footsteps to the stairway, awaiting a pat down. The guard leaned down due to his height and her lack of it, and raised her arms to her shoulders, telling her in Spanish to keep them raised, eyeing her latex-gloved hands, wary. He began his search. When he came to the weathered leather pouch tied to her belt loop, he pulled at it. She grabbed it and pulled it back.

"No," she said and leaned away from him. "You do *not* touch this."

"Gus," Yadi said, "please."

"No!"

The second guard tapped the one doing the searching and redirected his attention to the plane window with the face in it. The man there called their search of Gus off with a single wave of his hand.

Inside the plane, she followed Yadi down the aisle, the guard behind them ushering them forward in Spanish. He pointed, they sat, side by side, in comfortable plush seats. Yadi was thrilled, Gus was nervous. They heard the whoosh of a commode. A lavatory door near the back of the plane opened. Yadi leaned forward in his seat a bit too eagerly for the guard standing in the aisle. He shoved Yadi back down and kept him there until Balea Xolo dropped his girth into seat across from them.

"Oakley, you there?"

Cornell heard Texas FBI Agent York, his new local contact, in his earbud. York was reporting from a private airfield in Evadale, Texas.

"Come back, Oakley, over."

Cornell was elsewhere, at Liberty Municipal Airport, southeast of Evadale, fresh from his flight into a different Houston airport and his meeting with the local FBI office and his intro to Agent York.

"Oakley here, over."

"Friends in high places, Oakley?"

They were working the same case but from different angles. Cornell now had a major lead on teens Agustina Gómez and Yadier Rolando, new homicide suspects now in Texas, the girl looking for her immigrant father. When the two left Philly, La Ballena was still in jail. What was their interest in him? Was it them anticipating—knowing—he'd escape? Or was it the reverse, La Ballena wanting one or both of them to come to him regardless of where he was, for reasons currently unknown?

Moths to the light made the most sense. He was a powerful Peruvian, they were Peruvian, he was a god, they were his subjects, La Ballena supplied drugs, Rolando pushed them.

The local FBI and the Department of Justice had a more direct, higher-profile mission. Find La Ballena and return him to jail for trial. Cornell's new local partner, York, had been pulled that way and was executing on it.

Cornell heard the wind whipping Agent York's face and ears through the earbuds, taking the man's breath away.

"This is...there's some major attention we're getting here at this closed airstrip, Oakley. A Marine contingent just showed up. Ten men in three Humvees, full gear, body armor, the works. You know something I don't know about this operation?"

Cornell's fellow FBI agents, Houston locals, were about to execute a raid on La Ballena's 747 sitting at the end of a runway, its engines off, the aircraft quiet, stairs from a rear hatch lowered to ground level, its nose cargo door closed. The Peruvian strongman had escaped into the Texas scrubland after a major shootout, and per the Bureau's speculation, this 747 was queued up to be his ride out of the country. The US military, just arriving on the scene, had explained their orders to the agents. It was close to go time.

Yes, Cornell said, he knew the reason for the military attention on the Evadale end. The Feds had seen the La Ballena ambush site. A war-zone slaughter. Cornell was as busy on his end working his homicidal-teens case, but with a lower profile, one likely needing less effort to stabilize. The wife of a Texas Ranger had reported her truck stolen, the Starbucks exterior cameras showing the thief in the act. Great photos of him, good facial recognition that revealed him to be Yadier Rolando, one of Cornell's fugitive teens. The stolen pickup had passed a toll-booth camera outside the municipal airport, the camera revealing the license plate. The Texas Ranger wife's stolen pickup. Good law enforcement work.

Cornell, sitting shotgun in an idling Bureau sedan, with another Bureau sedan close by, tugged at his Kevlar vest, his subconscious validating his stakeout's importance. The air charter parking lot cameras said the teens' stolen pickup was here. There it was, in front of a hangar, close to three large, gleaming turboprops parked on the tarmac. Cornell's team, him plus three agents, waited on approval to rush one of the props, the only one showing any life.

Agent York came through in Cornell's earpiece. "Marines got the order, Oakley. We're a go here in Evadale, ready to rush this beast. Good luck in Liberty."

"Copy that, York."

———————

Gus held a can of unopened Pepsi in her lap from the plane's tiny galley. She sat quietly in her seat, coy, bordering on frightened, La Ballena in the seat across from her. Yadi was none of that, sipping a Texas beer from a bottle, exuding his tough, streetwise, macho-teen persona for this peruano businessman to experience and appreciate. Xolo sipped a beer as well, listening, his legs crossed. To Gus, Yadi would do anything, would help this man in any way asked, and apparently would say anything also, to make that happen, regardless of how contrived and pandering his words sounded.

"It would be an honor, señor Xolo," Yadi said in Spanish, confident, comfortable, legs crossed just like his potential boss, "if you would let me carry your message of good health and good cheer by delivering your wonderful products to your customers on every corner and to every bodega and school and church and countryside in every community in every state in this great big country of America." He uncrossed his legs, leaning forward for emphasis. "I will help you widen your reach, will gather more disciples for you, more young people, will spread your gospel of hope and love and fun, will lay down my peruano street rap, and this chica here will help me—"

"Stop talking, bocaza," La Ballena said, staying with the Spanish. "I have heard enough from you. I want to talk with her."

He'd called Yadi a loudmouth, which shut him down just before a hand on Yadi's shoulder from behind pulled him back against his seat.

Xolo placed his beer aside and folded his hands across his chest. He lowered his chin to them, his eyes searching Gus's then moving south, to her sneakered feet, then north to her jeans, her open coat, her black tee, her hands gloved in blue latex. Then to the short hair that framed her face, dyed reddish-brown, and back to her eyes.

"Agustina Gómez," he began, still in Spanish, "you are self-conscious of your fingers. You should not be. They are a wonderful gift. I am glad you came to see me. Thrilled, actually. Your friend here means well. He talks too much, boasts too much, which might get in the way of what I'll have him do for me in America, selling my product—"

Yadi responded by interrupting him with a happy "Sí" and a fist pump and a thank you.

La Ballena's stare shut him up.

"—but he must learn how best to conduct himself and know when to remain quiet, especially if he has you as his feisty young partner"—another Yadi fist pump, silent this time—"to keep him grounded and give him something pleasing to come home to. You are beginning to look like your madre, señorita. Your beautiful, but disrespectful madre. Such a tragedy. But let's not dwell on her. Indulge me, because I do not have much time. This plane, it is readying for takeoff.

"I will be giving your friend here a stake to work with in this country. I am returning to Perú. You can stay here in America and work with him, or you can accompany me to Perú if you wish. But I urge you to stay with him, as his partner."

La Ballena's guard, distracted, covered his earbud with a hand and retreated a few steps, squinting to listen to whatever he was being told. Gus saw alarm on his face.

La Ballena continued. "There is one more thing, señorita. The reason I am glad you came to see me. Your mother—if you remember, I coveted her stone talisman."

He glanced at Gus's waist where her fat, ancient, leather pouch was tethered.

"So wonderful a gift it would have been to me, so revealing a look into our country's past, so comforting, so therapeutic, and perhaps even magical. But she would not give it up. I recall that you used a gun to take it from me while I was busy teaching her a lesson. A gun, trained on me, by such a niña. I am sure, with you knowing her fate, that you regret that decision, maybe even more than she regretted hers. I would like you to return that bag to me now. Your gift to me for my benevolent offers to you and to your friend. Things will go best for you if you do."

An intimidating mention of her mother. A threat, to remind her of La Ballena's visit to their village, his destruction of her family, to instill the same fear of dread and loss and pain he'd left in his wake. To resurrect the misplaced guilt that came with her mother's rape and murder.

Gus, stiff, expressionless, analyzed him, her hands in her lap.

"Give it to me, señorita," he said, holding out his hand. "This is how you can make amends."

His fingers beckoned. She searched his eyes, searched Yadi's, then ended her hesitation by untying the leather pouch from her waist and bringing it to her lap.

"May I please hold it before I give it up, señor?" she said, her first words to him since she'd entered the plane. She searched La Ballena's eyes, hers unblinking, and waited for his okay.

His offer had disgusted her, incensed her, reminded her of his depravity, and yet it was all good, because him coveting the talisman put him right where she wanted him.

He nodded his approval.

She could never have gotten this close, La Ballena untouchable in jail, could never have had this chance without Yadi's acquaintance, his connection, his allegiance to this monster. Yadi, she knew, would never understand, would never agree, and after this, would not let her live.

She reached inside the pouch. When she had it in her hand, she raised her chin.

La Ballena was right. This was how she would make amends.

"I would rather drink my own urine, señor, than give my talisman to you."

Her hand exited the pouch with the small-caliber revolver from the pickup truck's glovebox. A twitch of the trigger sent a bullet into La Ballena's eye socket at close range, then two more trigger pulls delivered kill shots to the back of the head of his distracted bodyguard.

She jumped out of the seat, creating space between her and Yadi, and straight-armed the revolver at his head. "Give me the key fob to the truck, Yadi."

"Amor mio, you crazy chica, what have you done...!"

"Keys!"

He removed the fob from his jacket. She swiped it from his hand, but his other hand connected with her, pulling at her gun.

Bang.

She didn't know where the bullet hit him. He didn't follow her, she in her shaky feet scrambling up the aisle—"I'm sorry, Yadi!"—with her gun raised, past the flight deck with the charter pilots, their hands up, frozen in their seats. She reached the open hatch. Two bullets left. She now saw what had alarmed La Ballena's bodyguard. Peruano guards with assault weapons were crouched behind her stolen pickup and facing other men with guns a short distance away, behind two sedans. When she appeared in the hatchway, the standoff erupted into a gunfight.

Three peruano guards fired across the pickup's truck bed, the cartridges from their long guns spraying two vehicles with assailants behind them who were returning fire. A fourth guard laid down suppressing rounds that gave him room to retreat and enter the plane, with him vaulting up the short stairs to the jet's hatch.

Two steps inside the hatch, Gus shot him in the face, his body tumbling back down the stairs.

She poked her head out, saw the battle on the runway, the three peruanos spraying bullets at the men behind the two vehicles. FBI or cops or some other law enforcement people, people she was now sure had been chasing her and Yadi, just like Yadi had said they were doing, the two of them fugitives, no distinction between them, she as wanted by them as he was.

She couldn't stay in the plane—they would capture her. Gus hopped down the stairs, jumped the guard's body, and stayed low while rushing the pickup truck, the bodyguards taking and delivering fire. She opened the door, got in, and kept below the window, La Ballena's soldiers cursing her, grabbing at the door handle, but she'd locked it.

She didn't know how to drive. She did know that her foot needed to be on the brake for the truck to start, then on the gas pedal for it to move. She pressed the start button in the console. The engine roared, her foot moved to the gas pedal, her hand to the steering, her other hand to the shift, and her head just below the dash. The truck lurched backward amid screeching rubber and one front tire already shredded by bullets, then forward, with her stealing glances over her shoulder, the three peruanos left exposed in its wake. The truck thumped its way down the runway, away from what now became a rout, two of the three peruanos eliminated in a torrent of gunfire, one quickly surrendering to lie flat on his stomach, shot multiple times.

She and her ride rolled at too fast a speed, the truck swerving, Gus peeking over the steering wheel, going where, she didn't know, but she had her talisman and her backpack and she was alive, and La Ballena wasn't, because she, Gus Gómez, had stuck a bullet into his fat head. That made her giddy-happy, then weepy and sad. She prayed to her absent mami, describing her triumph to her, her vengeance, how she saw the bullet enter La Ballena's head and spray crimson against the headrest behind it, heard her own voice curse him, saw this murderer draw his last breath, saw and heard all of this, and it had first exhilarated her, satisfied her, but—

"I love you, mami, I miss you, mami, I am so scared, mami..."

Her vengeful act would never fill the void created by the monster who'd taken her caring, protective, heroic mother away from her. She swiped at her tears, thought of papá and baby sister Gaby, and realized too late that she should have already turned the steering wheel.

Cornell was below the hood of their vehicle, soaked in sweat under his suit, reloading his weapon in the attempt to arrest two teens in what his team had miscalculated as a lower-profile event. The only nod toward its higher difficulty, just in case, had been the Kevlar and the helmets and the weapons they'd been issued, Heckler & Koch MP5 submachine guns, typically used by FBI SWAT. One FBI associate was down, three including him remaining, all taking and delivering fire at armed thugs protecting a turbo-prop business aircraft. It was now a full-on siege. Much more than they'd bargained for, cartridges pinging the asphalt, penetrating metal, destroying windows, tires, the aircraft, with additional help on the way.

His phone vibrated, he couldn't answer, time only for a glance and a grunt—"a little busy here, York!" and a finish of his reload. He heard a screech of tires, unexpected, and peered past the rear bumper of their sedan. The pickup truck the armed soldiers were using as cover had moved, first in reverse, then slamming into drive, screaming away from the turbo-prop, leaving three thugs exposed. They went down in a rain of lead, two of them writhing and hollering in protest until they expired on the tarmac, the third whimpering in pain on his back until he tossed his gun and surrendered. Cornell heard the screech of tires stopping short behind him as more FBI arrived. He shielded his eyes from the sun then gestured to the new agent arrivals. "There," he pointed, "that pickup, it's part of this. Let's go."

They arrived at the pickup truck a quarter of a mile away, two tires left, the other wheels on metal rims, the engine running, the tailgate down, the vehicle sitting atop a runway marker impaling the underside. Cornell searched the horizon.

He pointed. "That bicycle, nearing the airport exit, that's her, one of the fugitives we're after—"

The two-wheeler was doing its best to speed away, the rider with a backpack, her tiny legs pumping, grinding, her effort waning.

"Agustina Gómez!" Cornell called, trotting after her. "FBI! Stop. Get off your bike and lay down on your stomach, now!"

Gus Gómez slowed to a halt, climbed off the bike, and lowered it gently to the ground. She turned to face her pursuers, her shoulders square. She was visibly exhausted, her hands at her side, except—

Cornell raised his long gun to his shoulder. "Put the gun on the ground, miss, and back away from it. Do it now."

Her cheeks lined with tears, her chest heaving, she remained still, her frightened eyes evaluating her predicament...she was taking too long...

"Gun—down—now!"

She leaned down, laid the gun beside her, and stepped back. She dropped her backpack, laid herself face down, and continued sobbing. An agent cuffed her hands behind her back while reading her her rights.

Cornell stood above her prone body. Such a small girl to have wreaked so much havoc—quirky, too, her hands gloved in blue latex, same as when the Philly cops had arrested her. He handed off his long gun, got into a crouch, and maneuvered into some semblance of facing her. Her sobbing had subsided, but her face was still soaked in tears, nearly kissing the runway, not able to wipe them away on her own. Cornell produced a hanky. "May I?" he asked.

She cried more, then said yes. "There were three of you," she managed, "I didn't have enough bullets left."

He dabbed her red eyes and cheeks, shaking his head. A feisty kid, but her bravado—to Cornell, it had no real malice in it, only desperation.

"Let's stay away from any more talk like that, Miss Gómez. It'll get you killed. These two agents are going to stand you up and escort you to the car."

Cornell volunteered to ride in the back with her, his associates in the front. Their vehicle returned to the bloodbath at the private jet. "I'm FBI Agent Oakley, and I've been chasing you since Philadelphia. I'm glad it's over. You should be, too."

More tears from the tiny teen, her head against the window, watching the small airport's scenery slip by. "It's over for you, señor," she said in English. "But not for me. I still have no family."

A large law enforcement contingent was gathered at the chartered aircraft. The pilots were out of the plane, were judged persons of interest only, unwitting about the details behind the charter, hired through a third party, but they were handcuffed as a precaution. One accomplice had surrendered on the tarmac, heavily wounded, as had one teenage male with a gunshot wound from inside the plane, both victims awaiting ambulances.

Cornell left his prisoner in the car with one other agent. FBI Forensics was investigating the scene inside the plane, where he joined them. Ten minutes inside was enough, the tally there two males shot at close range, both dead.

York had called Cornell twice more from Evadale Airport since his first interruption in the middle of the bullet barrage. Cornell, back outside, called him back. York sounded animated.

"Oakley! There you are. The 747 on our end is secure but damn it, there's no La Ballena. It's empty. No nobody. A one-hundred-percent false alarm. We're scouring this thing but, frankly, it looks like it's been abandoned. How'd you guys make out?"

"We got him, York. La Ballena. He was here. So were my two teen fugitives from Philly. A private air charter headed to Perú, but it never made it off the ground. One federal agent is wounded. We're squaring things away right now."

"Outstanding. Any word on who gets to take him back to prison?"

"Yeah, well, that's not how it went down. La Ballena is dead, was shot on the plane. The coroner will be here soon. We're piecing things together. One teen fugitive is wounded, the other, the girl, seems okay. As soon as I can get her into an office, we'll interrogate her. Join me when you can."

29

The conference/war room was still busy at the Turtle Bayou facility. So, too, were the other war rooms set up to address the moon-lander hijack. They were all tuned into a replay of bodycam footage from when a Marine sergeant and his squad had descended on the property at the end of Private Road 106 near China, Texas.

The hijacked semi was there, near a barn on a dirt road in the woods, camouflaged by heavy tree canopy. A high water table, deep tire tracks in mud, the semi's mudflaps caked in it, the road probably never saw much in the way of heavier trucks. Ranch and farmland spread out behind a two-story residence fronting an alpaca farm. Rice paddies, with bleating animals on the audio, the sergeant's video showed a dead alpaca in the front yard, then a dead man on the home's porch, fifties-sixties, Latino, a rifle under his body, plus a dead Latina woman next to him, a twelve gauge next to her, multiple gunshot wounds on her face and body.

When the replay finished, the Marine colonel at the Pentagon summarized the footage for his audience:

Two civilians dead from defending themselves, their livestock, and their property.

Light farm equipment, two SUVs, two pickups, all riddled with cartridges. Shell casings everywhere.

Bullet holes in the semi truck's outer skin, drippy red splotches surrounding the holes, more blood in the dirt, no body. "The ranchers got one of 'em soon after he exited the truck," the colonel said.

The semi was empty, which meant still no *Blue Spectre*, which meant the lander had acquired new transportation.

The security camera perches, hanging from the porch ceiling, barn, and mailbox, were destroyed, pieces of the perches scattered, the cameras gone.

An open book lay spine up on the porch table next the woman's body, the paperback held down by a Colt revolver. The sergeant moved the handgun out of the way and smoothed out the page for his bodycam viewers. Scrawled across it was one word in blue highlighter: *frito*.

"Fried," Emily Soo said. "In Spanish, frito means fried."

"It's also short for Fritos, as in the chip," Max said. "Maybe a deathbed clue."

"Marine recon copters are mobilized," the colonel said, finalizing his update. "The highways are under surveillance, plus there are two private airfields near China. We're starting there."

⸻

Max, Renee, and Emily remained huddled in their conference room like other NASA, military, and law enforcement types were huddling in DC, Houston, the JFK Space Center, the Pentagon, and elsewhere, awaiting the outcome of the newest Marine raid underway at another private runway a mile outside China. FAA records showed one hangar on the property with—

"A small cargo aircraft on the airstrip per the satellite imaging," the colonel said. "We can see it."

"Large enough to fit the moon lander?" Max asked.

"Specs for that model aircraft say yes. Tight, but big enough. A squad is en route. ETA three minutes."

Max sat up in his chair for a closer look at one of the screens, puzzled. He resisted pointing, poking Renee's arm instead. He spoke in a low voice. "The Houston Space Center feed. Look who just entered the room."

Mister Moon Rocks himself, the doddering Dr. Kirby. White lab coat, glasses, he shuffled in and found wall space at the rear of the NASA Houston group.

The live audiences all focused on the footage livestreaming from a Marine sergeant, one of six Marines storming a residence on the airport property. The house interior was a mess, tables overturned, shell casings underfoot, a ragged dotted line of bullet holes in the living room wallboard that ran from the front door through the dining room to the door to the utility room. The utility room door was splintered, revealing an overturned gun cabinet that had blocked it from opening. It had been a chase from the front of the house to the rear, interrupted by the barricade. The livestream moved to inside the utility room. A man was dead from multiple wounds to his face and body, a shotgun in his lap. The livestreaming Marine did an about face.

"Blood smear on the floor in the other room, beginning in front of the splintered door, through this room, and out the back door," the Marine said. "They dragged someone out." The Marine searched the immediate area. "His weapon's still here. It was one of their own." He turned, and the body of what was probably the homeowner was now back in view, seated on the floor. "Hats off to this patriot, God rest his soul."

Action now came from cameras on the Marines in position on the China, Texas, airstrip. A leader barked bullhorn orders at the cargo plane considerably smaller than a 747. The Marine colonel at the Pentagon over-rode his sergeant's audio for the viewers.

"They will rush the plane momentarily, folks. My friends at NASA, you should rest assured they will concentrate only on the flight deck and imme-diately behind it. Orders are to move into the hold only after they secure the front and to not shoot up any apparatus in there."

More footage streamed from the squad rushing the small cargo plane stairway and up the steps, no shots fired, no resistance. Six Marines were now inside the plane, moving from the flight deck to the after deck, then into the cargo hold. Packing straps and other discarded packaging materials and stray detritus lined the hold, but otherwise it was squared away.

"Do you copy my livestream, Colonel?" the Marine squad leader said. "There is no moon lander."

"Copy that, Sergeant," the colonel said.

The Marines entered the air hangar, still streaming their movements. Inside was a large box truck and an armored sedan.

"Fritos," Max said, voicing what they all saw.

Onscreen, the markings on the side of the truck affirmed they were in the right place, the red, yellow, and white logo for Frito-Lay, the chip company. "Like the alpaca-ranch lady told us," Max said.

The squad leader barked orders at the truck cab, demanding that any occupants in it exit with their hands behind their heads. After no response from the order, he gave the go-ahead. His weapon trained, a Marine pulled the door to the cab open and climbed inside. "Empty in here, Sergeant. There's a walk-through to the cargo space." A second Marine entered the cab. "We're going in."

Ten seconds later, the truck's rear door lifted open, the inside of the cargo area coming into view, but in shadows. Both Marines stood cradling their AR-15s in the middle of the open space at the rear of the truck. "It's empty, Sergeant."

"Mr. Fend," Max heard, raising his head to the speaker. The Marine colonel spoke into the camera on his end. "Please pick up. That's me calling you." Max answered his phone, the colonel greeting him with, "What the hell did they get, Mr. Fend?"

"Nothing yet, Colonel. Let's not give up on this. It's either still on the ground somewhere in the area or it's in the air. We just need to move on it, down here and up there."

"Yes, I get it," the colonel said, "but we don't know what we're looking for yet, and there are a helluva lot of planes up there. If there was another aircraft or more vehicles on that airstrip earlier, the satellite imaging will help ID them. We'll get this region carved up into imaging cross sections, but we might have missed a window if they did get airborne. We don't know the type of aircraft we're looking for. Again, what did they get?"

"The lander, Colonel. A billion-dollar moon lander. You should have the physical specs for it in your mail. Payload wise..." Max pulled up the *Blue Spectre* manifest PDF on his phone. It was attached to a classified email. "Ten consignments. Some cubesats, some experiments, one payload that's classified. No, make that two classified payloads."

Max read the list. "Emily. Where's Emily? I thought there were only nine payloads that went with it, this shows ten. One of them was added late. Why wasn't I—?"

"You were notified, Max," she said. "One late add, then it was scratched. Back to nine shipments. A compartment configuration issue aborted the tenth."

Max knew better than to argue with her. And after finishing a closer review of the revised manifest, he found himself preoccupied, instead now looking for—

"Kirby," he said, poking Renee. He searched for Dr. Kirby on a camera feed. "Where is he?"

He found him again, on the Johnson Space Center feed, Kirby's hands folded atop his gray head, an eccentric pose, his eyes unfocused, almost looking lost. Max checked the PDF again, then elbowed Renee.

"The manifest," he said, pointing at his phone. He zoomed in on the PDF. "Look."

Project #10. Name: N/A, classified 1.4(e). V. Kirby, NASA.

Renee thumbed through her phone, found the classified category, read him the official description for the category, but they knew it already.

"For scientific, technological, or economic matters—"

"Relating to national security," Max finished. "Not a surprise. But Dr. Kirby sponsoring it is. I wonder if he knows we had to pull it at the last minute."

The status, known by all now, was that *Blue Spectre* was in the hands of the Chinese. En route to where, and how, was pending. A breaking news story, impossible to keep quiet.

Max spoke again, this time meant for the entire Turtle Bayou conference-room audience, lest they'd forgotten. "Full onboard, self-contained AI capabilities. They tried to go the white-collar route and steal the specs and software online with Fifi Hu and failed, so they went after the apparatus itself, doing an end run around years and years and billions of dollars of development. Team, get ready. We might need to build another one."

"Max. Here's a thought," Renee said. "Can we turn *Blue Spectre* on?"

The room stayed silent a beat. This was where Ted Leonard, RIP during the *Blue Spectre* hijack, would have been the one to offer his input.

Emily spoke up. "Yes, we can turn it on. But maybe we should think that through before we do."

30

Cornell ID'd himself and spoke a few sentences to his teenage suspect in the FBI sedan. She didn't respond to any of it. He'd have to wait for the main event, interrogating her at the Houston FBI satellite office in Beaumont.

They passed a fast food restaurant, then passed another. "Hungry?" Cornell said.

"Sí, yes," Agustina Gómez said.

The Beaumont office was on one floor of the tallest building in the neighborhood, ten stories, aesthetically pleasing with charcoal-tinted glass panels on all sides. The three agents badged their way inside with their handcuffed escort, Cornell holding her drive-thru meal.

Miss Agustina Gómez sat at an interrogation table eating her McDonald's, her handcuffs and her latex gloves off. Matching her fingerprints to the ones taken in Philly had been an adventure, two digits too many, but otherwise the match was good. The backpack and leather pouch were in the corner of the room. She glanced at them frequently, chewing her french fries. Her next peek at the corner became a stare.

"Your belongings will be fine, Miss Gómez," Cornell said. "This is Agent York out of Houston. He and I have a lot of questions. You've been busy this past week with your boyfriend. We'd like to know everything you did and how you ended up in that private plane with La Ballena."

"He's not my boyfriend," she said. "Yadi's from Perú, like me, and I thought he was my friend, but he isn't."

"How so?" Cornell asked.

She swallowed a bite, took a sip from a drink, grabbed more fries and chewed, her eyes on the table, her look blank. Cornell waited. She chewed more. She took another sip. She grabbed another fry. More chewing.

"This is how this is going to work, Miss Gómez," Cornell said. He moved the sandwich wrapper and what was left of the burger and fries out of her reach. "You talk, we let you eat. Answer my question."

"Yadi killed an ICE person in Philly," she said, "then he killed another one at a detention center at Bowling Green. He told me he killed them because they were disrespectful. He said I'd be blamed for their deaths because it was me who wanted to go to the detention centers. He said we'd both go to jail if we were caught. He also said he'd help me find my father, but all he really wanted out of our trip was to meet La Ballena, to work for him."

"La Ballena was in jail until yesterday, in Livingston," Agent York said. "No one would have let your friend in to see him. It's a supermax prison."

She had her food back, ate more. "Yadi knew people who knew La Ballena. They were planning his escape. He said La Ballena wanted to meet me."

A look passed between Cornell and York. New territory.

"Why did La Ballena want to meet you?" Cornell said.

More fries, more drink.

"Miss Gómez?"

"Mi familia," she said. "I have not seen my father, my sister, or my uncle for three years. I don't know if they are alive or dead." She swiped another fry, chewed, blinked away a tear, then Oakley and York heard all of it.

About her father, a peruano cowboy. About her life without him after crossing the border into Texas. The border patrol cages, her only thirteen, the pain, the shame, the loss. Her Philadelphia existence, how fast she learned English, her life as a teenage girl in a big city.

Foster care. Panhandling on street corners. "...hundreds of dollars a day..."

Pickpocketing and pawn shops. Stealing jewelry from jewelry counters. "Sometimes a clerk puts it down and forgets," she said.

A scoff and a head shake from Agent York at the incompetence. "Idiots. That's jewelry store 101." Cornell simply nodded, appreciating her opportunism.

Her decision to return to Texas. The ICE detention visits. How she wanted to find the peruano family she was supposed to stay with when they first crossed the river into America. She *would* find them, and they *would* help her find her family.

"La Ballena wanted me to visit him because he knew me from Perú. Because he is a terrible person. Because he sells drugs and kills people and takes things from them and their families. Whatever he wants. He killed my madre in front of me! He attacked her, then he killed her. I saw my mami die." Another glance at her things in the corner.

"He wanted my pouch. The special stone that is in my pouch. It was my mother's, and she is dead because she wouldn't give it to him, and I took it, and I ran."

"Agent York," Cornell said, "what do you say we bring her pouch over here and let her show it to us."

York dropped the cracked leather bag in front of her. He raised his eyebrows at the smell it left on his hand.

"The leather is very old," she said, defending the odor. "The stone inside is older."

She slipped the stone out of the bag, gray-black and polished on one side. She kissed it, showing her reverence. She turned it over, the other side jagged, its surface raised, off-white, smokey gray in color. She raised the stone to her mouth again. This time she licked it. She put it back on the table, on top of the pouch.

"Can you tell us what that was all about, Miss Gómez?" Cornell said. "That lick?"

"A ritual of my people," she said. "Bones are porous. They make fossils feel stickier on your tongue. I know the taste, and I will know it when you return this to me."

"Fossils, like when dinosaurs died?" Cornell said.

"Yes, señor."

"You carry them with you?"

"Sí. To honor them, and to understand them."

York spoke, squinting his condescension. "So you're a teenager who steals dinosaur bones to use as swag?"

Agustina Gómez reached for the stone again and held it tightly in both hands. "I didn't steal it! It's from a creek in our village. They are *not* from dinosaurs. I know the difference. I want to be a paleontologist."

"You're saying these are *human* bones?" Cornell said.

"Sí. Human finger fossils. From the beginning of time. My madre, my people, we revere our amulets. We honor our ancestors. I know you will take this from me, and I won't be able to stop you. But I will want it back."

Done with Agent York's pomposity, she gave Cornell more of the rundown.

"I was lucky, señor. La Ballena was a terrible man. He destroyed our country and my family in the name of drugs. He is a murderer. I am in America only because La Ballena drove us out of Perú, and my padre and my tío brought us here. We were separated at the border crossing. When I heard you captured La Ballena and brought him to America, I hoped I could someday find him. God granted my prayers. He escaped, and Yadi brought me right to him."

Her jaw tightened, her fist clenched, readying them for her reveal.

"I shot him, in the face! For killing my madre! For wanting these bones. For ruining my family. Yadi tried to stop me. I shot him, too, and the guards." Her eyes widened with a sudden realization. "Where is Yadi? Is he..."

"He's alive, and he's in custody in the hospital," Cornell said. "He'll be interrogated, just like you."

She checked an interior window that had a view of the FBI office outside the one she was in, her look worried. "He will try to kill me, señor. Or La Ballena's people will try, if they ever get the chance. In here or outside."

"We won't let that happen."

"Okay," she said, nodding, "I believe you will do your best." A resigned Gus sipped her drink, folded her hands in her lap, and met their stares. "I am not worried. I have avenged the soul of my madre. I killed La Ballena and I spat on his body and I watched him die. It was worth it."

31

Max's phone buzzed with a text. Wilkes.

La Ballena dead in Texas. Call your friend Oakley. The media's got the story, but the FBI has the correct details

Max got Cornell's voicemail when he called him. He and Renee were stuck with learning more from the nationwide news on a TV in Max's Turtle Bayou facility office. It was an FBI press conference about the raid, the gunfight, dead Peruvians on a tarmac, and more dead bodies inside a small private jet. Liberty Municipal Airport, Liberty, Texas. Among the dead in the jet— La Ballena, the escaped Peruvian drug king. Reporters peppered the FBI spokesman with additional fantastic rumors that the agent was "unwilling or unable to confirm them at this time."

A teenage girl from Perú killed La Ballena?

She has six fingers? She wears fossils made from voodoo bones from the Amazon rainforest that are a million years old?

La Ballena's empty Boeing 747 sits on a racing dragstrip in Evadale, Texas? Bubblegum wrappers were in the cargo hold?

"That China Airways 747 at the dragstrip,'" Max said, opining, the presser ended, "I figure that was their way in."

"Whose way in?" Renee said.

"The moon-lander assault SOBs. The Chinese hitched a ride with La Ballena's commandos. They were working together. It all fits."

What did ring true was the speculation about the 747 and the Chinese gum wrappers. But the rumors about million-year-old fossils...?

The only ones he knew that were that old, and perhaps older, were from rocks no one was supposed to know about, found on the Moon.

Max and Renee's interest in this teenage girl off was now off the chart.

"This is nuts. Cornell. Where the hell are you?"

Max's second call to Cornell connected.

"Oakley. What do you want, Max?"

"Happy to see you found La Ballena." Max moved quickly into and beyond the kudos. "Great police work, you're a hero, you need a commendation and a raise. You also need to return your calls to your billionaire friends."

"So you saw the presser."

"Yes. Crazy stuff. Un-crazy it for me."

"I can't help with much of it, Max. He's dead. His bodyguards are dead, too. One surrendered, but he didn't make it. The girl we were chasing was with them. She's cooperating. Her friend survived, too, is recovering from a scalp wound, in the hospital. We're currently piecing things together—the chase, the stolen cars, the dead ICE workers. You called me why?"

"I want to interview your suspect. The teen girl. A matter of great importance."

"Sorry, but no. You can't interrogate her."

"An interview, Cornell, not an interrogation."

"Call it what you want. You have no standing here. No."

"National security gives me standing."

"Elaborate."

"I can't. It's classified. Look, we won't screw up your case, Cornell. It's just an interview."

"About what?"

Max should have had an answer for this, but he didn't. "Sorry, classified. We just need to talk with her."

"Let me take a stab at it, then. It's about your hijacked moon lander, right? I'll validate one rumor for you, Max, only one. The gum wrappers in that cargo hold were for Chinese bubblegum. How that info leaked, we're checking on that now, but that much is true."

"So you'll get me and Renee in to talk with her, then?"

"Fine, dammit, but the FBI needs to be part of it."

"No. Renee and me only."

"Max, you're not giving me much to go on here, bud."

"Classified."

Max prayed he wouldn't call his bluff. The CIA couldn't know about this request. Max and Renee were covert, and having them in there on official CIA business would blow their cover, so if the CIA gained an interest, Max and Renee wouldn't be included. Plus the issue about her having million-year-old fossils—current thinking was that was a scientific impossibility, and yet...

Neither Wilkes nor the CIA could know about her fossils. Apollo 17, sample 73001, its analysis pending—as far as Max knew, Max and Renee were on an extremely short list of people aware the sample contained fossils that defied their own existence, the list being the NASA administrator, the US president, Dr. Vernon Kirby, and the two of them. And those people might also be plenty interested in getting their hands on whatever "voodoo bones," ages unknown, this girl might have in her possession. The implications were mind-boggling.

"Can you make this happen, Cornell?"

"I'm Max Fend, Miss Gómez. This is Renee LeFrancois. A point of reference for you, so you feel more comfortable talking with us. La Ballena was brought to the US because I worked with our military to make that happen. The short of it is, I caught him."

An introduction to tee up her cooperation, if her cooperation could be had.

Her dark brown eyes showed a spark of interest. "I'm Gus."

Contact. A start. Excellent.

"*Goose?*" Max said. "You name is Goose, like the bird?"

"Yes. It is short for Agustina. Ah-goose-tina."

Padded folding chairs, lamps with shades instead of overhead lighting, and a conference table, the room's atmosphere was not any better than a doctor's waiting room, but it did have a see-through surveillance mirror. It was the best Cornell could do at making things private. She was a homicide suspect, so the FBI, in some capacity, had to watch the interview. Cornell had guaranteed he'd be the only observer.

Renee brought three dozen donuts with them, a dozen for the discussion in this room, the rest for the local agents and staff. If they could keep the bears fed, they'd be less likely to ruin their picnic.

"We were upset when we learned La Ballena had escaped," Max said. "We're happy he's been neutralized. The FBI's job, Gus, is to piece together what happened with you at the detention centers and on the plane. But we're not here about that. We're here to learn about your stone talisman. Have a donut."

Apparent to Cornell, and now to Max and Renee, was the pouch with the stone meant more to her than any of her other possessions. The FBI had let her keep it for now.

She had a fierce grip on the leather bag. There was no missing her supernumerary hands.

A headshake no to the donut.

"I saw them, you know," Gus said.

"Saw who?" Max said.

"The Chinese men. They were on the Perú airplane. Yadi and me were there when it was unloading. The first ones out were peruano soldiers and all their equipment. They wanted us to follow the soldiers off the runway in our truck. We did, but Yadi stopped so I could use a bathroom. That's when I saw the Chinese men. They had cars and trucks that came from the airplane. Doritos chips trucks. Two cars, two trucks."

Confirmation for Max and Renee that this was how the hostile assault teams got in. Good to know, and it was good to know also that she felt comfortable volunteering this info, but—

"Why are you telling us about the Chinese?" Max said. "Does the FBI know about them?"

"Because you are señor Max Fend. You built a moon lander. The TV news says the Chinese stole it. Maybe it was these men." She nodded at the mirror. "And now the FBI knows about them, too, señor."

So it was out there. It wasn't like they could keep so fantastic and deadly a heist a secret for long.

"Fine. Thank you, Gus. Can you show us what's in your leather bag now, so we can examine it?"

"Why?" Her eyes searched his and Renee's, her skepticism showing. "It's an old rock with bones in it. Why must you see it? Why does everyone want to see it?"

"The FBI says La Ballena wanted it, is one reason. Why did he want it?"

"It's because it is special to my family...and has been for forever. La Ballena said he thought it was magical. But he said that because he wanted it, because he takes things from people and kills people if they don't give them up. It is not magical. It's just a connection to my family's past. To my ancestors."

Tears welled, and her upset hung out there a moment, her nose sniffling.

Renee pulled up a chair to join her on the other side of the table, a tissue box in hand. "It might be more than that, Gus," Renee said. "Can you show it to us, honey?"

Gus accepted the tissues, dabbed her eyes, and evaluated Renee. She took a donut from the box and set it on a napkin. She brushed the crumbs off her fingers.

"Okay. You can look at it."

Gus pulled at the top of the pouch to spread open the drawstring. Her reverent, resigned look inside the bag preceded a pronounced exhale. She passed it to Renee. Max huddled up, and Renee took phone photos while Max held the bag up, Renee snapping all sides of it, all angles, from above and below. Gus ate her donut. Max returned the bag to the table and spread the top open as wide as it would go.

"I'm taking the stone out," he said.

Gus nodded, still chewing.

Renee snapped away with her phone, many photos of the stone in Max's hand as he turned it over and over. He set it on the table and produced a tiny magnifying glass from his Leatherman pocketknife, steadying it over the fossil side of the stone, he and Renee peppering Gus with questions.

How old?

"Beginning of time old, mami said. It was given to her mother by her mother before her."

Where was it found?

"Near my home in Gente de la Luna, in a creek bed. The creek is gone. The big companies ruined the land and the rivers and the creeks when they chewed up the ground and cut down the trees. These stones come from there."

Are there more stones like this, with fossils in them?

"Sí. I will study them when I am a paleontologist."

Renee smiled her approval. "You will be a good one, Gus."

Ten minutes of close scrutiny later, Max returned the stone to the pouch, satiated by the inspection.

"That's what this sample needs, Gus," Max said. "A paleontologist, to determine its authenticity, to understand how old it is, and to understand what we're looking at. More people will want to talk with you about it, and soon. These photos will be good enough for us for now. Thank you."

Max and Renee, back with Cornell on the other side of the mirror. Gus, still in the interview room, sipped at a carton of milk, three people watching her. She ate another donut.

"She's tiny," Max said. "Hard to believe she's gotten this far. What's next for her?"

"She stays here in a holding cell," Cornell said, "until the DA decides what to do with her. Charge her with La Ballena's homicide or her complicity in the other deaths. Maybe all of it, or maybe none of it. Not my call."

"How about letting her go for killing La Ballena in, let's say, self-defense?" Renee said. "She eliminated a monster."

"There's that, too."

"Max," Renee said, "she's going to need help in jumpstarting her life. She has no one. Worse yet, she could be a target. Are you ready to get on that when the time comes?"

"We'll work something out, Renee. Cornell, where's the other one?"

"Yadier Rolando's in the hospital, under guard. A head wound. He'll get to tell his side of things when they release him and bring him here for a chat. We'll compare notes."

"You need to keep him away from her, Cornell. Her fear of retribution is credible."

"Understood."

They took another glance at the Peruvian teen suspect before they left the surveillance room. Gus Gómez sipped milk and ate. She turned to the mirror and waved her hand, all six fingers of it.

"There's a certain paleontologist who should see these photos," Max said. "After that, Cornell, I guarantee he'll want to see that stone of hers in person and run tests on it."

"Not gonna happen, Max. Evidence."

"It needs to happen, Cornell. National security."

32

"Dr. Kirby's phone. If you're hearing this message, I'm not available or I didn't want to talk to you. Leave a message or don't. Choose your own adventure. I do, every day."

Max batted his eyes at Renee, the two listening to the greeting on speaker from the privacy of his Fend Aerospace office. He left a message for the curmudgeon scientist to please call him back. "I'm not crazy for wanting to talk with him about this, am I?"

"Debatable. But maybe the crazier the better, Max. You don't want to go any higher than him. We need to explain too much as it is, about how we know what we know."

The reason the 73001 lunar-sample report was never released, the bones found in the sample, the Cradle super-secret status—Max and Renee knew about all of it. What they were currently chasing might be crazier than all of it.

Max's phone rang. He checked the display. "It's him. Here we go." He hit speaker. "Dr. Kirby. Hi, Max Fend here, in my office. Renee LeFrancois is here, too. Thanks for calling back."

"Where's the moon lander, Fend?"

Okay, so they'd deal with Kirby's agenda first. "We'll find it, Doctor. The Feds and the military are running down the leads."

"That thing is so smart," the scientist said, "I'm surprised it can't find itself on its own. But it can't look for itself because it doesn't know it's missing, does it? Ha! Kind of like a Schrödinger's Cat paradox, but from the cat's perspective."

The tangled, rabbit-hole logic of a genius. Max passed on acknowledging it.

"We'll find *Blue Spectre* eventually, Doctor." He tried to sound convincing, but with the hours slipping by, the trail was turning cold, and while he and the FBI and the CIA weren't any less determined, they were losing confidence. "We're building another lander, just in case. I understand you added something to it at the last minute."

"And your team pulled it back. The late addition was our doing, the late subtraction was yours. Compartment space incompatibility or some horsepucky reason like that, Fend. We're lucky it wasn't on the lander, though, aren't we? I want my consignment back asap. Better that it stays with me until you guys say you're ready for it."

"Sorry you feel that way. Sure, we can make that happen. But tell me, Doctor, what is it? What's in the payload?"

It was worth a shot, Max's wink at Renee said.

"Classified," the doctor said. "Why did you call me, Fend?"

"You're a paleontologist, correct?"

"Among other things. A PhD in the seventies. Some South American digs, the African continent, the Middle East. Now I dabble in Moon rocks."

"Super. Right. Look, Doctor, Fend Aerospace works in many disciplines—"

Max explained the connecting tissue, Fend Aero being a diversified group, industries other than aerospace, etc., etc. Getting any more specific could come later if necessary. "Something that might be of major interest to you dropped into our laps earlier today. A stone with really old fossils in it. From Perú. When we meet you in person, we'll discuss how we got access to it. We'd like you to run some tests to date it. Renee is sending you photos of it now. Look them over, please. We'll wait."

A moment later..."In receipt, Fend. Hold on, I'm putting the phone down to examine them."

They heard him cough, heard gibberish that transitioned to humming, then a *Ha*, then another *Ha*.

"How quickly can you get over to the lab?" he said.

"You mean like tonight? It's already after ten, Doctor."

"I'm here. Lately I'm always here. Building 31, the Lunar Sample Laboratory at the Space Center, but you know that. Bring the stone with you."

"What? No, we don't have the stone, Doctor. We only have the photos."

"No stone, no reason for you to visit. Photos mean nothing. If you bring the stone, I let you in, I look at it, and we talk more. Otherwise, nope. Get back to me. Bye."

Max, in his office with Renee, made two unanswered phone calls to Cornell within ten minutes of each other. The third try, he waited patiently then left a voicemail. "It's Max, Cornell. National security situation. Call me. I don't care how late."

Ring. Max answered.

Cornell was agitated. "This better be good, you persistent SOB." Smooth, sexy jazz filled the background on Cornell's end, with a woman's cooing voice that wasn't part of the music.

"I need Miss Gómez's amulet, Cornell. "

"Max—"

"You'll need to secure that stone from her. You can blame me for breaking her heart, tell her I'll make it up to her, then sign it over to me. Tonight. If I have to make calls to get superiors involved, I will. I'll take full responsibility. I lined up someone to look at it. Plus it might help her case—"

"Max, calm your butt down. You won't be breaking her heart. I already did that. She gave it up to me and is crying it out in her cell. The leather pouch and stone are now in evidence."

Max and Renee traded glances, surprised.

"Understand this, Max. First, I did not just hear you threaten me, and I did not hear you tell me you would escalate. Second, the DA is leaning away from prosecuting her. We're talking about La Ballena here, a physically intimidating drug lord who a barely-five-foot teenager had to face down. There would have no doubt been a threat to her life in there somewhere, leading to a self-defense outcome. Meet me at the FBI Beaumont office, and I'll sign it out. You do what you need to do, then bring it back, whole and undamaged. You owe me, Max."

33

Almost one a.m. Dr. Kirby, white smock, gray head, tufted gray eyebrows, met Max and Renee at the entrance to NASA's lunar rocks lab. "Screw badging them, they're with me," the doctor told the guards. Max was wanded through carrying a brown paper bag, Renee with her laptop. Dr. Kirby hobbled away at a brisk pace that they were apparently expected to follow.

"I don't get it, Fend," he said, his ancient legs pumping. "Why come to me about this?"

"Are you interested?" Max said.

"Yes."

"Then you're the right person for us to see," Renee said.

A few lefts, rights, then a straightaway, they followed Kirby, humming to himself.

"This is me," he said and leaned into a facial recognition camera on an office door security pad. The door unlocked. "Move whatever you have to move if you want to sit. I'm not a hoarder. It's research."

They should have expected this. The "not-a-hoarder" hoarding was pro-level. A picture window on the back wall might look out into a lab or it might look at a brick wall, only the top few inches of the window visible. Detritus, binders, books, science charts the size of posters, framed photographs stacked atop each other, all were balanced on the credenza in front of the window. Another balanced heap, more like an anthill topped by more papers and gadgets, covered a desk, with two or maybe three over-loaded office chairs facing it. Dr. Kirby dropped a hand onto the pile on his desk, parted it, and found room in a box for what he'd just lifted off. Behold, there was wood underneath.

He opened a drawer and removed a magnifying glass and a pair of latex gloves. He pulled the gloves on. "Put the rock sample on the desk, please."

Max lifted a white cardboard box out of the paper bag. The bag had no markings on the outside, but the small white box inside did, preprinted with the word EVIDENCE in black, plus a date and other notes hand-written in black Sharpie.

"My goodness! From an evidence locker?" Dr. Kirby's eyes widened. "So it's part of a crime?"

"Yes, there's been a crime," Max said. "They're not sure who's respon-sible yet."

Dr. Kirby opened the evidence box and removed a zip-locked plastic bag with the leather pouch in it. The pouch out of the bag, then the stone out of the pouch, he examined it with the attention of a gemologist, turning it over in his hands, holding it up to the light, feeling the smoothness of the polished side and the ruggedness of the fossil side. He brought the pouch to his nose and sniffed it.

"Donkey hide, not cow. It's not legal to tan donkeys anymore..." He put the pouch aside, picked up the stone. "You know what I'm tempted to do right now, Mr. Fend?"

"Can't say I do, Doctor," Max said.

"I want to lick it," he said.

Max and Renee traded looks.

"Common practice. Because organic material breaks down, and the inorganic stuff that survives is stickier than the stone. Validates it was once organic. Don't worry, no licking for me." He went for his magnifying glass and moved in.

"This fossil is very interesting. Hmm. I should say 'fossils.' Yes. Ha! Do you know what these are? Or were?"

"Human bones," Max said.

"Good for you. Yes indeedy. Parts of an infant's open hand. But here, look at this! Oh my."

Renee was closest. He gave her the magnifying glass. When she leaned in to view the stone, the doctor pointed. "Do you see those three knuckles, at the base of three fingers?"

Renee said yes.

"And how two of the three fingers are the same length?"

"Yes."

"This infant had two digitus medius fingers on the same hand," Dr. Kirby said.

"English, Doctor," Max said.

"Two middle fingers. My guess is the baby had six fingers on this hand. Where did you get this, Mr. Fend?"

"From Perú. The Amazon rainforest. Can you determine how old it is?"

"Sure can. I'll run some tests and get back to you. Thanks for bringing this to my attention."

Stone back into pouch, pouch into plastic, plastic into box, the box to the desk corner. Dr. Kirby sat, leaned back, and folded his hands in his lap. "Will that be all for tonight?"

Max nodded an okay at Renee, that she should go for the kill shot.

"It can't be just carbon-14 testing, Doctor," Renee said. "Our guess is it's too old, that there's no quantifiable carbon-14 left."

"Excuse me? Why—?"

"Carbon-14 gets you only as far back as 60,000 years. Go farther back. Science tells us humans have been around for at least six million years. Try potassium-argon dating, Doctor. The decay of radioactive potassium-40 versus the decay of radioactive argon-40."

"*What?* Why that far back? That measures age in billions of years. What do you even know about potassium-argon dating? These are fossils, bones from a human skeleton that are now rocks, so *how* on *earth* could—"

He stopped himself mid-thought. He searched their faces, Max's, then Renee's...

Max's, then Renee's...

It hung out there, his last phrase, too precious, too opportunistic, dead air seeping into the clutter of his office, his mind, letting him analyze his own words, allowing the inference to make a connection. The connection Max and Renee had made, and the connection to what they knew.

If one fossil could be a billion years old per a lunar sample, from a celestial body that was once a part of planet Earth, then why not other fossils on the origin planet?

Max ended the suspense. "Yes, Doctor. *How* on *Earth*. Capital 'E' Earth."

"Apollo 17 Moon rocks," Renee said. "Now you know the need to understand the age of this stone better, Doctor, because this could be bigger than your unpublished analysis of sample 73001."

Billion-year-old fossils per the sample, unknown origin, unknown species, on the Moon.

And the impossibility of billion-year-old fossils from human bones, on Earth, in the Amazon.

Dr. Kirby's face blanched. "That Moon rock analysis is classified as top secret. How did you see—"

"Our moon lander *Blue Spectre*'s inquisitive AI, supplemented by superlative hacking skills," Max said. "No worries, Doctor. Renee and I alone know about your analysis, and we're not talking, mostly because we don't want to go to jail. This thing here, this fossil...Once the scientific community decides on the story this stone is telling, it needs to go back in the evidence locker, then back to its owner. How long before I can have it back?"

Dr. Kirby wandered the little aisle space that his office detritus provided, pacing, alternately rubbing his forehead and tenting his fingers, thinking aloud.

"I can't even...This is...this doesn't fit. It would change everything. From the Amazon? And the Moon? The Moon! After the collision that created it, that window of time when things were ripe for life. Ha!..."

"C'mon, Doctor, stay with us here," Max said. "How long will it take for you to do the dating? We need to give the stone back."

The doctor focused, pulling himself together, less scattered, more lucid. "Sure. Of course."

He reopened the evidence box to further admire the pouch, starry-eyed, apprehensive. Max sensed a reverence similar to what he'd seen with young Agustina Gómez.

"I don't know how long. I need to line up the equipment. A few days. I know where to find you."

"You'll take care good care of it, Doctor?" Max said.

"Sure." Dr. Kirby shuffled to a corner of the office and pulled a lab cart out of the way. He poked his hand through a stack of paperback journals with spectrometers and other scientific instruments atop it.

He spoke to himself, stroked his chin, and wheeled around. "No, it's in *that* corner." He crossed behind them. "Here, it's under this table with my micro-fridge." He moved another cart out of the way. "My safe. It's antique, but it works fine. As you can see, I don't throw many things out. The stone will go in there. The combination," he tapped his temple, "stays in here."

A black safe on wheels, with a combination lock and only one lever. Art deco calligraphy in gold across the front. *Kirby Safe Company, Chicago.*

"Any relation?" Max asked.

"Yes. That's me. Or rather my family. My parents. Extremely wealthy. Oil, then vacuum cleaners. A 1922 model manufactured during the first decade of the company." He dropped hard into his chair, the evidence box in his lap. "You're aware that some of the sample will be atomized during the dating process, right? When we're finished, it won't be the same as it is now. No way around it. I'll get Security to escort you out."

Yes, Max knew. Hell to pay with Cornell, something he hadn't been totally honest about. But it would be less of a concern to Cornell, now that there'd be no charges brought against Miss Gómez, no case to try, no need for the stone to be in evidence. Without a criminal case, maybe nobody would care.

Except Miss Gómez. She would care. An enormous loss to her if not enough of the stone—the fossil—were returned to her. He also had concerns that, depending on the results and regardless of its condition, she might get none of it back.

"Call me," Max said.

34

Beep, beep, beep...

Max raised his head from the pillow, orienting himself, listening to his stuttering phone, his eyelids heavy at 2:24 a.m. The calm, darkened Lake Anahuac, bedside to his hacienda rental, reflected a full moon, granting a mystical, magical view of the lake's rippling surface.

"It's Emily," Max grumbled, Renee asleep next to him. It was so déjà vu of sleep-stealing calls like this from Emily to his father Charles Fend back when Max was younger. Calls that could never wait.

"Mmglumph," Renee said, she even less coherent than her mumbling. She dozed off again. The phone beeped more.

Max answered, untwisting his sleepy tongue. "Hi, Emily. What is it?"

"*Blue Spectre* is on," Emily said.

Max dropped his feet on the floor, focusing. He'd been awakened mid-dream, a nightmare torturing him about the missing moon lander, unrecovered from the Chinese heist of a week ago. Was this still the dream? Maybe he'd willed this call to happen. He rubbed his eyes.

"I thought we decided to wait to turn it on, Emily."

"Correct. Its main GPS component turned on by itself. Maybe the AI did it. We have a location. I hesitate even saying where it is, Max."

"No patience for drama, Emily, it's two thirty in the morning. Beer me."

"It's on a slow boat to China."

At the Turtle Bayou Fend Aerospace hangar warehouse, 3:30 a.m., they had a lock on the moon lander. The signal came from the Gulf of Mexico, south of Florida. It was a ping from Maersk Line's *Stadelhorn* container vessel that carried twenty-foot-long equivalent intermodal capacity units, or TEUs, with a final planned destination Shanghai, China. If the signal could be believed, the lander was in one of the nearly 10,000 TEUs aboard the cargo ship, per the manifest.

Max was on a Zoom call with the district commander of the US Coast Guard, Sector Miami. The Department of Homeland Security had issued its orders, that the Guard should accompany the cargo ship as it entered the Port of Miami.

"Where what will happen to it, sir?" the commander asked.

"Where we will have a satellite play Marco Polo with the signal, find the right container, and have the local Maersk folks do what they need to do to open it, looking for contraband. I'll be boarding a jet momentarily, Houston to Miami, to become part of the effort."

"There are a lot of containers on that ship, sir."

"See you in under three hours, Commander."

Max, Renee, and Emily boarded a Fend private jet. US Navy personnel in a Key West installation had been alerted to be on stand-by.

Max settled into his seat on the jet, about to multi-task. Today was day five with no response from Dr. Kirby regarding Agustina Gómez's fossil. More than enough time to do what he was supposed to do. Max called him to roust him. The call went to voicemail.

Mailbox full.

"Probably full for years," Max groused. He sent the genius scientist a text.

Checking in Dr. Kirby. Max Fend. Call me

"Renee," Max said, free to talk, Emily in the lavatory, "would you want to look into using that system back door you used a few weeks back, to check on, you know, Kirby's Moon rock system hangouts?"

Specifically, the back door Renee had found into the Johnson Space Center's Lunar Sample Laboratory Facility's database. Where they'd first learned about the delay to releasing lunar sample 73001.

Her eyes widened. She curled her lower lip, her look at Max coy. "I didn't hear what you said, Max, because, you know," she reopened the laptop she'd just closed, "it would be better for you and me to *not* have heard what I didn't hear you say just now, should there be any repercussions about who knew what and when, and by whose directive. Follow that, Mr. Fend?"

"I didn't hear you," Max said.

"Good to hear." Renee went to work. First stop, the NASA lunar rocks catalogue, to get her bearings. Inside the catalogue, this amounted to breaking news.

"Max. The lunar sample catalogue's been updated, the analysis complete. Today, as a matter of fact. Hold on, it's...*What?*" She glared at her screen. "It's way different than the analysis we saw during our moon-lander demo at the lab. Different lunar mineral content in the sample. No backstory mention on the origin of the Moon. No mention of a fossil! Which completely invalidates what the AI saw on the NASA administrator's private network. And Kirby didn't sign off on the report. That spokesperson who gave us the Moon rocks lab tour, his assistant Karina Archibald—*she* signed off. Max, my guess is something's happened to Kirby."

Emily moved up the aisle and dropped into her seat across from them. "I missed the front end of that. What are people saying that our eccentric knucklehead Dr. Kirby did now, other than go on medical leave?"

Medical leave? Max hid his panic. "He released an overdue Moon rock sample analysis. Or rather someone on his staff did. When did he go on medical leave? Why wasn't I notified?"

"Max," Emily harrumphed, "we've been through this. When you read your emails from me, you learn things. We were notified a few days ago. An incident at the lunar rocks lab. He's being evaluated."

"For what?"

"The memo wasn't specific. They called it 'exhaustion.' It came from the administrator."

"*The senator?*"

"Susan Ignacio, yes, the one and only, our fearless NASA administrator. Dr. Kirby's in the Naval Medical Research Unit in San Antonio. Look, Max, NASA knew he was in decline. This shouldn't surprise you. Relax. And now I'm taking a nap."

Emily put on a sleep mask, reclined in her seat, and checked out. Renee gave Max a thumbs-up in silence, which meant she was "on it," would check on all of it, via SATCOM connections. Have laptop, will travel, and will hack.

Renee keyed, somewhat frenzied, at her laptop. As she found things through the NASA Lunar Lab system back door, she texted updates from her laptop to Max sitting next to her while Emily dozed across from them.

It's confirmed, Kirby's on medical leave. Confirmed he's in the Naval hospital his diagnosis incomplete. NASA announcement coming out tomorrow: Kirby retires from NASA after 52 yrs

She glanced at Max, her eyebrows raised, then she began keying again.

Following is from Kirby's NASA files inside the NASA Lunar Lab system. I did a search on fossils. Most recent matches were in a file named Cradle. Yes, you're reading it right. Password protected. Strong password. Some copy/paste info is in there. Here goes

A dwarf planet crashed into Earth creating Earth's moon 4.425 billion yrs ago.

3.5 billion yrs ago lunar volcanoes begat lunar atmosphere begat lunar magnetic field begat lunar watery habitat begat lunar microbes.

Strong speculation that Earth's moon supported life for millions of yrs before a catastrophic event destroyed the lunar atmosphere and made it uninhabitable.

Potassium-argon radiometric dating & mass spectrometry were used to calc absolute age of Apollo 17 lunar samples and Fend's Amazon stone fossil.

Sample 73001 lunar fossil, unknown species, absolute age is 3.5 billion yrs.

Fend Amazon fossil human hand survived test atomization mostly intact, absolute age is 3.4 billion yrs.

Sustainable life, Moon vs. Earth, chicken or the egg?

Renee stopped, rubbed her hands together and ran her tongue across her lips, her mouth parched.

"You look like you could use a drink," Max said. "Stronger than what we have onboard, so it will need to be either beer, soda, or orange juice."

"Juice."

Max returned with a pint carton of OJ and a cup. She sipped, then began texting from her laptop again.

Next texts are Kirby grappling with his sanity Max. Following questions and comments are his from the Cradle file

Did Moon develop intelligent life first? Moon was closer to Earth after the dwarf planet collision. Collision debris coagulated in 15K mile orbit, mass was added from more collisions, current separation Earth to Moon is 238K miles.

Did the cradle of human civilization start on the Moon in the window when it could support life? Did Moon inhabitants abandon a dying satellite when ecological conditions changed? Did Moon people learn space travel? Did Moon people colonize nearest fertile planet Earth, its mother?

The Magic 8-Ball and these fossils both say it is decidedly so. Ha!

Man as a species is 3.4 billion years old, not 6 million as science's current thinking suggests.

Remarkable.

I will be deemed certifiable. Maybe I am. But facts is facts.

Max stared at her after reading the texts, in awe of her, proud of her. He awaited her next few texts, knowing what they would say.

These fossils precede the accepted timing of the rise of Homo Sapiens by over 3 BILLION yrs Max. How could science be that far off. A world-changing revelation. That makes this information dangerous

Whoever he told with whatever proof he provided, they decided to move him out of the way

"Renee."

She was now hyperventilating. Max could see it, could feel it, sitting shoulder to shoulder with her, with revelations as stunning as these were. He laid his hand on her forearm, spoke in a low voice, Emily still asleep across from them.

"Deep, calming, cleansing breaths, honey, then give it a rest for a bit."

She closed her laptop, closed her eyes, and laid her head on his shoulder. Minutes later, her breathing had slowed to normal. She sipped some juice. She opened her laptop again.

I'm reentering the senator's private home network.

Don't argue Max I'm good now I'm doing it. Screw Jimbo her pitmaster screw

NASA Security. I can find my way in the same way we did looking for 73001. There's a cover up in progress

    We need more info

Emily snored, Renee keyed, Max went for a bottle of beer from the galley and returned, pacing the aisle in full ponder mode.

    Why cover it up?

    How sick is Dr. Kirby? Can we reach him?

    Where's what is left of Gus Gómez's stone talisman?

    How high does this go?

Max's phone pinged. More texting from Renee, more snoring from Emily.

    NASA Administrator knows. Top Secret file on Susan Ignacio's hard drive labeled Cradle. Password protection poor

    Kirby went to her with it. Her contemporaneous notes say he showed her the results of the fossil atomization and the sequenced age of the samples

    Life on Moon first then life on Earth

    Her calendar shows a meeting with President Vaughn at 6 am the day after she met with Kirby

    Max she has contemporaneous notes on the meeting with the president too. Here they are

    President concerned about repercussions and upheavals. Maybe worldwide panic over origins and age of the human race

    Ignacio: these fossilized human bones could not have survived billions of years in these rocks

    President: don't focus on why it couldn't have happened because it apparently did. Focus on what we need to do about it

    President: Aliens are real Senator. We have met the alien invaders and they are us

    Ignacio: Work needed to debunk that

    President: Fine get on it

    Max! She said "to debunk." Why not say to debunk OR prove correct?

    Ignacio to the president: what to do with Kirby

    President: He's had a good run

    End Ignacio contemporaneous notes on meeting with the president

    Begin Ignacio notes to self on what this would mean to Mars missions

These are incriminating, Max

Ignacio: Anticipate Congress spending would move toward more budget exploring man's lunar origin & suspension or slowdown of spending on Mars mission. Mars budget in jeopardy if Kirby info gets out

Ignacio's final Cradle file note: Check calendar & set up appt asap. Hedge the bet. Moon tourism futures

I have her calendar. Yesterday a 6 am meeting with her broker

Her broker! She's making it about the money Max

35

Touchdown at Miami International for Max, Renee, and Emily, and a fifteen-minute ride with a hired driver to Port Miami and an intermodal shipping container lot. The Maersk container ship sat dockside, a Coast Guard unit in the harbor. The cargo ship was ready for unloading. They found the only guy in a military uniform on the dock, the Coast Guard district commander. Max introduced them all to the commander.

"Maersk is fully cooperating, sir," the commander said. "They'll unload the entire ship right here if we make them."

"I'll be on with my federal contacts shortly, Commander," Max said. "Let's get the party started."

The Maersk captain brought Max and the Coast Guard commander up to Monkey Island, the top part of the ship, for the best view to watch the unloading. Renee and Emily remained ashore.

Max called Wilkes, asked, "How do we do this?"

"Simple. They unload one container at a time while our satellite monitors the GPS signal. When the GPS signal moves from ship to shore, we'll know that container is our guy. We're ready when you are, Max."

"Let's hope it's not in one of the bottom containers," Max said.

It was.

An exhausting 9,800+ intermodal container offloads later, per Wilkes,

"Stop the unloading, Max, we've got it. Have Maersk load that last one onto the semi that's about to make your acquaintance, then we'll double check the signal. The Coast Guard can tell Maersk the US government appreciates their cooperation. Sign for the transfer then get the hell out of there. You guys can get a good look at the box at a flight hangar at Miami International, then it will be on its way to JFK at Merritt Island, Florida. Good show, Max."

Thirty minutes by car later, people with federal clearances gathered inside a FedEx hangar at the airport. Max, Renee, Emily, the truck driver, a NASA Artemis manager from the space center, a Homeland Security agent, and an expert locksmith. When the last of the padlocks, slide bolts, cane bolts, and lockboxes was neutralized, Max got on the phone, on video, with Wilkes.

"Good to see your haggard face again, Wilkes. We're ready to end this nightmare and check on *Blue Spectre*'s condition. Opening the doors now. The moment of truth. Are you ready?"

"Do it."

With the handles unlatched, the locksmith pulled one rear door open, then the other.

All eyes lowered to the center of the floor. Bolted into the wood was a one-foot-by-one-foot electrical component. A *Blue Spectre* GPS module, still sending a signal.

No *Blue Spectre* lunar lander.

Emily verbalized what they were all thinking. "They're screwing with us. Our lander is in the People's Republic of China. It's gone."

Max walked inside and powered the GPS module down. "You copy, Wilkes?"

"Confirmed. The signal's gone," Wilkes said. "Signing off, Max. We'll talk later."

Emily phoned the assembled Fend Aero *Blue Spectre* employees back in Turtle Bayou for input-output, give-and-take updates.

"I gave them the news, Max," Emily said. "Everyone's terribly disappointed. They confirmed again that *Blue Spectre* is not transmitting."

"As in still not powered up?"

"Correct, Max. The only part that was functioning was that GPS module."

"Emily," he said, "I'm thinking we turn the whole unit on remotely to confirm that we know where it is."

"It's not entirely your call, Max. You'd need NASA approval and—" she looked in the direction of the Homeland Security agent, "probably approval from those guys, too. Plus it would ruin the surprise."

Max murmured colorful words that went well with his primal fist-pound of the interior of the container. His temper eased. "Fine. We'll make it work. We wait."

36

It was about to be a good news/bad news day for Agustina Gómez. Max and Cornell would deliver all of it to her, Miss Gómez still a guest at the FBI Beaumont office. The charges against her were never filed, and the word around FBI Houston and the satellite offices was she'd been officially released and was already gone.

News of her release was premature. She remained in an FBI jail cell with food and a bed, there temporarily while Social Services and ICE got their arms around what to do with her, because she had nowhere to go. Cornell and Max would speak with her shortly, to update her and to close the loop on what Max had borrowed. Something of major importance to her that would not be returned.

Cornell and Max grabbed one of the elevators in the lobby. When the elevator doors closed, Cornell went off. There were gestures.

"How the hell did you manage to lose my evidence?"

"I didn't lose it. It acquired top NASA clearances while it was being tested. Look, if it were key to a criminal case, we'd get what's left of it back, but the charges against her aren't happening, right? Plus it's tangential evidence at best. Those were gun deaths on that plane and at the ICE detention centers. No one stoned anyone."

"That's not how this works," Cornell said. "The Bureau does the Agency a favor, the Agency does one back. Your agency doesn't screw me by making me look naïve."

"I have no idea what agency you're talking about, Cornell. Fend Aerospace is working as a contractor for NASA here, no one else. Look, let me buy you lunch."

"You already owe me a lunch."

"Texas barbecue and beer. I've even got a driver today. We can drink and eat as much as we want, heavy emphasis on drink," Max suggested, then more seriously, "You need to walk away from it, Cornell."

"You screwed me, Fend."

"Last names now? Let it go, Oakley."

Cornell commenced with a slow, resigned headshake and stare at Max. "*You're* telling her, not me. It's going to crush her."

"I've got something that will go the other way. You lead, I'll clean it up."

The elevator doors opened across from the FBI satellite, a double-door entrance. Inside, eight desks filled a bullpen area, the interrogation rooms at the end of one hallway, two jail cells at the end of another. One enclosed office. Their teenage ex-suspect sat with a female agent in a glassed-in conference room next to the office, the room with a view of the desks in the bullpen. Cornell asked the agent with her to leave. He and Max grabbed chairs across from Miss Gómez.

"Hi, Gus. Mr. Fend and I have some news for you," Cornell said. "First, Yadier Rolando will be released from the hospital today. He's charged with two ICE employee deaths, one in Virginia, one in Pennsylvania. The DA's ignoring his claims that you shot him and La Ballena and his two guards on the plane. She has her reasons. Consider yourself extremely lucky.

"Second, ICE has found a community home for you to stay in near— where is it, Mr. Fend?"

"It's in Kingsville, south of Corpus Christie," Max said. "Near one of the King Ranch properties. The King Ranch is the largest ranch in the US What I can add to that is—"

Young Gus spoke up. "Gracias, señores, but I am not giving up searching for mi familia. I will go to every detention center in Texas on my own and—"

"Miss Gómez—Gus—stop." Max leaned in, wanting to wrap his

hands around hers, but he stopped himself. "I have some things to tell you. First, I need to update you on your stone. The testing NASA did on it—the stone, the fossils in it, they're not something they can return to you, not now at least, and maybe never. I'm so sorry, Gus. Your stone is gone."

She was speechless, touching the belt loop where she'd kept the leather pouch with her amulet tethered, her lower lip quivering. "No, no, please, get it back, *please*—"

"Gus. *Gus.* Wait, honey, please," Max said, "the other news is, we located your father."

"Papá? You found papá?"

Max explained, a rapt Gus listening. Her father's story was long, and Max would let the man deliver most of it himself. Óscar Javier Gómez. There were multiple immigrants in the ICE records with—no surprise— the same name. In short, her father had spent the last three years in Texas, New Mexico, and Mexico, in detention centers and shuttered prisons, sometimes as a day laborer, sometimes shoplifting his meals, sometimes begging, getting deported, crossing and re-crossing the Rio Grande, into and out of America, continuing his search for his daughter.

"The US will grant him asylum, Gus. Your search is over. He's on his way here right now."

"Papá!" Gus Gómez rushed to the glass, her face against it, eyeing a room busy with agents on phones and desktops. Then came the pacing interspersed with hugging Max and Cornell in between squees of excitement, until—

"Gaby. My pequeña Gaby. What about my little sister? And Tío Ernesto, my uncle?" Her eyes, alarmed and afraid, searched theirs.

Max stayed as gentle and as calming with his delivery as he could. "I am so sorry, Gus. Your father said your sister is gone, from Covid. He said nothing about your uncle." Cornell waved at the female agent waiting at her desk, coaxing her into the room.

The tears flowed, stemmed by tissues, tender words, consolations, and offers of more hugs, some accepted, some declined or ignored, with nowhere private for a young teen girl to turn to handle the pain, plus the joy, of the information she'd just received.

Max checked his phone. A text from Renee. "Her father is on his way up," he said to Cornell.

A moment later, Renee guided a short, gaunt Peruvian man with wavy salt-and-pepper hair through the front door to the FBI office. Gus bolted from the conference room, Cornell and Max following. She weaved her way around desks, elated, sobbing, and calling to him, but she soon stopped short.

A wheelchair entered behind Renee, a slumped person in it, the door held open by Agent York, guiding his charge into the office. The man's hands were cuffed in his lap, his head bandaged, his feet in leg irons, chains connecting them to his wrists.

"Yadi," Gus mouthed to herself. She remained frozen, her papá and Renee on the move around the bullpen.

Agent York arrived at his desk, Yadier Rolando next to it, his head still down. York removed his weapon from his hip and opened a desk drawer, would store it out of the way for the interrogation.

Yadi raised his head. Gus met his eyes. Yadi's face turned wild with rage.

York's gun, unattended, was a moment away from storage or a moment away from disaster.

Gus mumbled then screamed, "J-Jewelry. JEWELRY!"

Yadi grabbed then raised the weapon in his cuffed hands. Cornell left his feet and hurdled across the desks for a headlong tackle, his linebacker physique crushing Yadi and his wheelchair against the floor, knocking the weapon loose—except one cartridge had already left the barrel.

The bullet blasted Gus's papá off his feet before it penetrated the dimpled black door of an upright refrigerator.

Renee called 9-1-1. Max arrived alongside the elder Gómez and kneeled, Gus cradling her father's groggy head, Max moving aside articles of his clothing, checking for the wound. The angle of the shot...for it to hit the fridge, it had to have been a ricochet, but was it before it entered the victim's body or after?

The prone father opened his eyes, Gus hovering above him. He pulled her to him and hugged her tightly, speaking nonstop Spanish to his little girl, sobbing, invoking his wife and praising God, neither Gus nor her papá letting go of each other...

Max found no blood, no indication of a wound on him. On the floor next to Gus and her papá a leather pouch lay split, the stone it held freed from the pouch, its polished side chipped from the gunshot.

Cornell pulled Yadi out of the collapsed wheelchair by his neck. He stuck the barrel of a Glock in Yadi's ear and escorted the shuffling teen with the bandaged head back to a jail cell, the sheepish Agent York in tow, his weapon recovered.

Max and Renee got the father to his feet, and papá and daughter were shepherded to an office arm in arm to complete their reunion in earnest behind a closed door.

Max spoke to Renee. "Let me talk with that other agent, to let her know what's been set up for Miss Gómez and her papá, then we can head out. Cornell's got his hands full. He won't miss us." He gave the agent a number to call.

What was on the horizon for father and daughter per Max's intercession:

A motel for them to stay at for a few days, maybe longer, compliments of Max Fend. Assurances to ICE that runaway Gus Gómez would report to the Kingsville community home asap after. King Ranch, legendary home to prized Texas Longhorns and Brahma bulls across three centuries, agreed to give Óscar Gómez a tryout. A chance for him to become an American cowboy at the largest cattle ranch in America. And best of all, an expedited path to asylum in the US for them both.

At the elevator, Renee held Max's hand, pulled herself to him, and showed some PDA with a light kiss on his cheek. "I'm suddenly in the mood for a Hallmark movie, Max."

He returned her cheek peck, then searched her eyes, mischief in his.

"That won't do it for me. I'd be more interested in some wine, some Netflix, and some chill." The elevator dinged its arrival at the same time his phone danced in his pocket. Inside the elevator, after a longer kiss, he checked his phone. Texts.

"From Emily," he said. He read the first line. "Aw, damn it."

Dr. Kirby's gone. RIP. He died in the Naval Medical Center. Cause of death is pending. Preliminary indication is cardiac arrest. For once, read my emails to you.

Before you ask, there will be an autopsy to ensure no foul play because he had top secret clearances. I'll send his family our sympathies, Max. I knew him longer than you did

They shared looks. Renee said it first. "Tonight, no movies. Instead we feast on pizza, beer, then Naval hospital patient records."

37

Seven thirty p.m. The pizza was excellent despite having come from a Texas pizzeria. Two medium pies, one for her, one for him, delivered hot to Max's hacienda. Beer on tap from the well-stocked bar, chilled mugs. Renee had a time of it busting through the protocols established for the Naval Medical Center system, but she did get in. She found nothing out of the ordinary, no smoking gun, no suspected foul play over Kirby's death. Charts, readings, medications, tests, heart condition, mind condition. His cardiac arrest had come "from a secondary spontaneous pneumothorax," Renee read to Max.

"Meaning?"

Renee, reading more. "He 'likely blew out a bleb into his lung from coughing, which led to a quick cardiac arrest.' An internet search on 'bleb' says it's an air bubble."

Not suspicious in any way, just terribly inconvenient, for Dr. Kirby, and for her and Max, considering Kirby's revelations.

"Wait. The *Blue Spectre* demo we gave at the lunar rocks Eval Lab," Max said, squinting. "Didn't Kirby learn...?"

"Yes," Renee said. "The AI suggested a better pulmonologist to him than the one he had."

Renee noticed the security camera footage for the hacienda, top right quadrant of her laptop screen, had activity.

"Max. Two men in black just got out of a car in your driveway."

A Princeton Tigers tee covered Max's handgun in a side holster. He waited against the wall for the doorbell. When it rang, "Who is it?"

"NASA Cybersecurity, Mr. Fend," the lead guy said. He badged Max through the peephole. Even with the distorted view, the two appeared straight from *Men in Black* central casting, minus the sunglasses. "Special Agents Zampesi and Atkins. Is Ms. LeFrancois here?"

"You want to tell me what the problem is?" Max said through the door.

"We'd like to have a chat with her."

"Don't take this the wrong way, gentlemen, and please don't infer anything from this, but tell me if any of this involves a search warrant."

"It does not, Mr. Fend. Just a chat."

"Are you armed?" Max said.

"Yes."

"I am, too." Max opened the door. "Come in."

Max led them into one of the sitting rooms. Renee was busy moving pizza boxes and plates into the kitchen. She returned with a mug of beer. Her laptop was nowhere in sight. She sipped, Max talked.

"Have a seat, gentlemen," Max said.

"We'll stand. We'll get to the point. It's come to our attention that someone entered a NASA database over the last few days without proper authority. The database the Lunar Sample Laboratory uses for cataloguing research outcomes of Moon rock analysis."

Agent Zampesi, thin face, wide-set eyes, did the talking. Agent Atkins, stocky, intimidating, his expression grumpy, remained quiet.

"I'll be blunt," Zampesi said, addressing them both. "We think that person was you, Ms. LeFrancois. No idea why you'd be in there, but you were. We think you looked around, helped yourself to an eyeful, downloaded some notes, and left with some wrong impressions."

Max sidled up close to Renee in solidarity so there'd be no misunderstanding where his allegiance stood.

Renee hadn't flinched. "Oh my. I see. Does this have to do with Dr. Kirby?" she asked. Another sip of beer. "Because I did do some searches on the database after we learned of his passing, looking for statuses on our requests. We were working with him on *Blue Spectre* transit goods, quantifying the space they'd need onboard. We're still getting the specs around cubesat deliveries, experiments, and other commercial consignments the lander will deliver to the Moon, and retrieve from it, too. Fend Aerospace is a full-service lunar contractor, if you will."

Dazzle 'em with a few facts, Max was thinking, *do a pivot, and give 'em a commercial for the lander. Good show, Renee.*

"Ms. LeFrancois," Agent Zampesi said, "consider this the vocal equivalent of a slow clap. We did our homework. We know who you are. We cut our teeth in the same spaces and traveled in the same circles as your for-hire hacker contractors. A fact you omitted just now is, while you were snooping, you found a back door. One that's since been closed now that the system's developer, Dr. Kirby, may he rest in peace, is gone. You actually helped us by discovering that vulnerability. Thank you. We're not here for a sales pitch or to do any harm to you. We're here only to tell you to stay the hell away from the system. You got a free look, the only one you're going to get. No one will know about your transgression other than a few NASA elites. Not your superiors, not anyone. We're giving you a pass."

Renee jumped on one bit of info, something Max had picked up as well. "So Dr. Kirby was one of the lab's system developers?" she said.

"Yes."

Max knew what this meant. Agent Zampesi then voiced the answer to the question they wouldn't get to ask.

"Yes, the back door was his. He came and went as he pleased, apparently. One more important thing—another reason we're here. Dr. Kirby manipulated data, produced results and analysis without empirical study, and made conclusions without scientific corroboration. What you saw was the product of a hoax perpetrated by an eccentric old scientist who'd descended into a strong belief in the existence of UFOs and was also rumored to howl at the Moon."

Renee's hand had been verbally slapped, but Max's hadn't. He pushed. "We're waiting on Apollo 17 samples for shipment-compartment analysis. Any issues now that Dr. Hardy's gone?"

"Issues like what?" Agent Zampesi said.

"Are the samples where they're supposed to be, so we can borrow them?"

"I'll take this one." Agent Atkins, the quiet muscle of the duo, remained sour while he spoke. "Yes, Mr. Fend, they are where they're supposed to be, in the Lunar Sample Laboratory Facility. You'll hear shortly about your request, I'm sure. Ms. LeFrancois, stay out of the databases, or our next visit won't be a warning."

The front door closed, the agents gone.

They sat on a sofa, beer mugs in hand, pondering the message.

"We both knew he was off," Max said.

"He was eccentric, not crazy, Max. They're gaslighting us. Wait until they find out we were back in the senator's private network, too. I'll move around my files and my entire internet presence, and I'll work on a new laptop and put a stake through the old one. In case they come looking for it. Do you think they went to Wilkes?"

On reflex, Max checked his phone for messages and texts. The queue was large, but none of the connections were from Wilkes or any other familiar Agency names.

"No. We would have heard already." He massaged her arm. "Telling the Agency would mean bringing others into this top secret loop. My guess is Wilkes knows nothing about this, and it needs to stay that way. True or not, regardless of the implications about the NASA administrator, or even the President, no one can know what did or didn't just go down, Renee."

"Those samples are gone, aren't they, Max? I mean, we have our notes, our findings, Kirby's assertions, his testing, but without the physical proof, without the fossils—"

"My guess is yes, they're destroyed, or put somewhere where no one will ever see them, so no one gets a chance to tell a story no one wants to hear. It needs to be business as usual, even though our views might be forever altered. If we can even believe any of it was right."

A ping on Max's phone. An Emily text.

Max. Good evening. We did the math. We've waited long enough. By tomorrow morning it will be time to turn Blue Spectre on. What say you?

Max texted her back. *Assemble everyone for the morning*

Nine thirty a.m. inside the Turtle Bayou air hangar warehouse, in a large conference room.

Emily had a map from her laptop projected onto the hanging screen. The Fend Artemis program leads and department heads, plus Max, Renee, and Emily, sat at the long table, their necks craned, looking at Emily's map of the South China Sea, east of China, west of the Philippine Islands.

"Current time 9:45 a.m. central standard time here in Houston," Max said. NASA, Homeland Security, the US Air Force, and others were on Zoom. "That's 11:45 p.m. there. Are we ready?"

"We are a go, Max," Emily said. Max nodded. Emily stood to address everyone.

"Okay. The scenario with the longest timeframe for delivery is the Maersk Line or an equivalent cargo ship scenario. Considering time under-way, a cargo ship's snail speed, the weather conditions, and relying on our current speculation as to the destination, it would have arrived within the last twenty-four hours. If transport was by a faster ship or by air, it's been there for a while already. Regardless of the method used, this is the geography we want to show you onscreen at this moment. We expect it is, or will be, in this vicinity by now. We'll see if we got it right."

Emily pointed to the head of engineering, who was on his cell phone. He leaned forward, his phone to his ear, then he raised his head to the audience around the table. He gave a single thumbs-up. "*Blue Spectre* is now on and operational," he said.

They all watched the overhead map.

Five seconds turned into ten, ten into twenty.

Twenty-nine seconds after *Blue Spectre* had been powered up, a red dot glowed onscreen. The hoots, hollers, clapping, and high fives were deafening.

"According to the coordinates, *Blue Spectre* is transmitting from...the Wenchang Space Launch Center, on the island of Hainan, the People's Republic of China. Folks, our lunar lander *Blue Spectre* is now in the service of the China National Space Administration, and the US will know its every move wherever it goes, in China and anywhere else, even if—especially if— it does manage to get to the Moon. While it's operational, the AI will be functional for us as well as for them, and the Chinese will have no idea.

We're now calling this unit *China Blue Spectre*. Not all that original, but it works."

The clapping continued nonstop.

Max left his chair. He leaned over, close to Emily. "What do you think the Chinese are thinking right now?"

"Let's let them tell us," Emily said. "What they *should* be thinking, but I doubt they will be thinking, because they don't know," she was smiling, "is 'Trojan Horse.' They will question why the unit is now on and will look for what it was that someone on their end did to make that happen."

"Indeed. Well done, Emily." He hugged his diminutive chief of staff. "Thank you for talking me out of making it operational any sooner."

Max addressed everyone around the table. "Team. Can anyone tell me if the AI is functioning?"

Multiple yes responses. The unit's three cameras were operational, capturing the faces of the Chinese scientists poking at it, opening moon-lander compartments and doors, and pointing flashlights into the interiors, *ooh*ing and *ahh*ing in Chinese. The Fend team was already overwhelmed by the quantity of feedback the unit was sending.

"We'll need translators," Emily said. "Already the AI is responding to them in Chinese, and they seem delighted. Right now," they all listened to the audio for the video, concentrating on the language, "it's generating feedback about *kǒuchòu*. I hesitate saying this, but that translates to 'halitosis' in English, team. One of the scientists must have bad breath." The audience both in the room and on Zoom erupted in laughter. "See, each of them is putting his hand to his mouth, trying to smell what the AI is smelling. Wonderful."

Max closed out his clapping, the laughter quieting. "To have adapted already," he said to the group, "the unit must have evaluated its surroundings and gone with Chinese as its language of communication. Hell, this application is good. Kudos, Fend Aerospace team. Let's listen."

An elderly Chinese scientist turned solemn while patting the shoulders of his associates, the Fend team watching online. He spoke in Chinese, as a dignified teacher would to his rapt pupils, then all three scientists laughed.

"Emily, did you get that?" Max said.

"Here's the gist. He quoted an old Chinese saying. 'It takes ten years to sharpen a good sword,' or something to that effect. He's now telling them 'screw that saying,' they took years off their research and development by stealing the US's *Blue Spectre*."

Renee spoke. "Do you think they'll ever know about the rest of it?"

"We'll see. When and if they do, they will be in for a huge surprise," Max said. "But to do it, they'd need to completely dismantle the unit and break down the skeleton to get at the materials used to create the frame. In effect, to learn all its capabilities, they'd need to destroy it. The GPS module they left in the Maersk container was only one of *Blue Spectre*'s transmitters. The *entire unit* is a transmitter, every inch of it, as is its AI, which is embedded in the mixture of materials used to manufacture the parts. It's inside the unit's DNA.

"They'll learn how to turn it off, but it's guaranteed they'll turn it back on again and again. The genius of this is, if this unit ever gets to the Moon, it will be like we're there, too. But even if it doesn't get there, in the meantime the US will learn a whole helluva lot more about China's space technology."

"Max," Renee said, gesturing at her phone, "over here, please." He joined her in a corner away from the jubilation. They found enough quiet and privacy for Renee to show him texts.

"From my stockbroker. Fend Aerospace just jumped six points on the DOW," Renee said. "Over fourteen million shares traded hands. Analysts are making comments speculating that Fend Aero would soon enter the space tourism business."

"News to me," Max said. "Some new speculators must be looking to cash in." He discreetly searched the room, plus the faces on the Zoom call. "Hopefully it's none of these folks. Conflicts of interest for sure. But space tourism? Nope. Not on the drawing board at this point for Fend Aerospace."

"Max," she checked her texts, "the broker says it's multiple sales by multiple sellers, but all fourteen million shares were purchased by one buyer. Fourteen million going to one entity."

"Who was the buyer?"

"A holding company."

"Someone making a run at us?" Max thought aloud.

"My broker says no, doesn't look like it," Renee said. "Just a group of investors thinking Fend will offer private trips to Mars for people young enough and wealthy enough to afford them. And who like Fend's track record at getting its space projects done."

"Trust me, no Fend Aero private trips to Mars are on the horizon. Nor any to the Moon, either," Max said. "My guess is it's one investor. And like she told us, even though she doesn't know she did, she's hedging her bet."

38

Two years later, December 2026

"*Blue Spectre Two* rockets fired."

Commander Brophy was broadcasting from the Orion spacecraft to three other lunar astronauts and the entirety of the JFK Space Center, the Canadian Space Agency, the Japan Space Agency, the European Space Agency, and the Israeli Space Agency. The Starship Human Landing System, or Starship HLS, was on the Moon and presently a temporary home to astronauts Blanchard and Transom from the US and Canada, respectively, a white male, and a Black female, respectively, on the lunar surface for a planned weeklong stay.

"BS-2 Moon Lander is on her way down, landing area seventy-five yards southeast, over," Blanchard said. "We see her now from Starship. Steady as she goes. There's engine cut-off. And...touchdown."

Malapert Massif, the Artemis III mission's landing spot on the lunar south pole, was inhabited by *Starship HLS* plus separate CLPS lunar lander *BS-1*, as in *Blue Spectre One*, plus one unpressurized lunar rover, *The Senator Susan*. Blanchard and Transom were inside Starship, awaiting approvals for their first Moon trek. It was Day Two of their visit to the Moon, the first humans on the Moon in fifty-four years.

The front end of this Artemis mission was the successful launch and delivery of *BS-1* to the Moon four months earlier. The payloads for *BS-1*, which touched down 265 yards southeast of where *Starship HLS* landed, were drills, soil collection tubes, two college science experiments, two NASA experiments, and other NASA consignments of unknown specificity, some operational robotically, some awaiting the arrival of the astronauts to begin working with them. Among other tasks, the astronauts would drill to find samples of water and ice below the lunar surface.

The second CLPS lander, *BS-2*, had twelve commercial items with container space purchased by NASA and mega conglomerates like Mars Habitat, Red Planet Systems, and Martian Holiday Tours. The Artemis III team would be busy.

"Are you astronauts ready to ride *Susan*?" Commander Brophy said.

"Be sensitive to your audience, Commander," a chiding JFK engineer said. The elderly Senator Susan Ignacio, NASA administrator, was a RIP in May. Spontaneous astronaut humor occasionally needed filtering.

"Aye-aye, JFK," the commander said. "Roger that, my bad. Okay, the sooner we drill, team, the sooner we get things sorted out for later Artemis missions. Suit up."

Internal under-the-radar chatter included quiet rumors that the Artemis timetable had benefitted greatly from resolutions of program snafus unwittingly provided by, and unbeknownst to, the China National Space Administration. One example, a sixteen-month schedule improvement that came from the adoption of Chinese spacesuit technology, eliminating previous delays that had pushed the crewed mission back to 2027. Operation Trojan Horse continued to deliver until the Chinese powered off the source forever, having stolen whatever US technology they could and adapted it to their own, but never the wiser that this had been a two-way street.

The Senator Susan rover was on standby. Blanchard and Transom exited *Starship* and bounced a short distance over to her. "We are a go, Commander," and off they went, destination *BS-1*.

Payload container #1, the drills, payload #2, empty sample tubing for surface collection, payload #3, spectrometers…The planned drill sites were halfway between *BS-1* and *Starship*. They assembled the equipment. Drill bit extensions would allow them to reach as deep as seventy feet below the lunar surface in search of lunar ice and/or water, extrusion tubes at the ready for the extraction of the samples.

The first drill site was special. Regardless of the outcome, discovery of Moon ice or not, the Artemis program agenda included leaving behind a time capsule that might not be recovered by any being, human, whatever, ever. And yet, as was the nature of time capsules, this one was always meant to be discovered, in whatever millennia and by whatever space agency had a notion and the capability to do so, its secreted contents shared with the rest of the universe.

Day Three.

"This site is a bust." Astronaut and mining engineer Transom summed up the status of the drilling for Commander Brophy, her partner Blanchard preparing the drill for another go of it. "We need to search elsewhere. Let's make another few digs here to widen the site enough to accept the time capsule."

Two indelicate hours later, with the astronauts indifferent to the debris that the widened, seventy-foot-deep shaft had produced, they moved their small, wheeled hoist-and-crane system in place above the rear of *The Senator Susan*. They attached the pulley apparatus to the time capsule and lifted. After a short, bumpy ride back to the shaft, Artemis III's capsule, a common floor safe in black and dating from 1920s America, was ready for burial.

With the payload on the hoist, Transom spoke to her partner Blanchard and the entirety of the Earth and Moon, with Blanchard using a handheld phone to video the event.

"We dedicate this time capsule...to astronaut and senator Susan T. Ignacio, RIP, NASA's administrator at the time of her death...and to Dr. Vernon L. Kirby, a most esteemed NASA scientist, also deceased. The capsule's exterior is stenciled in small block letters in gold on all sides, in five languages. In English, it reads as follows, below the logo for the Kirby Safe Company, Chicago. *'These samples were returned for safekeeping. An origin story. Two planetary bodies, the Earth and its moon, one cradle of civilization, and it is memorialized here. The safe's combination is one right, two left, three right. Ha.'*

"Thank you, everyone. Astronaut Blanchard, let's bury this thing and get to work looking somewhere else."

———

Gus Gómez sat with her father in his pickup truck, a Ford circa 2004, as it bounced along an unpaved road near his employer, the King Ranch. Papá was her ride home from high school today. In between bounces, Gus watched these momentous, generational treks on the surface of the Moon in real time on her cell phone. Astronauts Transom and Blanchard posed for tripod camera footage in front of *Blue Spectre One*, Artemis III's first commercial payload lunar lander.

She spoke to him in English, commonplace for papá now, too. They'd come so far.

"Papá. Look. They're gathering rocks and dirt, and they're drilling for water. They just buried a time capsule. On the Moon, papá! Someday I will learn all there is to know about the rocks they are collecting."

Papá showed interest, but compared to Gus, his enthusiasm was more like getting new shoes versus a new car. Gus was giddy as she recorded the video. She laid the phone in her jeans lap, the event still in progress. This time, she spoke more to him, rather than at him.

"The work at the ranch—I know it is hard, papá. But you are a cowboy now, here in America, something you always wanted. You are making money. You are providing for us. I am so proud of you."

She reached for his hand and gripped it, giving it a shake, but his grip on hers was much tighter.

"No, no, my sweet Gus," he spoke her name in its parochial *Goose*, "I am proudest of you, mi niña. You will graduate from an American high school. And the newest news—our peruano friends, they are proud of you too..."

Acceptance at an American university. It was the beginning for her. Her papá was living his dream, and she would live hers, too. She could do it. She could get scholarships. She had a friend in a very high place; Max Fend had promised to help. A guardian angel whose people had stayed in contact with her, vouched for her, were shepherding her.

"Agustina,'" Papá said, his eyes filling. "I miss hearing your madre say your name. You are my Gus, but you will always be your mami's Agustina. If she could see you now, she and Gaby, they would be proud."

Baby sister Gaby. Gone due to the pandemic while in a detention center with her papá. Another wound that would never heal for either of them. She and papá wept a little more, then calmed themselves as they neared the ranch home they shared with another peruano family.

She gripped the pouch on her belt loop and held it so tight her hand cramped. In it, an old charm, the same as what Gus had possessed most of her life, embedded fossils included. Gaby's talisman, passed from papá to Gus.

She opened the leather, removed the stone, and licked the jagged side like she'd done numerous times before, tasting fossils from another hand that was beginning-of-time old. She cried a little more, the stone on her lap, next to her phone.

"We will be fine, papá. Our family, our ancestors, they are with us. We are from Genta de la Luna," she said, raising her chin. "We are the People of the Moon, and we are watching people walk on the Moon. This is so awesome. Ha."

Her laugh was tiny, a gasp squeezed through tears determined to expose themselves.

"The sky—it is not the limit for us, papá, it is only the beginning."

HIDING AMONG THE DEAD
Blessed Trauma Crime Scene Cleaners #1

PHILO TROUT:
Retired Navy SEAL.
Former bare-knuckles boxing champ.
Current crime scene cleaner.

"Couldn't pry me away...Bauer writes with authenticity...A knockout original story, with a host of equally original characters. Certainly not your typical crime fiction, and that's a good thing." —**David Swinson, author of** *Trigger.*

Philo Trout opted for a geographical fix for his checkered, violent career. His new life in Philadelphia as a crime scene cleaner is quiet—until he discovers some of his "clients" are coming up short on their organ count.

While he tries to outrun his past, one of his coworkers can't remember his own: Patrick, found brutally beaten, is now an amnesiac. When the connection between Patrick's history and the missing human organs emerges, Philo is determined to solve the puzzle.

The trail leads Philo into a dark conspiracy. A brutal organization will stop at nothing to protect their secret. Philo's past as a fighter might be his only route to the truth...

If he can survive that long.

HIDING AMONG THE DEAD is a dark and action-packed thriller by Chris Bauer. If you enjoy **Elmore Leonard** and **Breaking Bad**, then you'll love this edgy, heart-stoppingly suspenseful book.

Get your copy today at
severnriverbooks.com

ACKNOWLEDGMENTS

Andrew Watts, *USA Today* bestselling author. Max Fend, Renee Le Francois, Caleb Wilkes, Trent Carpenter are your characters, Andrew. Thanks for letting me move them around the chessboard again.

"The Spider and the Fly," a poem by Mary Howitt, 1829.

The Philadelphia Police Department, Office of Media Relations/Public Affairs.

Isabel Barton, author. Thanks for helping me get my Spanish mostly right. Whatever isn't correct here is this writer's fault, not yours.

Mark Bergin, author. I'll give you that your help didn't take much effort on your part, but it's still much appreciated.

Authors Jim Kempner and Beverly Black for saying you'd talk to me about stuff I was going to include here. I know, I never availed myself of your offers. Glad to know you were there if I needed you.

The Den of Drunken Monkeys, a honkin' tonkin' restaurant, Shepherd, Texas. I saw the pictures, I loved the vibe, and I knew I couldn't go wrong with the name.

Randall Klein, author and editor, for your review and your suggestions.

Janet Fix, author and editor, thewordverve.com, for your excellent edits and review.

The Bucks County (PA) Writers Workshop, chaired by Don Swaim. Always happy to have your encouragement and your feedback, team.

Bill O'Toole, MD for helping eliminate a medical mess before it could happen.

The Rebel Writers of Bucks County, PA: Rusty Allen, Dave Jarret, Jen Giacalone, Kathleen Madigan. Reasonability critiquers and gatekeepers all. I might have actually listened to you a little bit.

ABOUT THE AUTHOR

"The thing I write will be the thing I write."

Chris wouldn't trade his northeast Philly upbringing of street sports played on blacktop and concrete, fistfights, brick and stone row houses, and twelve years of well-intentioned Catholic school discipline for a Philadelphia minute (think New York minute but more fickle and less forgiving). Chris has had some lengthy stops as an adult in Michigan and Connecticut, and he thinks Pittsburgh is a great city even though some of his fictional characters do not. He still does most of his own stunts, and he once passed for Chip Douglas of *My Three Sons* TV fame on a Wildwood, NJ boardwalk. He's a member of International Thriller Writers, and his work has been recognized by the National Writers Association, the Writers Room of Bucks County (PA), and the Maryland Writers Association. He likes the pie more than the turkey.

severnriverbooks.com

Printed in the United States
by Baker & Taylor Publisher Services